BOOK OF BUSINESS

BOOK OF BUSINESS

—— A NOVEL OF THE LAW ——

by WILL NATHAN

Philadelphian Press, Inc.
Philadelphia

PHILADELPHIAN PRESS inc.

Philadelphian Press, Inc.
Philadelphia, PA
www.philadelphianpressinc.com

Printed in Canada

ISBN-10: 0-9791054-0-4
ISBN-13: 978-0-9791054-0-1

Author's Note:

A "book of business" describes clients who follow
a lawyer from law firm to law firm.

CONTENTS

BOOK ONE: CAUSE

BOOK TWO: EFFECT

BOOK ONE

CAUSE

1

San Francisco
{Early Afternoon, August 16, 1994}

August Bondoc never panicked. Never. But twelve million was twice what the jury had been asked to award. For a simple case of exposure, for God's sake, and live on Court TV.

Not content with jeopardizing his reputation as a trial lawyer, the San Francisco jury had even made fun of Bondoc's appearance, telling the media that Bondoc reminded them of Jabba the Hut. That had hurt. Possessed of a bulbous physique, Bondoc fought nature by assiduous exercise. He deeply resented, and normally punished, unflattering jokes about his appearance.

But now "evil fat man" quips were being hurled at him by a trial jury. Still, Gus Bondoc never faltered. He looked the TV cameras right in the eye—major network cameras, brought by the size of the verdict. Bondoc blamed California's anti-business culture. He blamed the public's hatred of lawyers. If institutions like Holliday & Bennett couldn't do business in California, Bondoc said, ominously wagging his finger at the red eye of the cameras, California itself would soon be out of business.

Well before the trial began, the shadow jurors and the hired shrinks brought in by Bondoc had all agreed that the Holliday & Bennett partners had shown no respect for the humanity of Nancy Frehen, the temporary legal secretary who had been subjected to the unexpected sight of a penis when she walked into her boss's office one day to take dictation. But Bondoc and his client had ignored these distress signals. As a result, defense of this case had already earned Bondoc more than three million dollars, with the potential for more money on appeal. As he faced the TV cameras and mouthed platitudes about his concern for the California economy, Bondoc's mind was three thousand miles away.

Other Holliday & Bennett cases were in Bondoc's office and, taken all together, the corporate law firm made up a large part of Bondoc's present book of business. But Bondoc was a survivor of the first order, and the fight that was probably already going on in New York was one he did not intend to lose. Suffering through a horrendous jury verdict, complete with unflattering jokes about his physique, was one thing. Losing Holliday & Bennett's book of business was quite another. The first was merely unpleasant. The second was unthinkable.

Stuck in late-afternoon traffic on the Bay Bridge, Bondoc mulled over what he considered his best shot at keeping Holliday & Bennett. He knew he would have to hire Gerry Frank to appeal the jury verdict. Frank was on everyone's A list, but, more important than anything else, Frank would never hurt Bondoc. Frustrated with the slow pace of traffic, Bondoc decided to call Frank's office from his car phone. The appellate lawyer picked up the phone himself after the second ring. Not many people knew this very private number, which was changed every few months.

Frank immediately sympathized. "What a shitty thing. You must feel terrible, Gus."

"Don't waste any tears on me, pal," Bondoc trumpeted. "Some jury screws somebody somewhere every day. Don't confuse me with someone who actually cares what twelve assholes think." Frank was used to Bondoc's bravado when he was down. He said nothing. After a moment, Bondoc got to the point. "Listen Ger, here's why I'm calling. That lunatic jury is getting in the way of client control here. There are people in New York who are going to start calling for my scalp, and this is a client that has paid me a lot of money."

"How can I help?" Frank intoned, his solemn voice projecting the equivalent of a deadpan expression. The two men had been friends since law school, and Bondoc's pretense that the verdict hadn't hit him in the ego was vintage Gus. Just as Frank expected, Bondoc announced, "I'm going to bring you in for the appeal, Gerry, so cover my ass. How about it?"

"No problem, Gus. That's what we're here for." One bad, dirty joke later, the call was over.

He must really be hurting, Frank thought, idly plugging his cell phone back into its charger. Frank always covered for any lawyer who brought him into a messy appeal. That was how you built up an appellate practice. If you didn't criticize the lawyers who screwed up, then they kept on coming back. By contrast, appellate clients on the losing end of trials were typically one-time dance partners who started angry and poor and finished angrier and even poorer.

Holliday & Bennett wasn't Bondoc's only disappointed law-firm client. Representing large law firms was one of the few growth industries in the Bay Area legal community. In the '90s, the largest firms had grown to hold more than five hundred lawyers. For them, yearly revenues of over three hundred million dollars were commonplace. And such firms sued and were sued just like any other deep-pocket business.

August Bondoc had been introduced to John Epimere, a senior litigation partner at Patton, Welts and Sims, in the late '70s. An important client had insisted that PW&S, and Epimere in particular, run a case Bondoc was then defending. Rather than fight Epimere for control of the case and client, Bondoc almost immediately began investing considerable time winning over this quirky, autocratic man. And, within a very few years, Bondoc's blossoming relationship with Epimere paid big dividends.

For reasons people could only guess at, Epimere used his considerable influence within PW&S to have Bondoc made the firm's unofficial outside legal counsel. By 1994, PW&S had long since lost its preeminence in the Bay Area legal community. And, like many another failing enterprise, PW&S's appetite for litigation had steadily increased as its prestige and economic fortunes fell.

In the early '80s, during boom times, PW&S had leased large amounts of expensive office space in downtown San Francisco. In 1991, it hired Bondoc to sue the landlord for racketeering. What PW&S really hoped to do was to use Bondoc's lawsuit, and its lurid racketeering charges in particular, to bluff the landlord into reducing PW&S's rent. Unfortunately for PW&S, the landlord was a Wall Street villain of considerable backbone. Bondoc, on the other hand, made more than a million dollars in legal fees before the last appellate court ruled that PW&S had no case. At Epimere's insistence, PW&S had stuck with Bondoc all the way through appeal. But now that the racketeering case was over, Epimere was being forced to retire. And PW&S hadn't hired Bondoc to defend the counter-charges claiming the racketeering case was a hoax.

Looking for the big kill, Bondoc had invested more than four million dollars of his firm's time and money to prosecute a malpractice claim against an investment bank for giving bad merger advice to a Silicon Valley computer firm. The case had been thrown out of court before trial and, unless it was reversed on appeal, Bondoc had not only just lost three big cases in a row, he hadn't even been paid for this last one.

But Bondoc never flinched. Never bled. And, when he pulled his black Porsche into the driveway of his large home in the exclusive Piedmont district of Oakland, he studiously ignored his dark-haired wife's anxious stare.

"You O.K.?" she said.

"Never better," said Bondoc.

"What about the client?" said Peg Bondoc.

"Never better," repeated Bondoc.

"Come on, Gus," said Peg, "save that stuff for the office. I know you're hurting. It won't matter if you admit it to me. I won't tell anyone."

Bondoc felt his rage nearly overcome him. As far as he was concerned, it had been his first wife's insistence on knowing his "real" feelings that had caused their divorce. His thin, intense second wife was usually less intrusive, much easier for him to manage, but she had never as fully engaged him as the sloppier, happier Sammy had. He had really loved Sammy. Bondoc's mind raced. Goddamn jury. Goddamn penises. Goddamn TV. Goddamn wife.

He controlled himself. "If I say 'never better' Peg, 'never better' it is, O.K.? That's the way it has to be. Please let's not discuss the damn trial. It's bad enough I've got to go back into work later tonight."

Peg had just gotten back from Palm Springs that morning, hoping her husband would finally start acting like a human being again now that Frehen was getting close to the end. She couldn't deal with Gus's work habits lately, had even started suspecting he must be fooling around. But now was not the time to probe anything sensitive. She kept quiet, served dinner, and watched him drive off two hours later.

2

New York City
{August 17, 1994}

There were seven people in the New York meeting. After
listening to the expected buzz of recrimination, Ben Laidlaw, the Holliday & Bennett partner who had hired Bondoc,
spoke out. "Look, gentlemen, we did this to ourselves. Blaming Gus Bondoc won't help anything. You're all acting like
a bunch of old biddies."

Alice Greenberg immediately glared over at Laidlaw.
"Sexism is what's basically wrong at this firm," she said, "and
I personally don't think people like you are ever going to
change, Ben." Greenberg was thirty-five, heavyset, severely
dressed. Laidlaw was fifty-six, trim, silver-haired. He had a
well-deserved reputation for treachery, but he was also known
as the ultimate company man, loyal above all to the firm
chairman, Thomas G. Gilhooly, Esq., which august personage
was, at this point in the meeting, staring out a massive picture
window at a truly magnificent view of the Manhattan skyline
as if no one else were in the conference room with him.

General Counsel Ed Zbrewski had the front line responsibility for supervising August Bondoc, but, as usual, he hung

back, saying nothing. Zbrewski was short, completely bald. He had been on the firm's three-person executive board longer than anyone else in the room.

The three visitors present for the meeting sat and stared at Laidlaw. In the silence that followed Alice Greenberg's outburst, one of these three began typing notes, obliviously punching away at his laptop down at one end of the enormous white-marble conference table. That sepulcher-like object dominated the main conference room of Holliday & Bennett's World Headquarters Office on the sixtieth floor of 40 Wall Street in New York City. There were eighty-three separate branch offices of the firm, located in sixty different countries, employing over fifteen hundred lawyers. And all of this was managed by the seventy-eight people who worked on the sixtieth floor. And everyone on the sixtieth floor worked for Laidlaw, Greenberg and Zbrewski. Under the ultimately watchful eyes of Gilhooly.

Sol Weiner, who had just cost Holliday & Bennett twelve million dollars, was not present. He was back in Holliday & Bennett's San Diego office, safely tucked away from the fray. Weiner had been a firm-wide scandal for more than ten years. Lonely, driven, a true workaholic, he was famous for having forgotten his then wife's name during a speech he gave on "Family Values" at a firm meeting in Buenos Aires.

Weiner was a personal disaster, but a legal gold mine. In 1993, more than half the firm's six hundred million dollars in annual revenues came from the Hong Kong office, where more than four hundred and fifty Holliday & Bennett lawyers serviced those actively seeking sanctuary somewhere else. Unlike most refugee populations, the Hong Kong Chinese had money aplenty to pay for the best legal advice on where to go and what to invest in once they were there.

The son of German Jews trapped in Shanghai during WWII, Weiner spoke any number of Chinese dialects. He was both an Oxford-educated English solicitor and a Berkeley-educated American lawyer. Holliday & Bennett's US-bound Hong Kong émigrés had wanted Weiner, and only Weiner, from the first day they set foot stateside.

Holliday & Bennett knew that, absent a miracle, its cornucopia of legal business would end in 1997 when the Crown Colony's franchise expired. Hanging on to its Hong Kong clientele once they had successfully emigrated was seen as vital to Holliday & Bennett's long-term survival. Like other international law firms, they'd already had their share of US office failures in the '90s. Los Angeles, Dallas, even the firm's high-profile Washington, D.C. office—all had closed over the past three years.

Blinded by its growing need for Weiner's book of business, Holliday & Bennett ignored increasingly vocal complaints made over the years by women employees working in any sort of proximity to him. Weiner forced his attentions on whatever female person was handiest once the thought of sex occurred to him. Since he was always at work, this typically happened while he was sitting at his desk. In 1989, Weiner had exposed himself to a cleaning woman late one December evening. She had been paid off and sent back to Costa Rica, far from probing plaintiffs' lawyers and their questions. Only four of the seven people sitting in the room were aware of the earlier flasher incident and how it had been handled. No one else knew anything, not even Bondoc. It had, of course, been kept out of the trial.

"'Jabba the Hut,' that's what the jury called Bondoc," Greenberg muttered, refusing to sit. Dark haired, unattractive, she was known throughout the firm as a tough infighter. "A wimp, that's what Mr. Laidlaw here got us for a trial lawyer. A guy who I now find out hasn't had an actual jury trial in ten years. Ten years. Out of all the lawyers in California, we have to pick this guy."

It was at this point that the Chairman asserted himself. Like Weiner, Gilhooly was licensed as an English solicitor. He had left Great Britain and lived in New York for the past twenty-five years, becoming so thoroughly Americanized in the process that he summered in Maine and wintered in Palm Beach, never considering Tuscany. His social X-ray wife, a born-in-the-wool English Lady, complained bitterly to her friends on both sides of the Atlantic that she could not get Tom to leave the US. Just this year, he hadn't joined her at the opening of the London Theater Season in the West End—though she suspected, and not without reason, that infidelity, rather than any aversion to air travel, was the root of that absence.

Weiner was Gilhooly's personal nightmare. Many of the remaining six people in the room felt Gilhooly's decisions over the years to bury Weiner's sexual peccadilloes were what had caused a twelve-million-dollar verdict to come crashing down on the firm. And Gilhooly felt those same people were not just after Bondoc; they were also after Gilhooly.

"Alice," he began. "Please, just sit down and be quiet. You're not a trial lawyer. Gus Bondoc did a fine job at trial. We all watched him on television right in this room, and we all said so at the time."

What had actually happened was that Gilhooly, who had never tried any sort of case in his life, had nonetheless dictated Bondoc's every courtroom move, including the content of Gilhooly's own live testimony in front of the jury. Everyone at Holliday & Bennett knew Gilhooly was trying the case by remote control. Until now, no one had dared to criticize the Chairman, even indirectly. Certainly, Bondoc had understood the protective coloration he got within the Holliday & Bennett hierarchy by religiously taking Gilhooly's "advice" on courtroom strategies. In practice, this had meant denying the firm ever knew anything was wrong with Weiner.

"The Weiner case isn't the only thing on our plates this afternoon," said one of the three visiting partners. "Excuse me for interrupting, Mr. Chairman, but three of us came out here from San Francisco for the sole purpose of discussing the other case Mr. Bondoc is handling for this firm. That case is potentially much more serious than the Weiner matter—the numbers are bigger, at least, and what we need to focus in on is whether Mr. Bondoc is the right lawyer for the case. The Weiner matter is history; other than an appeal, there's not a lot we can do about it. The Applied Bio matter, the sixty-million-dollar Applied Bio matter, that's something where the outcome's still in the future."

The speaker was Stan Wolmann, the head of Holliday & Bennett's San Francisco office. He had been the office manager charged with baby-sitting Sol Weiner in 1989, when Weiner had frightened the poor Hispanic woman who emptied the trash nearly to the point of hysteria. Wolmann once ran the Holliday & Bennett office in Caracas, was fluent in Spanish, and, thank heaven, had happened to be working late when the incident occurred. He had reached Gilhooly at his club in Manhattan. After a hurried consultation, the two of them had arranged for the return of Ms. Francesca Hernando to her native village in Costa Rica, from where she had, some years earlier, illegally emigrated to the US. To the amazement of her fellow villagers, Ms. Hernando arrived home fifty thousand dollars richer for her brief exposure to Weiner.

All this was done in two days, and Nancy Frehen's greedy, inquisitive lawyer never detected the faintest whiff of cover-up. After first enduring Gilhooly's effusive thanks for his presence of mind in rescuing Weiner from what could have easily turned into a criminal matter, Wolmann had persuaded Gilhooly to get Weiner out of the San Francisco office. Now, on the heels of the $12 million verdict against Weiner and the firm in San Francisco, Wolmann had come to New York believing he still had some unspent credit with Gilhooly left over from the flasher incident. He intended to use that credit to dump Bondoc from the Applied case. With him were the two Holliday & Bennett San Francisco office partners who had been responsible for the firm's work for Applied, up until the relationship had gone sour and Applied's president, Louie Habash, had hired Ben Carpuchi to sue Holliday & Bennett for sixty million dollars.

As soon as Wolmann paused for breath, Homer Rhodes, the more explosive of the two Applied lawyers, jumped to his feet sputtering. "Right lawyer for the case my ass. Bondoc just cost us twelve million dollars for a little weenie wave, and he was up against an unknown. Carpuchi is suing us, me, for sixty million dollars. And Carpuchi is a monster. There are dead corporate bodies all over California that Carpuchi has personally brought down, killed, and eaten. Bank of America, General Electric. Man, you don't have to be a genius to say you want a new lawyer after what's happened to Bondoc this week."

Wolmann winced. Sad little Tom Martin looked up from his computer and winced as well. Martin had worked on the Applied fiasco under Rhodes. Now his career at the firm was entirely bound up, along with Rhodes', in the outcome of Applied's legal malpractice case against Holliday & Bennett.

He had heard Rhodes say "It's our ass" at least a hundred times. And it sure is, thought Martin, looking around the table.

Wolmann agreed with every word, but he knew the approach was wrong. Rhodes didn't have a clue that the Chairman had scripted the firm's whole defense of the Frehen case, so that attacking Bondoc was tantamount to attacking Gilhooly. What was worse, Gilhooly would never assume that Rhodes didn't know what Gilhooly's role in the Frehen case had been. Gilhooly would therefore interpret Rhodes' and Greenberg's attacks on Bondoc as some sort of conspiratorial power grab, a bid to cut short his ten-year term as Chairman. "Probably thinks I'm ready to start blackmailing him over the cleaning lady," Wolmann thought to himself. He silently cursed Rhodes.

Rhodes had sworn he would keep his mouth completely and absolutely shut during this meeting. Wolmann had made him swear to it before he agreed to bring him along, and only Rhodes' "But it's my ass, my career" outbursts day after day in Wolmann's office had gotten him that conditional invitation. In contrast, bringing Martin was easy. All the guy did was work, take good notes, and make no trouble. How the two, Rhodes and Martin, had gotten so closely bound up in a fix like this was unknowable. And now Rhodes had as good as kept Gus Bondoc on the payroll in the Frehen case, and probably saved Bondoc's ass on Applied too.

Wolmann was furious and impotent at the same time. He looked over at Zbrewski for help, knowing Ed would have seen the whole thing. Sometimes, at annual firm retreats over the past eight years, Wolmann would watch Zbrewski watch Gilhooly and be sure Zbrewski could read the Chairman's mind, if not everybody else's. The meeting went on for several more hours, but Wolmann was right—as far as Zbrewski was concerned, it had ended as soon as Rhodes openly insulted Bondoc's handling of the Frehen case.

Zbrewski himself abandoned any thought of getting rid of Bondoc. At least not while Gilhooly's still around, Zbrewski thought, turning the politics of that larger problem over in his mind. There was nothing set in stone about ten years; the Chairman was subject to recall at any annual meeting by two-thirds majority vote. Ten years was tradition, nothing more.

3

{January–June 1994}

The job application she gave Bondoc, Nimmer & Sourwine that March stated that Gina Costello was twenty years old, came from The Bronx, New York, and had attended Hunter College for one year. She had no prior job experience.

As often happened, Gina Costello was first hired by the Bondoc Firm as a temp. She came to work while the law firm's word-processing department was staging one of its periodic revolts. Her performance under the resulting pressure was such that the firm's personnel administrator offered her full-time employment two days into her temp assignment. No effort was made to check any portion of her job application. And, once she was listed as a full-time employee, she immediately enjoyed access to all of Bondoc, Nimmer & Sourwine's various computer databases. As was the case at most civil law firms, internal computer security was nonexistent at Gina's new workplace.

In early January 1994, Gina had been working late at a South Bronx newspaper. The paper's editor, Pierre Esclemond, had gently rejected her latest clumsy attempt at seducing him, explaining that he couldn't bring himself to take advantage of a juvenile crush. Gina, equally stubborn, argued that she knew what she wanted. Then she threw her arms around Pierre and began kissing him as passionately as his unresponsive attitude would allow. He pushed her away.

"God, Gina, now you've gone too far. I'm not going to do this. I'm too old. I don't want you. I can't believe you want me. It's not even healthy for a young girl like you to want someone like me."

"I love you, and you're such a jerk not to enjoy it, Pierre. How many ugly old black men get offered what I'm offering you? You crazy, mon," she'd shot back, forcing a smile from Pierre.

Pierre Esclemond was fifty, and he was ugly. A former Haitian refugee, he was a naturalized American citizen who had published the weekly *Haiti Today* newspaper for nearly twenty years, bringing news of home to the refugee Haitian population of New York City and the rest of the US.

Esclemond had published his controversial views even while he was an illegal alien in constant danger of being deported back home, into the arms of Papa Doc and his secret police. *Haiti Today* had opposed Papa Doc and his weak but equally vicious son, Baby Doc, throughout their terror-filled reign.

As editor-in-chief (not to mention *Haiti Today's* sole employee on more than one occasion), Pierre had been mugged, shot at, and had his apartment fire bombed. When his criticism of the regime still didn't stop, a single-car accident the NYPD termed "suspicious" resulted in the death of his wife. Then, in 1986, Baby Doc had fled Haiti for France, and Pierre's shooting war with the Duvaliers had ended.

That night, when they'd both calmed down, he'd taken Gina out for dinner. He'd wound up telling her as much as he knew about how the Duvaliers had bled Haiti's treasury dry from the 1950s through the 1980s. How they'd hidden what they'd stolen (mostly the cash residue of US aid that never reached the population) in Europe, so that it was all waiting there when Baby Doc went into self-imposed exile. Gina had been quite attentive. She was particularly interested in Pierre's theory that Baby Doc had lately taken to laundering these stolen assets through legitimate businesses in the Silicon Valley. "Once the money hits these new high-tech companies as venture capital, it becomes practically impossible to trace," Pierre had said. "And what's worse, Baby Doc is probably making a good dollar just as an investor. What I'd give to have someone inside one of those California law firms laundering the money. Especially somebody who understands computers the way you do, Gina."

Gina had started programming at age fourteen, using computers to work up detailed asylum applications for refugees passing through the Catholic Charities office her mother ran. At the paper, she'd handled everything from billing advertisers to laying out the front page. When, two months later, she headed for California without telling Pierre, *Haiti Today* missed three weekly publication dates in a row, all due to "computer difficulties."

Gina's father, Tony Costello, had been the first person from his extended working-class Brooklyn family to go to college. After Tony graduated from Georgetown's School of Foreign Service, he had gotten a job at the State Department. As a freshly minted, very junior FSO, he'd been given Haiti as a first assignment. Once there, Tony met and quietly married an attractive embassy receptionist named Eugenia Estime.

The light-skinned daughter of one of Haiti's few prosperous business families, Eugenia saw marriage to Tony as an escape from an arranged marriage with one government official or another, the usual price of Papa Doc's allowing a family like hers to keep its various import licenses in place for another few years. To solidify her position, Eugenia had quickly gotten herself pregnant. But when Tony and Eugenia's relationship became public knowledge, Eugenia's family was furious. Her father complained bitterly to his own government, which, in turn, complained to the US Ambassador. Tony was expelled by the Haitians and fired by the State Department within the same twenty-four-hour period.

Gina was born in Haiti's one passable hospital four months after Tony left the country. Despite active opposition from her family and no word from Tony, Eugenia spent the next several years fighting both the US and Haitian governments to allow her and her child to enter the US. Finally, in 1979, Eugenia and her by-then-four-year-old daughter arrived in New York.

Once there, they found Tony comfortably ensconced in Bay Ridge, selling Hondas and unwilling to admit he and Eugenia had ever been legally married. The only hold she had on Tony, Eugenia soon discovered, was Gina, and then only as a dirty secret. In the urban village to which Tony had retreated after his disgrace in Haiti, he'd be shunned if word got out about a black child. And without his neighborhood connections, the job at the Honda dealership would evaporate. Not to mention the effect on his sex life. No self-respecting Italian girl would touch a guy with a black kid.

As far as Tony was concerned, his relationship with Eugenia had already cost him his chance to break out of his Brooklyn neighborhood and into a larger world. Now she was showing up like a bad penny, all set to make him an outcast right where he lived, and his first thought was how he might scare her into taking the child and returning to Haiti.

In the end, however, Tony was too middle class for violence. The Italian kids who hurt people didn't go to Georgetown to learn how to do it. Or, for that matter, to Brooklyn Prep. They went to Boys or Madison, and they usually didn't graduate—just vanished out of high school and into the life. So Tony informally agreed to pay child support, and Eugenia started life off in the US as a Black single mother of an interracial female child.

In Haiti, Eugenia had been white. Her skin was not very dark, and her black hair hung straight to her shoulders. She had been a prize in Haitian society on account of these things, and had been brought up to hold the rankest kind of racial prejudices against those with darker skin, kinky hair, or more pronounced African features than hers.

Eugenia did not pass for white in New York, however, and Gina stood out as an obviously interracial child. They had little money, especially when Tony remarried five years after their arrival and, in consultation with his new wife, thought it safe to cease making the child support payments. In the North Bronx, where they lived, the shock of the racial animosity she suffered on Gina's account gave Eugenia more sympathy for the Haitians illegally arriving in New York in their thousands than would a lifetime spent in Port au Prince as the wife of some government official or businessman. Eventually, her fluent English and grasp of the French patois used in Haiti led her to a job with the New York Archdiocese. There, like everyone concerned with the welfare of Haitians in New York, she fell under the influence of Pierre Esclemond.

In the closing days of Baby Doc's rule, people began to disappear in Haiti. Eugenia's family was not spared the terror. She had never reconciled with her parents, and their deaths robbed her of the opportunity to do so. Pierre was a source of both information and comfort during that period—his own wife was gone, no doubt killed by the same forces, so his sympathy with Eugenia's predicament was all the more genuine.

Needless to say, Gina's fellow students at Mount St. Ursula High School thought her attachment to the Haitian refugees extremely odd. The consensus there was that the starved, bug-eyed Haitians who washed up in rags on the Florida shoreline and were then transshipped to New York to clean out grease traps, catch rats, and empty medical waste—such people were subhuman.

By the time she was a high-school senior, Gina cared more about Haitian politics than any events in her own country. And after high school, she didn't want to go anywhere or do anything but work for Pierre Esclemond. His defiance of the Duvaliers, and the disregard for his own life that went with it, as not so modestly reported in his paper, had put him in a category by himself. When he told her about Baby Doc's bank accounts a year later, she took it as her cue to move to San Francisco. The man who had helped the ex-dictator protect the money he'd stolen was August Bondoc.

Gina's first few months as a spy at Bondoc, Nimmer & Sourwine brought her quick success. After failing to penetrate the firm's modem connection with Wells Fargo (the bank had adequate security, although the law firm didn't), she soon found the accounting manager's password. It was written on a post-it stuck to the woman's computer screen, under the printed legend "don't forget." Having established on-line access to the firm's banking records, Gina then hacked into the firm's internal listing of all its individual lawyer passwords and picked out those of the highest users. Then, ostensibly working overtime on briefs she had already finished during her normal shift, she spent each night trolling through the firm's billing and deposit records, logged in as one associate or another. In this way, no one saw any spikes in computer usage, and no one saw Gina at all.

Not that anyone ever looked. Security was truly non-existent at Bondoc, Nimmer & Sourwine; the managing partner, Nimmer, didn't have a computer. Avoiding outright revolution in word processing was the only immediate concern of those staff members otherwise charged with managing the firm's computer operations.

Her first research project was simple enough. Within her first few days of work, she had learned how the firm assigned client numbers to cases. Some of these case numbers involved matters that were obviously associated with the Duvaliers, matters like the case brought against Baby Doc by a blind Haitian refugee named Henri Manigat. Manigat had obtained a multi-million-dollar judgment from a Bronx jury after testifying that the last thing his eyes had ever seen were the two black thumbs that gouged them out. Those thumbs belonged to Baby Doc himself. The man had not collected a dime of his verdict, but he had recently found a California lawyer to represent him for collection purposes. That lawyer was making a nuisance of himself, trying to conduct discovery regarding the Duvaliers' possible investments in Silicon Valley. Bondoc was wearing the man out, at substantial expense, and someone was paying Bondoc's bill.

It wasn't quite that simple, of course. She knew there was no guarantee that the bank accounts from which Bondoc's money came belonged to the Duvaliers, as opposed to some untraceable front. Even if the accounts were theirs, and even if Gina could identify them, they were most likely emptied each month. But it was a start, and she thought herself very clever when her database was able to identify three or four definite places where a determined asset trace might find hidden treasure.

In May, she'd sent her first asset identifier printouts by federal express to Pierre, right from the Bondoc office. Then, at lunch the next day, she'd called him from a pay phone and explained what they were and what she'd done to get them. That was the first time she'd had any contact with him since she'd gotten on the plane to California in February. Before that call, her mother was the only one who knew she'd gone to the Bay Area. Gina knew she could "go to jail, pulling a ridiculous stunt like spying on a law firm," even before Pierre began yelling at her over the telephone. All she said back to him was that she hoped he would do something with what she'd sent him, not just act like another nervous, overprotective parent.

"I can't promise anything, Gina," Pierre had said. "The people on that so-called Good Government Commission are mostly as crooked as everyone else. It's a sinkhole. I can't believe you're naive enough to think this is worth risking yourself for." He paused, then laughed. "You crazy, mon."

But Pierre soon promised to help her, in return extracting from her a solemn promise to cease her spying until they talked again. She heard nothing for nearly six weeks.

Then, late one evening in mid-June, Pierre showed up at her apartment. He was literally shaking with excitement, shouting as soon as she opened her door.

"They got sixteen million dollars, Gina! Sixteen million dollars! And they may get more!"

Gina was shocked, delighted, frightened. Sixteen million dollars was a lot of money—enough to make the Duvaliers demand an investigation, to cause her law firm to recheck her resume, to attract the kind of outside computer consultants who would know how to uncover Gina's illegal entry. And Pierre was exclaiming their accomplishment a few feet from the door of one of her neighbors, who worked as Bondoc's personal secretary.

Mildred Conroy, whom everyone called Millie, had told Gina about the vacancy in her own garden apartment complex when Gina had started work. The one-bedroom was cheap, safe, and very close to Millie's identical flat. Inevitably, once Gina moved in, Millie became a full-fledged pest. Pierre, unaware of who might be listening, caught the full blast of Gina's paranoia.

"Why not tell Baby Doc my home telephone while you're at it, Pierre," she hissed, keeping her voice down. "Just what do you think you're playing at here?"

Mortified, Pierre stepped through the door and into her small living room. Gina, meanwhile, walked up and down the sidewalk in front of her apartment, satisfying herself that no one had overheard him. She came back into her apartment grim-faced. Pierre sat on the small foldout sofa bed, looking anxiously at her.

"Jesus, Gina, I don't know what I was thinking."

"It's all right, Pierre. But I'm practically living on top of a partner's secretary, and the woman has developed an intense curiosity about my personal life. Now tell me more— quietly."

Pierre then took her through his first contacts with the Haitian Good Government Commission, how he'd talked with a young consular official who had been particularly recommended by Pierre's various contacts in the Aristide regime, and who had shown only mild interest at first. "All he really seemed to want to know was who you were," Pierre said.

Pierre paused, looked over at Gina to gauge her reaction, then went on. "He was just a kid himself. But he knew who I was, knew the paper, and so he said he'd check it out."

Almost immediately, Pierre had begun hearing rumors from his stringers in Port au Prince that the Aristide government's ministry of foreign affairs was holding an unusual number of meetings with the Swiss envoy. Swiss accounts belonging to members of the Duvalier family, which could be proved to belong to members of the Duvalier family, were said to be the subject of the talks. The Haitians, reportedly, had threatened to publicize Swiss dealings with the Duvaliers, just as Jews were trumpeting Switzerland's relations with Hitler.

Pierre had immediately gone to see his government man, but the Haitian official volunteered nothing. Only his continued interest in the identity of Pierre's source had made Pierre realize that Gina's information must be important to someone. The story had first broken in the mainstream US press that afternoon. According to the *New York Post*, sixteen million dollars belonging to the Duvaliers had been seized from four numbered accounts located in two Swiss banks. These funds represented only a small part of the estimated seven hundred million dollars stolen from Haiti by the Duvaliers. But its recovery represented the first instance of any success by the Haitian Good Government Committee. No explanation as to how the accounts had been uncovered was reported, nor was there any acknowledgment of Pierre. "But it's obvious what's happened—your information did this," Pierre told Gina.

It was true that the government man Pierre had returned to after the first rumors emerged was less than forthcoming about the value of Gina's information. But Pierre already knew the reason for the man's lack of candor, and now he kept it to himself. The Haitian Good Government Committee, in the time-honored tradition of Haitian politics and culture, was intent on withholding the finder's fee Pierre had bargained for before turning over Gina's materials.

Pierre had instantly realized how foolish he'd been. He'd accepted flimsy, unwritten promises of future payment from the Haitian government from a man in a white linen suit. Now, unless he could credibly promise the government man additional information, he'd never see a cent of it. And Pierre desperately needed the money.

Gina didn't know that *Haiti Today* had been unprofitable for most of its existence, and constantly in danger of being seized for debt. To prevent private creditors from shutting him down, Pierre had filed for bankruptcy twice over his twenty-year career. With that tactic, and by using political contributions from the Duvaliers' opponents to pay those same creditors pennies on the dollar, he had been able to keep publishing. But he was headed for a third bankruptcy, one he doubted the paper would survive now that the Duvaliers were gone. The money he might have gotten for Gina's printouts—hundreds of thousands, even millions of dollars—tantalized him.

He had no idea what Gina should do next, though. The Swiss bank accounts had been found through dumb luck, and it was pure chance that they'd led to anything more than sixteen cents. He only hoped she had some other ideas.

4

San Francisco
{August 17–19, 1994}

The San Francisco law firm of Treister & Sullivan was down to five lonely partners. Up until the twelve-million-dollar Frehen verdict had hit, Shane Sullivan had been pushing a deal to combine Treister & Sullivan with Gus Bondoc's firm. But Bondoc's humiliation now threatened to derail Sullivan's plan.

Treister and Sullivan rarely fought, but the Bondoc deal had divided them from the start. Robert Treister, the senior partner, had always been lukewarm toward the merger. And he had, by far, the more prized book of business. Treister's negotiating skills had made him a fixture at most major Bay Area real estate and commercial loan closings. His clients were repeaters.

Sullivan, like Bondoc, was a civil litigator. Civil litigation clients tended not to come back.

In the early '90s, corporate America had come to realize that it was being eaten alive by the very defense lawyers who were supposedly protecting its interests. Auditing legal bills, negotiating fixed fees, use of mediation, and extensive anti-consumer lobbying at both the state and federal levels became the order of the day for most corporations. As a result, Treister's practice was healthy, and Sullivan's was suffering. In the year before the Frehen verdict, Treister & Sullivan had shrunk from twelve to eight lawyers, with nearly all of the loss coming on Sullivan's side of the law firm. A merger with Bondoc, who, with clients like PW&S and Holliday & Bennett, had miraculously escaped the plague otherwise infecting law practice on Montgomery Street, was a critical step for Sullivan.

Treister & Sullivan's conference room was on the fortieth floor of the Embarcadero Center, where it enjoyed a panoramic northern view of the San Francisco Bay. That view had cost plenty, and there were still three years to go on a lease that required rent payments at nearly twice the rate obtainable in the current market. Treister's ego had been actively engaged in selecting their address.

"I'll walk right out of here," Sullivan was saying. "None of us guaranteed the lease on this art museum. As far as I'm concerned, the Rockefellers can have the art and this so-called corporation along with it."

"Shane, you know perfectly well that almost everything here that's at all valuable is mine and not the law firm's," Treister replied with some heat.

Sullivan knew exactly what belonged to Treister, but he was playing on the older man's lifelong abhorrence of the irrationality of the courts. "A Bankruptcy Judge gets to decide what belongs to whom, Bob," he said. "Any of us start taking stuff out of here, then the firm stops paying the rent and we're all buying into a world of trouble. And if we ever do wind up in court with a bankruptcy on file, then I hope you can find all your title documents. And explain away who's been paying to insure it all these years."

Talking right through his hat, thought Gil Levy, Sullivan's younger partner. Levy had never seen Sullivan try to bullshit Treister before, had never seen Sullivan try to bullshit anyone, for that matter. Normally, the problem was trying to keep Sullivan from telling too much of the truth.

"I hate threats, Shane," said Treister, looking ferociously at Sullivan. "I don't know why I have to listen to such things in my own office. Especially from people I'm in business with."

Sullivan, saying nothing, looked around the room. It was dominated by a fifteen-foot light-oak conference table, built on site while the room was being constructed around it. Next to him, underneath an oil painting depicting darkly lit goings-on in a seventeenth-century counting house, sat Levy. Gil was Sullivan's sole remaining litigation partner. Thirty-six, sloppy, overweight, and routinely obnoxious to almost everyone but Sullivan. The staff hated him with a particular vehemence, but Levy got the job done.

The Treister side of the firm was seated further up the table, grouped together. Andy McGlynn was Treister's Levy. In terrific shape, McGlynn was sitting close to Treister; he looked like a bodyguard. White shirt, cheap tie, commuted three hours a day from some godforsaken suburb into downtown. Then there was Joe Sarone, Treister's first partner. Lazy, fifty-six, never had a client of his own, probably never would. Dead weight. Treister had said he wanted to dump Sarone with or without the Bondoc deal. The problem was that Joe was competent, even if he wouldn't work himself to death for you. And competence was an elusive quality— for more than two years, Treister had been unable to find a replacement for Sarone who satisfied him. Sullivan blamed Treister's recruiting problem on Treister & Sullivan's shrinking size, something the Bondoc deal would cure, and Treister had gone along with this thinking.

After the Frehen verdict hit, though, Treister's equivocal noises began. At this partners' meeting, a week after Bondoc had faced the national TV cameras, Treister began by announcing he was "still considering" the Bondoc merger. Sullivan had responded by threatening Treister with dissolution and bankruptcy. Sullivan knew Bondoc. If Bondoc sensed Treister's loss of confidence in him, he would kill the deal.

Mainly, Treister and Sullivan never bothered having formal partnership meetings. Between the two, they had the only significant books of business. No one questioned the way they ran the firm. But the Bondoc merger was something else—fearing catastrophe, all three junior partners tried to reconcile the two men. A hum of conciliatory voices filled the conference room. But neither Treister nor Sullivan spoke again. Both just sat, staring. Ten minutes later, a secretary knocked softly, then opened a door and said "Mr. Treister, Mr. Atwood is on the telephone."

Martin Atwood was Treister's most significant client. He was famous for having used several hundred million dollars of insurance funds to fund a rich man's shopping spree—airplanes, art galleries, gourmet restaurants, expensive homes, and radio stations were all purchased with Banker's Life monies. Making arrangements for liquidating Atwood's exotic menagerie of assets and then dividing the proceeds up with Banker's Life had provided Treister & Sullivan with enough revenue to guarantee it two spectacular years. When Atwood called, Treister took his calls immediately. There was always a chance Martin would come back.

Later that day, Treister and Sullivan met alone in Treister's glass-walled office, the closest to the unobstructed bay view the whole building was designed to capture. Its floor and walls were filled with pieces of exquisitely carved antique Georgian furniture, interspersed with unusually patterned rugs Treister had purchased himself on trips to Africa, India, and the Orient.

But the most impressive paintings and sculptures were all on loan from Atwood. After his last run in with Banker's Life, Atwood now felt safest having his lawyer hold those objects d'art Atwood was particularly fond of for the all but indefinite future.

"Are you in or out, Bob?" said Sullivan, ignoring what he'd heard in the meeting earlier that day.

"I'm still considering the matter, Shane," Treister said.

"You've been considering the matter for months, Bob, and you know damn well I thought we'd gotten beyond that."

"I never said I'd do this deal, and I've never said I wouldn't do this deal. You know that's true."

"I know I've never seen you have such a problem making a decision before. And I'm going to tell Bondoc you've got cold feet. I'm not going to keep leading those people on over at his firm, pretending we've got agreement over here and putting all this time into this deal just so you can remind me you never said yes or no. I mean really, what the hell is that?"

"I'm not going to be rushed, Shane, and I'll tell you this, I'm not going to be provoked either. Whatever problems we have here, we're going to work them out together. Cooperatively. We're not going to get in a fight."

As Treister talked, Shane Sullivan relaxed. He liked and admired Treister, and he appreciated Treister's talent for diffusing antagonism—he'd seen it work dozens of times. At least Treister could remain under control. His calm reassured Sullivan that the situation might yet turn out as he hoped it would.

Gus Bondoc had his own meeting that same Monday. He had shown up to work the day after the verdict, faced down the media, called Gilhooly and Zbrewski, and made a special point of working a full day. Then he took Friday off for an impromptu long weekend. He and Peg had biked furiously all over Sonoma, and he showed up Monday feeling refreshed and genuinely good. By then, rumors were spreading between the secretaries and paralegals that Bondoc's firm would collapse, that Bondoc himself was being sued by Holliday & Bennett. Younger lawyers at Bondoc's firm were openly questioning how Bondoc would pull in new cases after such a public disaster. Kelly Nimmer, the partner who ran Bondoc's firm for him, brought the bad news in.

Nimmer thought of himself as being exquisitely sensitive to Bondoc's personality, and he expected the worst. Mass firings of the disloyal junior lawyers. Some sort of witch-hunt at the staff level. So what he got back from Bondoc surprised him.

"We'll have to talk to everybody together, Kelly," Bondoc said, half an hour into Nimmer's narration of the various panicky rumors rampaging through the law firm.

Nimmer stared at Bondoc open mouthed. "OK, Gus," he replied warily. "We can do that, but who's going to talk? And what are they going to say?"

"I'm going to be the one to talk, Kelly, and I'm going to convince whoever's willing to listen that the sky isn't falling. Now look, I don't like this shit anymore than you thought I would when you walked in here expecting me to fire the whole goddamn bunch. And you're absolutely right in thinking I hate having to explain my business to a bunch of dopey secretaries and kid lawyers. But this Frehen thing is all over TV, and if we fire people for gossiping, then the TV people will just report on that too. And as far as I know, all we need to do right now to hang onto Holliday & Bennett is stay out of the news."

"Listen, I phoned Gilhooly early this morning. From my house to his, 4:00 a.m. California time. And he not only takes the call, he tells me right off that he figures they're after him as much as me. Now that's obviously a good thing for us. So then I told him about hiring Gerry Frank for the appeal, and Gilhooly's on board there all the way. And just now I've talked to Zbrewski, and I think even that SOB is headed back into his cage. It's three in the afternoon in New York and he just finished an executive committee meeting. And I'll tell you what, Zbrewski sees where Gilhooly's going with this. So there won't be any problem from Ed unless he decides to try to push Gilhooly out of the whole goddamn firm, which he probably thinks might be worth a try. But Gilhooly watches Zbrewski the same way Zbrewski watches Gilhooly. Those guys are two scorpions in a bottle, and that battle's not today's fucking problem for us. Get the office together. Say in one hour, in the big room. We'll all have tea and sympathy and I'll be Mr. Nice Guy."

San Francisco's north waterfront was dominated by broadcasters and advertising agencies; the neighborhood was quite removed from the downtown high rises largely occupied by the hundred or so corporate law firms that made up the conventional Montgomery Street legal community, and Bondoc liked it that way.

"Half those firms in those big towers are already on their ass, and the other half will be there soon. Businesses into TV, CD ROMs, Video games, stuff like that, that's the future, nobody like that's going out of business," Gus had told Kelly and Teddy Sourwine the day he'd found his alternative to life on Montgomery Street. Found it by just jogging along the Embarcadero, the road that circled downtown, following the curve of the Bay.

As usual, no one tried to talk Gus out of anything Gus appeared to want. So, later that year, Bondoc, Nimmer & Sourwine headed out for new territory north of Broadway, where no respectable law firm had gone before. One advantage was the use of the elaborate "big room" where Goody Silberman Advertising, the building's owner and main occupant, put on its multimedia pitches for new business. There was room for nearly a hundred people in the auditorium.

Bondoc stood facing his audience from a raised stage at the front of the room. Behind him towered an enormous, darkened TV at which a number of lower level employees stared, expecting a show.

"Thank you all for interrupting your busy day and coming to this meeting," he began, not waiting for everyone to finish arriving. He was the goddamn boss, he thought, and when he called a meeting for 3:00, people had better show up. My time is involved here, and there sure as shit isn't anybody here who can't be replaced.

He still had his Mr. Nice Guy smile on, though, and he looked kindly at his audience. Bondoc had spent the last hour studying a list of names and faces, and now he greeted many of the people filing in late by name. Names he noted for future reference.

"We called this meeting to talk about the verdict in the Frehen case and what it means to all of us. Kelly tells me a lot of you are upset about what happened, and that some of you may even be worried about your jobs. And what I'm here to do is to tell you my opinion of what happened, and then to answer any questions you may have as honestly and completely as I can. Bondoc, Nimmer & Sourwine isn't just my firm, you know—we're all in this together. Each and every one of you is an important member of this law firm."

Ha, thought John LaBelle. Sitting well back in the audience, he recalled Bondoc's much-repeated line at shareholders' meetings over the last ten years: "The only reason anyone has for being here is to make me money." Screw you Gus, thought LaBelle, I just hope this hurts as much as it should.

"Now first, we lost this case," Bondoc went on. "We shouldn't have lost, because the Holliday & Bennett firm didn't do anything wrong. Certainly they don't deserve to pay any twelve million dollars in damages for what happened to Nancy Frehen." Bondoc hesitated, then involuntarily repeated himself. "Twelve million dollars."

LaBelle thought he saw the Big Boss wince at the second "twelve million." Carefully maintaining a somber outward demeanor, he grinned inwardly. Seeing Bondoc wince made his early return from vacation after the Frehen verdict more than worthwhile. I guess I really must hate the guy, thought LaBelle. So why are you still here, said a familiar voice in his head.

Bondoc went on. "I mean, nothing probably happened to Nancy Frehen to begin with. She says that a Holliday & Bennett partner exposed himself to her, but she never proved what happened. It's just her word against Mr. Weiner's. And believe me, everybody knows she was unstable. She couldn't type, couldn't spell, and couldn't cope with any type of normal job pressure. She was just out for the money, pure and simple. She knew the lawyers who sued for her before she ever went to work for Mr. Weiner, and the whole thing was most likely a setup right from the start. And now she thinks she's won because she got twelve jurors to agree with her. Well, that's wrong. This isn't over. There are a whole lot of stops on this train before anybody gets off with any twelve million dollars. First the trial judge has to agree that this verdict is just. If he wants to, he can order a new trial in front of a new jury just like that."

Here Bondoc snapped his fingers. Immediately, everyone looked at the TV, instinctively assuming it would be startled into life by Bondoc's conjuring trick. Bondoc looked back at the screen, then stared straight ahead. His annoyance was palpable.

"This is a live performance, people, put on by management just for you," he said, blending equal parts menace and sarcasm into his voice.

The audience forced a collective smile at this comment, then focused its attention back on stage. No one there doubted Bondoc's ability to bite.

"And then there's appeal. What's happened here is so bad that I just know the Court of Appeal is going to take it very seriously. And I'm not the only one. Gerry Frank agrees with me, and Holliday & Bennett has agreed to allow Gerry to work with us on the post-trial and appellate matters."

Out in the audience, wires in the heads of the brighter lights among the associates began to glow. This was hard information. Many had assumed Bondoc's reputation as a trial lawyer was trashed for good and all. But if Bondoc wasn't fired for losing this, he must be something special after all. Being a survivor was what mattered.

Bondoc stood on stage, watching the announcement of his political triumph over Ed Zbrewski sink in with the younger lawyers. All had high IQs, but few had the street smarts to be considered partner material. Most just kept hanging on, afraid to go elsewhere for fear there was no elsewhere to go. Bondoc never lied to anyone about their career prospects. But working on their insecurities, he often held them in a long-term, profitable inertia while they continued to bill two hundred hours a month for the firm. John LaBelle was his longest-standing victim, but now LaBelle was outliving his usefulness.

"Now there's a lot more I could say about why the jury did what it did and how we might have tried to convince them to look at things differently. But I'm sure you've all seen all the jury interviews. And I just think we got the wrong jury to hear this case. These particular jurors were out to get lawyers and people with money in general, and the evidence and the arguments didn't mean much to them. So I don't feel any sense of personal failure in this, and neither should any of the team members who worked so hard on this trial. It's just one of those things. Now, are there any questions?"

This was the tricky part. He knew some people were volatile. LaBelle had been on the so-called verge of resigning for the last ten years. Embarrassing Bondoc at a meeting like this one, after such a serious reversal, could prove irresistible to someone like that. On the other hand, thought Bondoc, it would end the agony of indecision about LaBelle's leaving the firm.

But there were no tough questions. Just a bunch of softballs, expressions of sympathy for the client, cheerleading for the "trial team," even compliments on Bondoc's tie. About the only thing interesting was LaBelle's failure to ask the sycophantic question required in a meeting like this one. That guy must really be out looking for a job, thought Bondoc, maybe even found one, to stay quiet in a meeting like this. Maybe the son of a bitch really thinks I'm the one who's finished. In an instant, he decided that LaBelle had to go.

5

Richmond, California
{June–July, 1994}

Pierre and Gina had stayed up all night. Sitting together on her tiny living-room couch, they'd come up with nothing.

Pierre, like everyone interested in the Duvaliers, knew that high-tech stocks fascinated Baby Doc. But Gina had seen no indication that Bondoc, Nimmer & Sourwine was handling any of the money, and she had no way of knowing if any of the firm's Silicon Valley clients were Duvalier investments.

"You'll have to get close to someone, Gina. I know it's asking a lot. But it may well be the only way to get any further. And I think this man Bondoc is the obvious choice. He's the only one who ever sees Baby Doc, the only one Baby Doc would trust."

"I can't understand you, Pierre—this whole California thing wasn't even your idea. Now all of a sudden you want me to do Bondoc? What happened to all this concern about my having a normal life?"

She stood glaring at him. "For someone who wouldn't touch me himself, you sure have some funny ideas about me and this lawyer. I'm lonely and I'm scared, Pierre."

She paused. It was after seven a.m., and she had to get ready for work. If she didn't get to the El Cerrito BART station by eight a.m., she'd be late.

"I want to go home and see my mother, Pierre. And I want to get out of here before they realize what it looks like I just did. I sure don't want to roll around in bed with some big-shot lawyer who doesn't care whose money he takes. I can't believe you'd suggest this to me. Me, remember? The baby who thought she was in love with you?"

At 9 a.m. she called in sick. They spent the rest of the day together. By the time she drove him to the San Francisco Airport she'd agreed not to do anything sudden, to keep thinking of ways into the Duvaliers' records, and to consider getting closer to Bondoc.

"But I'm not getting involved with him sexually, Pierre. I still can't believe you'd even ask me to do such a thing. I think you crazy, mon." They'd both laughed at what had become their own special bon mot, and then Pierre was gone.

"Duvaliers' Millions Grabbed By Swiss," read the *San Francisco Chronicle* headline on Gus Bondoc's East Bay breakfast table at 6 a.m. that same morning.

"That's just great," said Gus to Peg, "Jean Claude sees spies everywhere, and now this." Jean Claude Duvalier, one-time absolute dictator for life of the Republic of Haiti, hated the name "Doc." No one around him used it in either public or private. Bondoc's whole book of business was based on his exquisite sensitivity to such idiosyncrasies.

"But what could have happened, Gus? Once money went into any of those European fünds," Peg said, using the Swiss-German pronunciation she'd heard her husband laughingly emphasize whenever the subject of shadowy Swiss money came up, "I thought it never came out." She had been to Europe several times on "fünd" business, taking the Orient Express to Venice, then waiting at Lake Cuomo while Gus attended meetings across the Swiss border in Chiasso. Each trip had been a delightful combination of shopping spree and intrigue.

"Well, the Swiss aren't as reliable as they used to be. Someone like Jean Claude can't expect to get the same protection as an ordinary Colombian drug smuggler or American Mafioso. Too many civilians killed too publicly for even the Swiss to ignore. If his accounts are identified, he's on his own and he knows it."

Gus read through the rest of the scanty, misspelled *Chronicle* article, then slowly read and reread the *New York Times* account of what had happened. It was almost eight-thirty before he left for work.

His last words to Peg that morning were "I don't know how the Haitians figured out where the money was—the newspapers are acting like it was an act of divine retribution. But Jean Claude's going to want someone he can lay his hands on."

No one made the connection between the seized accounts and Bondoc, Nimmer & Sourwine. Large sums were transferred out of Switzerland and into Liechtenstein and Cook Island banks. One Swiss bank officer who had worked the affected Duvalier accounts was struck by a hit-and-run driver and badly injured. And the sixteen million changed hands and disappeared down the maw of Haitian officialdom. Pierre got nothing, and, fearing a public protest would bring Baby Doc's goons down on him, kept quiet about it.

Baby Doc's Swiss bank problems weren't the only thing occupying the attention of the lawyers at Bondoc, Nimmer

& Sourwine that June. The week Pierre visited Gina was also the week that the Frehen case was set down for trial in San Francisco Superior Court. Jury selection would begin the third week of July.

Other than corporate takeover work, there is nothing quite like trial preparation in a big civil case with an unlimited budget in the last month before actual trial. The frenzy of busywork, little of which actually impacts the trial, resembles nothing more than a mass anxiety attack. Associates work eighteen-hour days preparing elaborate memoranda anticipating every evidentiary contingency, partners spend their weekends suggesting revisions to these memoranda, and somehow time passes. Staff are on duty at all hours, and overtime opportunities are limitless. This was how Gina met Gus.

She hadn't actually decided she was willing to come on to him, as Pierre had so clumsily suggested. She'd been sexually active since the semester when both sex ed and driver training were taught, but kinky she was not, and sleeping with some old guy was definitely kinky as far as she was concerned. Still, Gina had gotten a thrill she couldn't describe out of tracing Papa Doc's money, and now her hacking efforts had hit a wall. Nimmer, angered by some minor bank overcharge, had switched out of Wells and over to a Japanese bank whose electronic transfer methods included a dedicated terminal kept in a locked room.

She had wound up routinely working a noon to 11:00 p.m. shift once preparation for Frehen went berserk in early July. 11:00 p.m. actually meant 1:00 a.m. most nights, with the firm buying her a cab ride home to Richmond. One Friday night, however, after she had gone out to the front of the building, the cab didn't show. It was 1:00 a.m., she was locked out of the office, and the security guard inside the lobby had disappeared. Then she saw a black Porsche exiting the underground garage to her left. She ran over to the small two-seater.

"Help," she said, smiling down at Gus Bondoc.

Bondoc had noticed Gina's striking good looks several times since she'd come to work in his office. Law-firm employees tend to be plain or fat or both, self-selecting for their ability to withstand stress rather than to catch the eye. Now, looking up at her, he felt a real tug of physical attraction. It embarrassed him, and he blushed in the confines of his too-young sports car.

Before Bondoc could speak, Gina plunged ahead.

"Oh, Mr. Bondoc—it's you. Thank goodness. I'm Gina, from word processing. I'm stuck—my cab never showed and that security guard is probably asleep somewhere. I don't even know if there's anyone left upstairs, and this neighborhood gives me the creeps at night. Can you give me a lift to BART?"

Bondoc automatically reached for the door opposite him and swung it open, muttering something inaudible in the process. Gina ran around the front of the car, her trim body briefly outlined in the headlights, and jumped in next to him.

Bondoc was never sure what happened next. He wound up driving Gina home, that much he remembered, it being ridiculous to drop her at the train when she lived so close by, on his side of the Bay. But how he wound up inside her apartment, screwing her with most of his clothes still on, that was all a bit of a blur. When, finally, he left her and went home at 5:00 a.m., he could hardly believe he had let himself go like that.

For her part, Gina hadn't decided to make a pass at Bondoc until she'd sensed the older man's tension in the car. He was so nervous he hardly spoke. There was none of the bland self-confident presence he projected at the office during the workday. Gina had dated high-school boys with more self-assurance. She thought about what Bondoc really was, then—taking money from Baby Doc, not caring where it came from or who had been hurt for it. She thought of the day all the Haitian bodies had washed up on Florida's tourist beaches. Infants, mothers, whole families. She thought of grabbing the wheel and crashing his car, hurting him back, killing him if she could, killing herself too if that's what it took. But she did nothing, just chatted. At her apartment complex, she asked him to walk her to the door.

"At this time of night, my neighborhood isn't any better than the one around the office, Mr. Bondoc."

He'd agreed easily, apparently sensing nothing out of the ordinary. Then he'd come in for coffee, for "the drive home." She'd made up her mind to try by then, and the event proved much less troublesome than she'd expected. Bondoc's ego was such that he found nothing odd about a twenty-year-old woman's sudden, intense sexual desire for him. In response to her overtures, he'd taken her roughly, selfishly. Once done, however, he looked up at her, stunned. "Jesus, Gina," he muttered, almost to himself, but distinctly. "I haven't come like that in years."

Funny, she thought, even bad sex put you on a first-name basis. It would have been dangerous to share any whimsy with the panting, partially dressed Bondoc, however, so she said nothing. She just rolled off her couch and headed for her small bathroom, hoping he'd leave before she returned. Instead, she had sex with Gus three times that night, each time slightly more satisfying than the last. Only after she'd managed one small, genuine orgasm, at about 4:30 a.m., did he agree to leave. Her earlier, faked cries of pleasure hadn't fooled him one bit. As far as she could tell, Gus Bondoc seemed to be making a study of her emotional make-up.

Like a blind man sliding his sensitive hands over a raised-terrain map, he was feeling not for pleasure, but to obtain an object, to get to a point. It scared her, finally, Bondoc's emotional intrusion during what anyone normal would see as just casual sex. It was a male intuition, nothing queer about what Gus had going for him in bed, but so strong it might as well have been feminine. Her last thought before sleep was how difficult it would be for her to get information from a man for whom she couldn't successfully fake an orgasm in over three hours of intercourse.

She called in sick that morning. First she was warned her pay would be docked, as she had not enough accrued good time since Pierre's visit to take sick leave. And then she got the inevitable follow-up call from Millie Conroy. "It'd better be good if you're going to stay away long while the Frehen trial is so hot. Word processing is nuts, just nuts, as usual."

You don't know how good an excuse can be, thought Gina, wishing she were back in The Bronx. That was the start of it, her "thing" with Bondoc, just two weeks before the Frehen case was set for trial.

That fifty-five-year-old Gus Bondoc wound up obsessed with twenty-year-old Gina Costello had very little to do with Gina herself, young and desirable though she was. Job pressure was closer to the mark. Bondoc was no superman. He knew ordinary people instinctively didn't like or trust him, and he had a keen insecurity about his ability to affect the "common touch" so necessary in civil jury work.

As a young prosecutor in the '60s, he had compensated for the aversion jurors felt for him by so repulsing them with the details of the grotesque crimes he alone in the DA's office had the stomach to try that the defendant never had a chance. Sitting through eight months' worth of repetitively horrible evidence about long-dead bodies buried in cornfields was not something anyone but Bondoc saw much future in. But by working cases no one else wanted, Gus had become a winner in the DA's eyes. And when he eventually left for private practice, he left with a sterling trial lawyer's reputation.

Bondoc had used that reputation to bluff his way out of countless difficult civil cases well short of making an opening statement to a jury. The truth was that of those lawyers practicing in his specialty area of business litigation, few had ever gone to trial as lead counsel in a serious civil case. Trial-advocacy seminars, internal litigation-section discussion groups, peer-review meetings: all these ersatz things were shields for something a client was never supposed to learn. Montgomery Street's brand of trial lawyers were not trial lawyers at all. Instead, they were "business litigators."

And "business litigators" filed motions and took depositions and reviewed documents and billed hours. But they did not try cases; they settled them. The rare case that made it to court was an aberration, recognized as such by everyone involved, particularly the unfortunate trial judge witnessing a fifty-year-old litigator trying his first jury case with all the aplomb of an elderly pastor trapped in a bordello.

Bondoc knew the angst his reputation as a "real trial lawyer" engendered among his less experienced colleagues in the "business litigation community," and he had played on their anxieties year after year. But now, with Frehen, the inevitable had happened. He had a fanatic on the other side, a guy who'd barely gotten out of some night law school, an ex-cop for God's sake. And behind him, writing motions and keeping the case from being disposed of on any legal pretexts, there was the ponytailed former poverty lawyer who had all the cherished academic credentials possessed by the type of men with whom Bondoc usually jousted.

Bondoc saw his humiliation coming, even if the enormous cash flow generated by defending Holliday & Bennett distracted him for the time being. Then a twenty-year-old girl had entered his already tangled life, something that had never happened to Bondoc before. And, very soon, Gus stopped being in charge when it came to Gina.

Through pre-trial preparation and on into trial itself he continued to sleep with her, calling at odd hours to come over, eventually just arriving unannounced whenever he had the opportunity. Gina's warnings about Millie Conroy's presence in the Richmond apartment complex seemed to make no impression on him, though he never actually encountered Millie there. After trial had begun, he'd moved into a hotel nearby the courthouse. When the pressure of daily trial preparation became overwhelming, Gina began sneaking into his suite. But not without objection, and not every time he begged her to come. Faking orgasm was no longer a challenge, and Bondoc's gratitude for perfunctory sex had become humorous to her.

But she still had no idea how to tap him. If she asked about Baby Doc, her face would betray her in an instant. Lying still and pretending he wasn't fucking her while he went ahead and fucked her just the same hardly seemed like purposeful self-sacrifice.

It was only after she stood him up one night, and got away with it, that she realized the power she had over him. If getting information out of him is too much for me, she thought, at least I can make his life miserable.

6

Superior Court in and for the City and County of San Francisco
{Afternoon, August 15, 1994}

As the Frehen case approached climax, Bondoc watched Jack Rose pace back and forth in front of the jury box. They were in the punitive-damages phase of the Frehen case, and, despite earlier premonitions of disaster, Bondoc was now convinced he was riding a winner. The week before, the same jury had awarded Ms. Frehen the grand sum of $14,500 in actual damages for Sol Weiner's pathetic act of indecent exposure.

Bondoc knew Rose had mortgaged his house to pay living expenses during the long build-up to this trial. Rose's wife was in the audience, hanging on his every word, probably wondering how she would pay next month's bills once the jury had finished off her husband's case with a good laugh and a knowing wink. Bondoc was enjoying himself enormously, and allowed his mind to wander to the happy thought of meeting Gina in his hotel room as soon as court was over for the day. Peg was in Palm Springs, and not due back until trial was over, though he assumed she was watching Rose's performance on Court TV.

"Money," Rose intoned. "Money is all Holliday & Bennett is about. Don't be fooled by their phony apologies—if they thought it would save them money they'd apologize for the Holocaust. The only way to get them to change their behavior and start treating working people with respect is to take their money."

The apology had been Bondoc's idea. He'd convinced Gilhooly that the Chairman had thought of it on his own, of course. But the net result was that Sol Weiner had come right out of the box telling Ms. Frehen that he was so sorry he'd done anything she'd felt was out of line, and that he accepted all responsibility for the trouble it had caused. The apology never actually acknowledged that Weiner had intentionally exposed himself, of course. At Gilhooly's insistence, both Weiner and Holliday & Bennett never admitted that anything wrong had ever taken place. And neither the apology nor the denials could explain away the other angry female victims of Weiner's sexual appetites who had flown to San Francisco to testify against him. But the fact that Rose was so obviously bothered by his apology tactic delighted Bondoc. This case was going to make him a hero to every fanny-pinching man in America.

Rose built to a crescendo of wishful thinking. "How much?" he asked. "How much is enough? How much would be too much? Give Nancy six million dollars. More importantly, take six million dollars away from Holliday & Bennett. Don't give me any more; the Courts won't let me keep it anyway. But give me six million dollars and your job is done."

This guy is certifiable, thought Bondoc. He'd asked for half a million in actual damages, and instead all he'd gotten was pocket change. Now he's telling the same jury how much not to give him. He wondered if Rose would simply go crazy after losing the Frehen case, turn into a new Dan White, the infamous ex-SFPD detective who'd shot the Mayor and a gay city supervisor to death in the 1970's. Dumb shit never should have taken such a stupid case in the first place. How could he expect to beat the kind of legal team a firm like Holliday & Bennett would put into a courtroom? How could he think he could beat me?

7

Huntington Hotel, San Francisco
{Evening, August 15, 1994}

That same evening, Gina was supposed to wait for him in the hotel, taking a rear booth at the Big Four Restaurant if she got there first. Earlier in the day, he'd seen to it she was ordered out on some minor errand to the East Bay just so she could pack a bag and spend the night with him, here in the most elegant of all San Francisco hotels—the Huntington, on Nob Hill.

It was 7:00 p.m. by the time Bondoc got to the Huntington. Jack Rose had finished talking at 4:30. The jury was dismissed promptly, but Bondoc still had to go through the daily routine of meeting with his trial team and calling Gilhooly for a lengthy rehash of the day with that luminary.

Now, finally, with Peg gone and the Frehen trial all but in the bag, he was free. But there was no Gina at the Big Four, and, as the evening wore on, no Gina period. After several calls to her apartment, and an hour-long wait in the Big Four's dark mahogany bar, Gus went up to his room. He was furious with Gina, but he was even more furious with himself for getting so distracted during a trial. Gina never showed. All Gus Bondoc had for company the night before the disastrous twelve-million-dollar Frehen verdict was a dirty movie and his right hand.

8

Richmond, California
{Late Evening, August 16, 1994}

The evening of the disastrous verdict, his mind swirling with thoughts of the jury's hateful comments, the resulting problems of client control, and a wife he knew was on his trail, he arrived at Gina's place around 11 p.m. By then, she'd gone to sleep in front of her television. The doorbell was broken, so he had to knock furiously to wake her up. It was at least five minutes before she came to the door, five minutes for Millie Conroy to peer around the corner and figure things out for herself.

When he was finally in, he said nothing. Just sat down on the couch and looked at her. She saw his need then, knew she was safe from him if she just played the whore. So she sat down on the end of the little couch, stripped off her shirt and jeans, and looked at him wordlessly. He fucked her right there, of course, the world's greatest lover. Then, after accepting her hollow excuse about BART trouble the night before, he was gone. He had been with her less than an hour.

What a switch from that first night, Gina thought as she showered, determinedly washing all traces of him off herself. No phony stories about BART trouble, or faking orgasms then; not when Gus was paying attention. Now he's genuinely freaking out, and I'm more than likely the only one who knows it. And what can I do?

Then her thoughts turned mean. How about ruining his life? How about pushing this disgusting prick right over the edge? What is it I really want out of this? Gina wondered, tossing and turning her way toward a fitful, unsatisfying sleep.

9

{August–October, 1994}

Several days after his initial confrontation with Treister, Shane Sullivan called Kelly Nimmer. After first telling Nimmer how sorry he'd been about the Frehen verdict, asking how Gus was, and making the other required remarks about the vagaries of jury trials, Sullivan admitted that Treister was reconsidering the merger.

The day before, just one day after the abortive partners' meeting at Treister & Sullivan, Sullivan had decided to try shock therapy, walking into the older man's office unannounced.

"Since you won't decide, I'm going to do it for you, Bob. I'm not going to sit around here while you play some mind game that makes you right and me wrong. All I want is for you to fish or cut bait."

Treister had looked up coldly at Sullivan, who hadn't sat. Then, in a voice just short of a yell, Treister said, "So what's changed between yesterday and today, Shane? Twenty-four hours more, that's enough time to expect me to make this decision? Now look, no fooling, I want you to back off and just go back to work for a while. And," he said, biting off each word, "I want you to stop pushing me on this. Do you understand? *Stop.*"

Sullivan had met Bondoc in the mid-'70s, when Bondoc, working on a contingent fee, had sued Bank of America. The Bank had been represented by the hundred-lawyer firm that had employed Sullivan out of law school. Sullivan's bosses had regarded Bondoc as equal parts ambulance-chaser, liar, and thief.

But Sullivan hadn't taken the grave warnings he received about Bondoc from his senior partner at all seriously. That partner was the same man who'd eaten his first McDonald's hamburger the year Sullivan joined the firm, an experience he pronounced "darn good" to an excited audience of other McDonald's virgins. What did a guy who hunted ducks with a shotgun for fun on weekends know about somebody like Bondoc? Bondoc, who was young, funny, and thoroughly charming to Sullivan.

Besides, Sullivan had thought at the time, these old fossils represent every robber-baron corporation they can lay their hands on, so how is it that Bondoc's such a no-good bastard? Bondoc was the only lawyer in the Bank of America case who knew anything about its complicated facts, and the only one who had any appreciation for the pyrotechnics that Sullivan would light off from time to time to make his own presence known.

Eventually, Sullivan's skepticism toward authority resulted in a need for new employment. When Sullivan told him he was quitting, Bondoc came through. For the next three years, the two men had worked closely together— "Bondoc's sorcerer's apprentice" one client had called Sullivan back then, and the description was fair enough.

As Bondoc's student, Sullivan quickly learned the value

of having more manic energy than any of your opponents. He also grew used to the knee-jerk hostility and suspicion that the older man routinely encountered in going up against the San Francisco legal establishment. And almost imperceptibly, he was being drawn away from the mainstream of commercial life, into a netherworld of set-ups, deliberately broken agreements, and embezzlement.

Gus's ego, meanwhile, never allowed self-doubt to enter his mind. He could roll in scum, but it could never sully him. That same ego eventually drove Sullivan away— Bondoc simply refused to allow Sullivan to grow out of his apprenticeship. So Sullivan left Bondoc.

Fifteen years had passed, but Sullivan keenly remembered how Bondoc smarted in defeat, how his personality craved both praise and loyalty, how he admitted no one but himself into the calculation of what it was appropriate to do or say when things got tough. Once Gus heard Bob was out, even wavering between in and out, Bob would be out but good.

But Gus Bondoc had other things on his mind when Kelly Nimmer came in with the news. At nine the night of his speech to the firm, Gina Costello had telephoned him at home. She'd insisted he come over to her apartment in the low-rent East Bay city of Richmond, and the visit had quickly led to sex. The call was so unexpected that he hadn't even brought a condom. His vasectomy prevented any possibility of a paternity suit, but the thought of disease had been nagging at him for the last two days.

"Sullivan just called, Gus. Seems like he and Treister are fighting with each other. Sullivan says that Treister's out of any combination with us."

Bondoc stared blankly at Nimmer, silently trying to recollect a context in which to place his statements.

"Kelly," he said at last, "I haven't thought about that deal since the verdict. But when I talked to Shane before the jury came in, he didn't say anything about any problems. And he's got to be the most guileless lawyer on the planet."

"That's it, Gus—Sullivan says Treister's out, but he wouldn't come out and say why. It's like he's afraid to say that Treister's been scared off by the Frehen thing, like Sullivan thinks he can put the deal back together again if he doesn't let Treister make you mad. On the other hand, Sullivan's telling me that he forced Treister's hand, told him to make a decision or he'd tell us that the deal was off. It's a mess, and a stupid way to try to put a deal together, I'll tell you. There isn't much to like in Sullivan."

Bondoc thought about Sullivan. People with weak or submissive egos like Kelly Nimmer simply couldn't handle Shane, and disliked him for it. But Bondoc's emotional balance wasn't disturbed by Sullivan's personality; at times, he even enjoyed seeing others squirm in Shane's presence.

"Well, so what? We don't need those guys, Kelly. Forget it. Why even talk about it anymore?"

"Hold on, Gus," said Nimmer. "Sullivan we don't need, but Treister is a whole different thing. Don't get down on me for saying this, but this Frehen thing is bad. You never should have tried that case. There was too much publicity and too much chance of getting a black eye, just like you did. The fees were great, and I know you'll hang on to the client. When it comes to that stuff, you're the best, Gus, but there's such a thing as reputation. We have to figure out how to pay the rent while you rebuild, and I'm telling you that Treister's book of business is enough to make me put some more effort into this deal. Hell, we may even be able to get Treister without that fucking Sullivan."

It was startling to hear Nimmer make so much sense. Bondoc had relegated Kelly to the role of friendly, helpful village idiot a few years into their partnership, after realizing that Nimmer was not up to handling the flood of PW&S's high-level dirty work. But Nimmer, Bondoc suddenly remembered, had always been a shrewd judge of character. He tried to put it together. Thoughts of Gina Costello, next to him on a couch, casually peeling out of her work clothes, suddenly flooded his mind.

Sitting across from Bondoc, Nimmer didn't have a clue about Gina. No one did. For all of Bondoc's assumptions about his young mistress's promiscuity, she was as chaste as a nun as far as the office was concerned. The others who had tried her, including one particularly aggressive female partner, had gotten nothing more than a smile and the brush. Nimmer will freak out, Bondoc thought. I'll know what's out in public view when he loses his lunch.

"I can't deal with this right now, Kelly—I've got too much else to think about. You do what's right to keep the deal alive with Treister. When you want, I'll deal with Sullivan. He's easy if you know how."

After learning of Sullivan's call to Nimmer, Treister responded by calling every consultant, merger broker, and headhunter he could think of, putting the word out that Treister & Sullivan was on the verge of a split and that his profitable transaction group was looking for a new home. But it was still necessary to deal with the firm's acutely threatening lease liability.

More than one San Francisco law firm had been forced to file for bankruptcy on account of an overpriced office lease. The pattern was well known. First you downsized in response to a diminishing book of business. While this was healthy, it made people nervous and was terrible for morale. People you didn't want to lose started looking. If they were good, they found new work. When good people left, it made the remaining good people even more nervous. And when you were left with only those few employees who were both good and loyal, you still had to pay the same rent. It was the one expense you couldn't reduce or walk away from. In a legal economy where you weren't the only one suffering, a bad rent just ate you.

The saving grace, for some lawyers, was the professional corporation. It's rumored that, in kinder, gentler times, lawyers were uniformly good credit risks. Supposedly, the old-fashioned lawyer would sell his house and beggar his family rather than breach a contract. No one presently alive has ever met anyone like that, but many landlords don't require their lawyer tenants to be stuck personally on leases. Treister & Sullivan and Bondoc, Nimmer & Sourwine both carried the fine-print designation of "a professional corporation" at the end of their names, and nobody at either firm ever personally guaranteed anything.

But Treister had stepped over the line between law and business years before. A bankruptcy by a law firm with his name on it would jeopardize his banking relationships and his connections to other investors. Both groups, being themselves truly old-fashioned, would look at a bankruptcy of any sort as evidence of Treister's financial irresponsibility. With Treister and Sullivan at odds, control over a bankruptcy filing was in doubt. Of all people, Joe Sarone held the swing vote. Treister had been dumping on Sarone for too long to rely on him now. Short of bribing the guy with a pledge of lifelong employment, Treister was in a box. And there was always the risk that Joe wouldn't believe any promises of better days or, even worse, that there really weren't replacement tenants, at any price. Once Sullivan and Levy walked out the door, even Treister wasn't going to pay $60,000 a month for three more years just for the sake of his business reputation.

After his own consultants confirmed the likely benefits of a merger with a larger firm like Bondoc's, Treister began to reconsider his position. A few weeks after Sullivan's call to Nimmer, Treister himself called Bondoc.

"Gus, it's Bob," he said.

"Well, hello, stranger. And how's your nasty Irish partner?"

"As usual. Right now he's not talking to me, but I hear he's out looking for a new job. Is he still talking to you guys?"

"You know, Bob, I'm not really sure. Kelly's the one doing all the talking to Shane, and I'm not involved except to guide things in a certain direction, if you take my meaning. Anyway, things have really been hectic around here."

Like trying to juggle his nights at Gina's with his so-called home life. Peg knew, or at least he thought she knew. She said nothing, though.

"Whatever," said Treister. "Look, Gus, I've been thinking about what's happened here. I know I've been cold to this deal, and I know Shane's been hot for it. But I also know that you appreciate that I've got a client base that's worth having, and that I've wanted to be cautious about where I land with it. My partner is an impulsive man, and sometimes, even when he's right, he scares people off."

Bondoc was fully alert now. If this deal went through, he was going to have to depend on Treister to help him deal with Sullivan. Not to mention all the other restive lawyers at Bondoc, Nimmer & Sourwine.

"So what are you saying, Bob?"

"You know what I'm saying, Gus. You knew when you

picked up the phone."

"So you're in?"

"You bet I'm in."

"What about Sullivan?"

"If he's ever a problem for either one of us, he's out."

"Done," said Bondoc.

"Done and done," said Treister.

Later that day, Treister walked into Sullivan's office and hinted at a willingness to reconsider the Bondoc deal. As expected, Sullivan virtually gushed with forgiveness and fellow feeling, promising Treister that he would do everything possible to preserve their partnership.

"I've hardly been able to sleep I've felt so bad about what's happened. If there's any way to put this deal back together, I'm going to do it. You know I don't want to be alone in a room with Gus Bondoc. I tried that fifteen years ago and left wearing a pair of suspenders and barrel. I want you to run interference for me over there, Bob. You're the guy I trust, not Bondoc or Nimmer or any of them. I'm not stupid. Without you, there's never been a deal with them for me."

Treister nodded and smiled at the younger man. Fuck you, Shane, he thought. If Gus Bondoc wants to eat your lunch, I'll gladly ring the dinner bell.

A month later, formation of the combined firm of Bondoc, Treister, Nimmer & Sourwine, a professional corporation, was announced in *The Recorder*. The old Treister & Sullivan offices were put up for sublet, the losses absorbed by a combined firm of more than thirty lawyers. When Sullivan's name was deleted from the letterhead to "avoid upsetting the younger partners," Bondoc and Treister both told him to be patient, to wait until after things "settled down;" it would all be put to rights. Sullivan had to live with it.

10

The Bronx; New York City
{September 7, 1994}

Pierre was not himself. That his paper had fallen on hard times was nothing new. But with both Duvaliers gone from Haiti, the paper wasn't just broke—it was fast becoming irrelevant. I'm in a mid-life crisis, he thought. But there was one more dragon for him to slay: the one in a white linen suit who had cheated Pierre out of a very substantial finder's fee.

Since their last meeting, Pierre had kept away from Mr. Edouard Jones, waiting for fresh information to arrive from California. Matters came to head, however, when Jones arrived unannounced at the paper one bright blue September afternoon.

Pierre led the man, dressed today in jeans and a torn T-shirt, into his small private office. There was no one else on the premises. Jones didn't sit down when Pierre offered him a chair.

"These are my work clothes, Esclemond," he said, "and I'm half inclined to start our little meeting by breaking both your arms to show you just how serious I am."

Pierre was genuinely startled. Not even the Duvaliers

had tried violence here, at the paper's offices—they were too afraid of the outcry from the American Congress if Pierre's freedom of the press was muffled in too obvious a manner.

He had a gun in his desk, of course. Everyone below Fordham Road had a gun somewhere. But as Pierre's eyes darted to the drawer, Jones's right hand, wrapped up in a chain, smashed into Pierre's face. The older man fell down as if struck by lightning. His shattered nose gushed blood onto the filthy concrete floor.

Jones waited patiently for Pierre to come around. Then, once he was sure the prone figure was sufficiently conscious to hear him, he spoke, trying to affect a reasonable tone of voice.

"Now look, Mr. Esclemond, you're not dealing with the Duvaliers anymore. Nobody hates us. We're the good guys. The government people here, the feds, the cops, they all want us to hunt Baby Doc's money down. You complain about me, the file gets lost. And eventually, so do you.

"You can't pop out of the woodwork, turn over a sixteen-million-dollar rock, and then expect to be left alone. Now stop playing hard to get and tell me what else you've got before I call for a car and take you someplace private for a more thorough interrogation."

"What about the money from the last time?" Pierre managed to gasp from under the gobs of blood and phlegm that seemed to be drowning him.

"Give me something new and we'll talk about money," said Jones. "You're smart enough to know we'll pay something for a continuing source."

But he had nothing new—this was why he'd been avoiding the man standing over him for the past several months. The one thing he hadn't understood was Jones's willingness to put on some old clothes and come in here to beat the hell out of him.

Muggers in The Bronx killed people every day. Why not Pierre? And why not by Jones? While Pierre hesitated, Jones casually kicked in his testicles.

Only a few minutes had passed since the two of them had first entered the office. Pierre didn't know when anyone else would arrive—probably not for several hours. Plenty of time for Jones to take him away.

For the first time since Gina had phoned him from San Francisco, Pierre was truly afraid. He found himself talking despite every good wish not to.

"My source is still inside," he said. "But she hasn't got anything new. She's working on something real good, but there's nothing concrete. That's why I've stayed away—that and the fact you didn't keep your word about the money."

"She," said Jones, "so it's a 'she,' is it? And where is 'she' located? And what's her name? And does 'she' know about the finder's fee you've got going here, or is 'she' doing it for free? Come on, Esclemond. Start answering some real questions."

Pierre realized at once that he'd put Gina in jeopardy. Despite a rising sense of panic, he stared defiantly up at his attacker. "Fuck you, Mr. Edouard Jones. You've gotten your last free ride from me. You hurt me bad enough, I go to the cops. You kill me, you get nothing. I've spent the last twenty years expecting a beating like this. You don't scare me, you cheap thug."

Jones kicked high up on his chest this time. Pierre felt at least three of his ribs crack; he thought he was having a heart attack. Fortunately, so did Jones—he held back when he saw the look on the older man's face. Killing Pierre was off limits, and now Jones turned and left. Over his shoulder, he said "Call me when you're feeling better, old man."

Pierre passed out. When he awoke, it was to the sound of a siren screaming. He was headed to the hospital, and it took considerable persuading to get the attendant to turn the siren off and take him home instead.

"No health insurance, mon," he said. "They won't treat me right anyway. I'm not dead, I'm not going into some stinking dunghill of a public hospital, let them get me sick with their germs. Just take me home, I pay you for the ride, cash only, no taxes, OK?"

"But you been beat bad, mister," the very polite Hispanic attendant said. "We can't just let you take care of these kinds of injuries on your own. If you die, we'll be sued for sure. You need X-rays, pain pills; you're probably going to have to stay in the hospital for a few days. And what about the cops? Someone's going to have to make a police report."

"That's just it," said Pierre. "I know the guy who beat me up—he's a collector for someone I really owe money to. If I try to get anyone into trouble over this, it'll just get worse for me. You know how it is. Anyway, it's my own damn fault for betting money I didn't have. I been beat lots worse than this before. Who called you people, anyway?"

It turned out an advertiser who'd come in to complain about a misprint had found Pierre unconscious. Knowing there was no reliable public ambulance service outside of Manhattan, the man had telephoned a private ambulance whose card he kept in his wallet. The man had left once the ambulance pulled up, so no police were involved yet.

It wasn't until Pierre agreed to pay three hundred dollars for a ride home that he got his way. No cops, no paperwork. Just home, and then in bed for a week. Or two.

11

San Francisco; Novato
{September 22, 1994}

Gus met with John LaBelle in a private conference room adjoining Gus's office. An hour earlier, the Treister merger had been publicly announced in the main conference room; the new Treister & Sullivan lawyers formally presented; and the synergy of the deal praised to the skies by all concerned. LaBelle had been loudly enthusiastic about Sullivan rejoining Bondoc, telling anyone who would listen what a terrific litigator the incoming partner was.

Now Bondoc was telling LaBelle that Sullivan was, in effect, LaBelle's replacement. That, after fifteen years, Gus would like LaBelle to clear out. To make things perfectly clear to all concerned, Sullivan would soon be moving into LaBelle's cherished corner office, the vestigial symbol of LaBelle's otherwise entirely faded status within Bondoc's firm.

"Sooo," Gus exhaled, "that's it, John. No use crying over spilt milk. We both know it's not working anymore. And with all the rest of the changes going on around here, it's just time to split the blanket, that's all."

LaBelle listened in disbelief. Sure he'd hated Gus for years. Bitched about him humorously, and sometimes not so humorously, to everyone he knew. But he'd stuck it out. Been there longer than anyone, longer even than Kelly Nimmer. Worked himself to death for his partnership. Never let up after he'd made partner.

As much as he hated his professional life, he'd been comfortable in it. Being fired made him see he'd never have left on his own. Just gotten older, hung on. Even worked on things like the Duvalier matters, which, ten years ago, he'd have told Gus he wouldn't fool with.

He left Bondoc's office in shock, then spent several hours alone in his office, doing nothing. That night, at home with his wife in the Marin suburbs, he could barely repeat one word in ten of what had passed between him and Bondoc. LaBelle's wife, Carla, was an ex-assistant DA in her mid-forties. She'd stopped working to stay home with their only child, a three-year-old who'd been conceived in a test tube after the couple had suffered through years of infertility problems. When she'd quit the DA's office, she'd been confident her husband would never leave his well-paying San Francisco job, no matter how miserable it made him. But she'd never considered the possibility that he'd get unceremoniously dumped.

"You didn't talk back to him, did you?" she said after John stopped trying to reconstruct what had happened.

"I don't think so." he said. "The best I can remember, once I figured out where he was going, all I did was listen. And for once he didn't beat around the bush. Just Sullivan's in, you're out, and thanks for the memories."

"My God," Carla said softly. "Fifteen years, a thousand weekends, a million late nights, and that's all that evil man has to say? We must be able to sue him for something, huh?"

"White male lawyers who sign twelve-page employment contracts don't normally get much when they sue, honey. Bondoc is a prick, but he's a paranoid, well-organized, very smart prick. Suing him, it's like trying to eat a porcupine— way too crunchy."

John and Carla's home was in the northern Marin town of Novato. Its cathedral-roofed living room looked out on a horizon only partly spoiled by the presence of dozens of nearly identical structures. Their only child, Claire, played quietly at their feet, oblivious to any tension in the room. After John repeated the word prick twice in quick succession, however, his wife spoke sharply to him. "Keep that up and you'll be hearing her talk that way before you know it. All my nieces and nephews were spouting that filth before they were her age."

This was Carla's most vigorously enforced house rule. She'd worked in a criminal-justice system where the words "scumbag" and "defendant" were used synonymously by both courts and lawyers. She wasn't going to allow her Claire to join in this vulgarization of common discourse.

John made no attempt to defend himself. Instead he went to the refrigerator, got out two bottles of German beer, twisted off both caps, and handed her hers.

"Drink up, for tomorrow we go broke," he said quietly.

"Not funny," Carla snapped back. But then she relaxed, drank down a long swallow, and smiled over at her husband. "We'll get through this somehow, John. We love each other, we've got our kid, our credit's in good shape." Then, turning ever more practical as the news sunk in, she asked, "How much time do you get to find another job? Or is it two weeks notice and a Timex? Is that what the boss man has in mind?"

"Oh no, nothing as sudden as that. They need me to

transition in Sullivan on that malpractice case against Holliday & Bennett, and that'll take a few months. If it goes to trial on schedule, I may even last until after the trial."

"Do you think Bondoc will actually let someone beside himself try a case like that?" his wife asked him.

"Until Jack Rose ate his lunch last month I'd have never thought it. But even Bondoc must be afraid of getting creamed again so soon, and Holliday & Bennett is about the most unappealing client to take in front of a jury you can think of. Assholes who think their shit doesn't stink."

"Great, John. Keep it up. I don't mind being poor, but I do mind having a foul-mouthed child." Then, looking at her husband quizzically, she said, "What about Sullivan? I know you like him, but do you think he was in on this?"

"Not the guy I knew fifteen years ago. He's as guileless as Bondoc is devious, and that's saying a lot."

"People change, John," his wife said. "No one stays a plaster saint, even if they start out that way."

"Shane's no saint. But he just comes right at you. He doesn't sneak around or dissemble. I don't think he could do that kind of thing even if he wanted to. Bondoc's the one replacing me in the lineup—Shane's just the new guy. It's not his fault Bondoc wants me out. He hasn't been around for fifteen years, for Pete's sake. Besides, we're friends."

"Well, how's it going to work?" Carla pressed on. "They didn't part so well last time, did they?"

"Shane walked out upset, that's true," her husband said. "But within a few months he and Gus were back on speaking terms. He just kept his distance from us. Didn't want referral business, only came in when we asked him to because something needed explaining. Bondoc was always singing his praises around the office—'Why can't you do it like Shane would?' He ragged on me and Sam and Deirdre with that one for years. Now, I don't know. I don't know why Shane's back. The rumor is his practice is in trouble because Treister's biggest client dried up on both of them. And coming into our shop with your tail between your legs is not a good thing for somebody with a strong ego. They've already cut his name out of the firm, you know. Did it today after the merger was announced. At least that's the backroom gossip Kelly Nimmer's secretary is peddling."

"Well, good luck with that kind of a start," Carla said. "But we've got to look out for ourselves. You've got to find another job, not procrastinate while you help this guy get ready to try some unwinnable case and Gus Bondoc rakes in the legal fees. Agreed?"

"Agreed," John said, picking up his child and turning toward her bedroom. "Our eating comes way ahead of worrying about what happens to Shane Sullivan."

12

San Francisco; Novato
{October 18, 1994}

John LaBelle found out Gus Bondoc and Gina Costello were lovers the way people always find out things in an office. Millie Conroy wasn't blind and she wasn't deaf, and she'd known about Gus's many trips to Gina's apartment almost from the beginning. Even though Millie had worked for Gus for well over twenty years, he'd never given her a ride home to any of the cheap apartments she'd lived in, didn't even know which side of the Bay she lived on in any given year. All Gus knew about Millie, Kelly Nimmer often joked, was that she was where the coffee came from.

But Millie was loyal. She liked her job and she kept her mouth shut. She even stopped bugging Gina for fear Gina would complain about her to Gus. Then Gus fired John LaBelle, her one true friend at Bondoc, Nimmer & Sourwine. She'd been both Gus's and John's secretary in the early days of the firm, and she'd followed John and Carla's struggle to conceive over the years. She thought of Claire as if she were her own child. Every Christmas she sent her an elaborate handmade sweater, each year's bigger than the last.

So one day, shortly after Shane Sullivan had taken up occupancy of John LaBelle's corner office and news of LaBelle's departure had circulated through the secretarial pool, she asked John to have lunch with her. LaBelle had mixed feelings about Millie. He knew very well that she was someone whose life was lived through others. Her interest in his family life bordered on the unhealthy. She was also nosy, opinionated, and as big a rug for Gus Bondoc as he'd ever been—working late nights, not putting in for overtime, fawning on the boss. Since he was leaving anyway, he had more than half a mind to cut her dead and break his connection with her.

But John was much too good-natured to hurt Millie's feelings. They wound up eating lunch in the back lot of Pier 23, surrounded by tourists wearing the sombreros the restaurant passed out on sunny days. There, Millie told him. She said she'd known for months. She just wanted John to have something on his side of the table if Gus tried to strong-arm him out of the firm without making sure he'd found a good job, one where he could support Carla and Claire. "I don't want Carla to have to go back to work, John, not while Claire is only three. A child needs her mother at home at that age."

Carla was actually dying to get back to work and had plans to hire an au pair that fall, but John didn't mention that. Instead, he quietly examined Millie in minute detail about every reason she had for believing Bondoc was sleeping with his young word-processing employee. Millie had no idea how they'd met, but after observing Bondoc drive into their apartment-complex parking lot one night she'd kept careful note of all goings-on for the past several months. She told LaBelle about Bondoc pounding on Gina's door the night of the Frehen verdict. She hadn't been getting much sleep, she said, trying to keep up with those two.

By the end of the lunch hour, neither of them had eaten much. LaBelle was dumbfounded. Gus Bondoc was the most cold-blooded, reptilian human being he'd ever known, physically ugly and thought of as asexual by his colleagues, men and women alike. And yet, somehow, he'd gotten a healthy-looking woman employee, barely out of her teens, to screw him day and night for months. And no one even knew it was going on. That amazed LaBelle, who knew the office gossips were usually as adept as any secret intelligence service. Millie, meanwhile, was glowing with a newfound sense of importance. She looked at LaBelle and said. "You know I'm risking my job telling you this, John. It can't come out it was me who told."

"Relax, Millie," LaBelle replied. "It's not going anywhere beyond this table. And it'll come out on its own soon enough—these things always do. What I'm curious about is this Costello woman. Who is she? And why would she want to get so involved with Gus?"

"Well, I've checked her personnel file, and there's nothing strange there," said Millie. "But you know, right after she moved into that apartment I found for her, there was something odd. I know you're going to think I'm a terrible snoop when you hear this, though." Millie stopped speaking and looked across the table for reassurance.

"Come on, Millie—I've known you for years, and we're still best friends," John said. Snoop doesn't begin to cover it, he thought to himself, imagining Millie lurking in the bushes outside Gina's apartment.

"Well," Millie relented, after studying John's face, "one night a strange black man came into the complex. And there aren't that many blacks where I live," she said, somewhat proudly. "I know all of our black tenants by sight. And this black man didn't really know where he was going, and banged on a couple of other doors, asking for Gina. I opened my door a crack so I could hear better, and when he finally got to Gina's apartment I heard some of what they said to each other before they went inside." She stopped, waiting for a prompt from John.

"And?" he said.

"And, this black man, she called him Peter, or maybe it was Pierre, he said something about millions of dollars, that 'they'd caught sixteen million dollars.' Anyway, it was something about a lot of money, and then Gina dragged him inside. I couldn't hear anything else, even though I went out and stood by her door for a while."

And probably used a stethoscope, John thought. "Do you think it had anything to do with work?" John asked her.

"Who knows," Millie said. "I mean, she's just in word processing—those people don't have any inside information, do they?" Word processors were the etas of office life, kept in their own pen, never socializing with the rest of the staff, left to pound away at an inexhaustible supply of briefs and transaction documents.

The significance of Pierre's words didn't immediately occur to either John or Millie. Millie read romance novels on her BART ride into work; John took the sporting green with him on the bus every morning, leaving the rest of the *Chronicle* for Carla. Neither had seen the news articles about Baby Doc's missing money. It wasn't until John got home to Novato that night that he got an inkling of how serious the situation with Gina might be.

He'd called Carla from the office right after lunch, dropped the bombshell that Gus was almost certainly having an office affair, but refused to go into much detail despite his wife's considerable urging that he tell her the whole story right there on the phone.

"I just can't, hon," LaBelle said, "Sullivan's on my ass for about fifteen different things in this Holliday & Bennett mess. And besides, I don't want someone bursting in here while I'm talking about Bondoc's love life. I'd be out on the street within an hour."

He didn't say his phone might be tapped. He didn't even really think such things were possible. All the same, as soon as he hung up, he was sorry he hadn't called Carla from his cell phone. Back home, Carla found herself entirely distracted. She cancelled her hairdresser appointment and put the baby in a stroller. There must be some way to use this, she thought, starting out on a long walk, some way to get Bondoc back for being such an asshole to my family. She needed to get every scrap of information from her husband, maybe even have that awful Millie Conroy come up for a meal and let her slobber all over poor Claire.

By the time John got home from work, shortly after seven, she had the baby down and two cold beers waiting on the kitchen table. John looked annoyed when he realized Claire was already asleep—this was usually his time with her—but one look from Carla and he realized he'd better just drink his beer and tell all.

And Carla enjoyed it right up until John got to the strange black man boasting about having caught sixteen million dollars of somebody's money.

"Jesus, John," Carla burst out profanely, "sixteen million! Don't you remember? Sixteen million is what Baby Doc lost last summer, when the Swiss gave up some of his money to the Haitians."

John looked at her blankly.

"Oh, excuse me, I forgot, all you know is who won the last 49ers game. For a Princeton grad, you certainly are well read, aren't you?"

"Look, Carla—just because I'd rather read sports than the rest of that local rag they call a newspaper out here, don't make me out to be an idiot. If the *New York Times* ever makes its way up to Novato, maybe I'll take an interest in world news again."

"OK. OK. You know I think the *Chronicle* is just the *Enquirer* in drag. But they do run articles from the AP every once in a while. And back in June there was a story on the front page about how the Haitians had found some of Baby Doc's money in Switzerland and embarrassed the Swiss into giving it up. And I swear it was sixteen million dollars. I just know it was."

John started thinking rapidly. He was pretty sure Gina had been working for the firm since at least April—he remembered noticing her in the hallways around springtime. How much time did someone need to infiltrate the firm's computer system? What kind of security was there, anyway? He thought about Kelly Nimmer's aversion to computers. Not much security, he concluded. But why Gina, and why Baby Doc? Gina wasn't exactly white, but Haitian? She looked more Sicilian than anything else. And Costello, that was an Italian last name, wasn't it?

Then John wondered if Gus himself was somehow mixed up in ripping off Baby Doc. He'd lose his law license, even if he evaded jail time. And knowing the Duvaliers, Gus's physical safety could suddenly become very questionable.

Carla was staring at him now. "Are you thinking what I'm thinking?" she said.

"I don't know," her husband said. "But if Gus is mixed up

in Baby Doc's sixteen million dollars disappearing, then he's in a world of hurt."

"Of course he's mixed up in it," his wife replied, "He's sleeping with someone who probably made it happen, and that's all Baby Doc or any other garden-variety thug like that is ever going to want to know. Your friend Gus Bondoc is headed for the fall of his life, and we don't have to do a thing. Personally, I hope he winds up dead in an alley." Carla's background as an Oakland DA had given her enough exposure to such various types of street mayhem that the idea of Baby Doc's having Bondoc killed was not at all remote.

"Shit, Carla, all he did was fire me. I don't hate him that much. And I'll tell you something else, no way is he a perp here. Gina's got him buffaloed, that's all, and he has no idea she's the source of any problems for Baby Doc. She's a nice looking twenty-year-old woman, that's all, and all Gus is guilty of is going out and rolling around in some new pussy."

Carla looked at him sharply. "Watch your mouth. Gus is disgusting, and he's a moral cretin to boot. If you had more backbone, you'd hate him as much as I do."

"But I don't want it on my conscience if Gus gets hurt," John said. "I don't care what he's done to me. He doesn't deserve that."

John's willingness to forgive Bondoc for just about anything had driven his wife to distraction for years, caused row after row when he refused to stand up for himself. And now he'd been fired and he was still protecting the bastard, she thought. The dirty scumbag. What do we care what happens to him?

"Do you love me?" she said. "Do you love Claire?"

"Of course."

"Then don't do anything sudden. Get some advice from another lawyer, someone you really trust. Maybe Sullivan, if you're sure he's really OK, but remember this thing is so bad it could be dangerous for anybody who knows about it. And make sure that Millie keeps her mouth shut. She never should have told you. I wish I didn't know. And don't play private investigator, stay away from this Costello woman, don't do anything except maybe ask someone else what you should do. And then talk to me before you go off the deep end. I mean it, John—screw the pooch here and Claire and I are out the door."

13

Peg Bondoc wasn't an idiot. Even without living next door to Gina, she'd figured out what was going on between her husband and his new mistress within a few weeks of the affair's beginning. All it took was a call to a private investigator and she had all the particulars she could possibly want. The real question was what to do about it.

She rarely confronted Gus. In return, he let her raise their two kids pretty much as she chose, never criticized her spending, and let her pick what they watched on television. But despite Gus's apparent domestic passivity, Peg knew he possessed a very controlling personality.

Sammy, Gus's first wife, had foolishly picked at his reserve, and she'd been manipulated into an unwanted abortion and an eventual divorce for her trouble. Peg knew Gus would be furious if he found out how she'd satisfied herself he was having an affair. The marriage wouldn't last a month if Gus ever discovered that he'd been followed to Gina's apartment, and that Gina's apartment manager had been bribed into copying Gina's rental application for Peg's investigator.

So she'd done nothing with her proof—no angry scenes, no tears. Just life as usual while she waited for things to blow over. She was sure he'd never done this to her before, and all she could think was that the Frehen case had pushed Gus around the bend.

By late October, however, Peg was losing heart. Gus was seeing Gina three or four times a week, making little effort to explain his absences. And Peg was beginning to consider Gus's involvement with Gina a real threat to her marriage.

He must think I know something, she thought. Surely he can't think I'm so stupid I don't know what he's doing. Maybe not with whom, and maybe not why, but the rest is too obvious not to call him on it. I've got to do something or I'm going to wind up in divorce court anyway. And the kids don't deserve that; somebody has to hold this marriage together, at least until they're in college.

Gus and Peg's two children, Thomas and Elizabeth, were both high-school students. As the children neared graduation, the divorce rate in both their classes approached 50 percent. The kids whose parents split nearly always had their grades and test scores drop badly. To Peg, divorce meant second-class colleges and second-class lives for both her kids. That was what made her as angry as she'd ever been in her life.

The same week Millie Conroy told John LaBelle about Gus and Gina, Peg confronted her husband about where he was spending his evenings. Since Gina had listed Bondoc, Nimmer & Sourwine as her employer on her rental application, Peg decided to put Gus on the defensive by unexpectedly showing up at his office just before lunch. Gina was in his office dropping off a long memorandum from Sullivan about the Applied case when Peg brushed Millie aside and walked in unannounced.

"Hello, Gus, want to have lunch?" Peg said, studying Gina, who got flustered and left. So that's what she looks like, thought Peg. Cunt.

Gus looked up from Sullivan's memo, saw Gina retreat, and then stared at Peg. "What's going on, Peg? You never said you were coming in this morning."

Peg looked him right in the eye, "You know what's going on as well as I do, Gus—you and that girl. So the only question is, do we talk about it here or do we go to lunch and talk it over there?"

Peg wasn't speaking loudly, and even with the door open, Millie probably can't hear this, Gus thought. But Peg was so angry she was liable to start raising her voice any minute. Christ, what a situation, right in the office. He suddenly realized his affair with Gina was over. He wasn't going to have a choice about it.

Wordlessly, he got up from his desk, grabbed his suit coat, and led Peg out of his office, down the hall past the row of view offices and the conference room and into reception. "I'm taking Mrs. Bondoc to lunch, Jean. May even do some shopping," he told the receptionist as he kept walking towards the elevators, Peg in tow. Normalcy, just keep it steady, don't panic. No scenes, no publicity, for God's sake. He could just imagine the effect a well-publicized office affair would have on his book of business after the Frehen disaster. Even Gilhooly couldn't save him from Zbrewski then. Holliday & Bennett would be history, and he'd be a laughingstock. Probably be part of a Jay Leno monologue. Fucking Peg, he thought as he pushed the down button, what does she care what I do? Who the hell does she think she is, messing around with me like this?

They walked over to Fog City. There were booths there,

so even though it was crowded, there was still some privacy. Short of going home to talk, this was as safe a place to discuss something sensitive as Bondoc could think of.

"I'm not going to deny anything, Peg," he started out. "But whatever I'm supposed to have done, do you mind telling me why you're forcing me to discuss this with you in the middle of a working day? What good does it do to drag out my private life in front of the people at the firm?"

She ignored him. "Who is she, Gus? And what's so special about her that you'd pull a stunt like this on me and the family?"

He ignored her, instead asking Peg the one question she'd hoped to avoid. "What do you mean, her? You know who Gina is, that's certainly obvious. What I'm curious about is how you know so much about her without asking a single question all these months. What've you been doing with your time, Peg?"

There was real menace in his voice now, just as she'd feared. Gus was no stranger to surveillance. As a young lawyer just out of the DA's office, he'd spent every breakfast for a few weeks monitoring an opposing lawyer's CB radio frequency, listening to the guy discuss one crooked thing after another on his way into work. Eventually. Gus had enough to make a call to the US attorney, and Eddie Fitz had been arrested for dealing in illegal Indian artifacts. Disrupted Eddie's trial preparation but good, Gus had. Made obtaining a cheap settlement easy.

Only one thing to do if it comes to this, she'd decided. Kick him right in the balls. "One more stupid question, Gus, and I'm going to finish lunch with my divorce lawyer. And he's going to make a call to the newspapers. So let's talk about what's left of this marriage or shake hands and come out fighting. Get it?"

Gus got it. Over the next hour, the two of them made a deal. Gus was finished with Gina. She'd be permitted to stay on the job if she wanted; even Peg understood how expensive firing her might be for the firm. If she became difficult, she'd be offered a normal severance package, sweetened by a much larger private settlement from Gus. Gus wouldn't stray again. Peg's kids would still have a mother and a father and would score in the 1500s on the SATs. Neither Peg nor Gus knew what Gina had really been up to. Nor did they know Millie Conroy and John LaBelle were aware of the affair. To them, it was all done, simple as that.

14

{November, 1994—March, 1995}

Edouard Jones was on his own. The sixteen million his government had recovered from Baby Doc had slid down the throat of Haitian bureaucracy. No word of thanks had been passed on. He was regarded with contempt by them—an amateur who'd failed to protect himself.

Now Jones intended to get whatever additional scraps of information he could. And this time he would sell that information to the highest bidder. Altruism, especially accidental altruism, was for fools, and Mr. Jones was not going to be fooled twice.

Beating Pierre Esclemond half to death had been reckless. But Jones was not a trained investigator. In Haiti, when Jones's father, Colonel Francois Jones, wanted information, he beat it out of people. If that didn't work, he murdered them and found someone else to question. People in Haiti knew this, so they rarely refused to talk. Jones admired his father very much.

While he now knew Esclemond's source was a woman, he didn't know what to do with that information. Going back and beating the old man again was one solution, but Jones worried that he'd kill Esclemond before he'd get what he needed from him. That would leave no link to the source, and such clumsiness would not meet with his father's approval. He could call his father in, but that was dangerous. Jones did not want to be left with nothing again.

The week after the beating, while Pierre was still holed up alone and untended in his Bronx apartment, Jones hired Kroc Associates to investigate what he described to them in a letter on Haitian Consulate stationery as "information leaks negatively impacting on certain Haitian citizens who I do not wish to further identify but in whom the Haitian Consulate has an interest." This high-sounding letter, along with his diplomatic credential, were sufficient to allow him to engage the Kroc firm without paying a retainer and install a surveillance team around Esclemond's apartment.

Within two days, Pierre was observed leaving his apartment to place a telephone call from a local bodega. A day later, the bodega's owner was paid three hundred dollars, and Gina's home number was retrieved from his phone records. The Kroc office in San Francisco was then sent to watch over Gina's apartment.

By mid-October, Jones knew the identity of Gina's mother; knew her connection to Esclemond; and knew she was sleeping with Gus Bondoc. And Jones knew Bondoc was Baby Doc's lawyer on the West Coast.

His first thought was that Bondoc had betrayed Baby Doc to the Haitian Good Government Commission for a share of the sixteen million. But the sexual relationship didn't make sense—it tied him too closely to Baby Doc's betrayal. According to Kroc, Bondoc was cunning enough to understand that.

Not that it mattered—Jones had struck gold, and he

knew it. Whether he blackmailed Bondoc or went to Baby Doc, he stood to recover much more than a finder's fee. His father would envy him.

That same fall, Shane Sullivan moved into John LaBelle's corner office with the bay view. His friend LaBelle had been moved to a much smaller office, with no view of anything, a few days before. Sullivan was notoriously insensitive to office politics and hurt feelings, but even he realized that LaBelle had suffered a serious loss of prestige. But everything had been arranged before Sullivan got there, and LaBelle's old office was one of the few large enough to make the point Sullivan felt he needed to make. If he wasn't a name partner, he sure and be damned was a senior partner. The existence of his insecurity in this regard did not hit him for several months.

Sullivan found LaBelle's detailed memo on *Applied Biological Medical Devices Corporation v. Holliday & Bennett* waiting for him in his new corner office. Trial was scheduled for April, barely six months away. Sullivan told his new secretary to hold his calls and shut his door.

Several hours later, he thought he had a good picture of what had gotten Holliday & Bennett into the litigation. Homer Rhodes and Tom Martin had taken a small royalty dispute between Applied and one of its inventor/physicians and escalated it after they'd uncovered evidence that the doctor had been communicating with one of Applied's biggest competitors. The case was sufficiently speculative that Sullivan suspected Rhodes' advice to prosecute was motivated more by a desire for hourly billings than any strong belief in the merits.

Apparently Rhodes had always been able to settle his weaker cases gracefully. And for several years, during the case's pre-trial phase, Dr. Thomas Dolan, M.D., had done nothing out of the ordinary in defending himself against Applied. He'd employed the small law firm he used in all his affairs, and they'd dutifully followed Holliday & Bennett associates all over the country, taking depositions, building up huge files and equally large bills.

The more than ten million dollars Applied had paid Holliday & Bennett over the years leading up to trial had all been justified by Rhodes' predictions of a sixty-million-dollar judgment against Dolan, a man worth several times that. LaBelle's memo said the firm's working assumption was that a settlement of at least twenty million could be negotiated before trial--a result Rhodes was confident Applied would accept as a victory.

Nothing turned out as expected. Four months before trial, Dolan hired a new lawyer. That new lawyer ignored one settlement proposal after another. Growing desperate, Rhodes turned to the court-appointed retired judge for help. He tried to convince Dolan that Dolan had to settle, that no sensible person in his position would trust a Bay Area jury. But every time Rhodes agreed to something Dolan appeared to want, Dolan asked for another concession.

It became obvious even to Rhodes that Dolan had been stringing him along—there was no choice but to try Applied's case. But because he'd always considered settlement inevitable, Rhodes didn't begin his trial preparation until settlement discussions began to break down. Applied's experts were hired late, and haphazardly. One of them had a widower father who suffered a stroke, lingered for a month, and then died. The distraught expert showed up at his twice-continued deposition unprepared and near hysteria.

Dolan's new lawyer gleefully took advantage of the

situation. After shedding the requisite crocodile tears, he asked for exclusion of the expert's testimony on damages. Two days later, the court granted Dolan's request.

Still, losing the trial hadn't been easy. The trial judge was so thoroughly poisoned by his retired colleague's reports of Dolan's treacherous refusals to settle that, by trial time, he was ready to see to it that Dolan regretted the decision to press on. That judge began the trial by harshly interrupting and criticizing Dolan's lawyer during his crucial opening statement.

But then Rhodes refused to take Dr. Dolan on early. Sure, losing the expert was bad, but nobody ever won a case with experts. The bold move, the right move was to put Dolan on the stand first, right after he'd gotten steamed at the trial judge for trying to screw him so openly. Cross-examine Dolan forcefully enough and what the jury sees first is an old man mad at the world for no apparent reason—someone who doesn't like the trial judge any more than the judge likes him.

But instead, Rhodes took the coward's approach and stalled, probably thinking that the trial judge's hostility would scare Dolan into settlement. The first five witnesses were fillers, the trial boring, and soon the trial judge moved past his impatience with the case.

By the time the case got down to its merits, Dolan was calm. He made a respectable showing on direct. Despite his all too obvious arrogance, the jury liked him. When he insisted he hadn't agreed to suppress medical technology— Rhodes' basic charge—they believed it. Rhodes crossed him in a thorough, workmanlike way, but he never got to Dolan.

After a four-month trial, the jury cut Rhodes' throat in two hours. Two days later, Holliday & Bennett was fired, their last and largest invoice left unpaid. Applied sued Holliday & Bennett for legal malpractice within the year. That case had remained dormant while Applied pursued an appeal against Dolan.

The decision on appeal had come down a year ago, and it was a disaster for Holliday & Bennett. Applied's appeal briefs focused almost entirely on the exclusion of experts as grounds for reversing the jury verdict.

"Pure set-up," Sullivan told Bondoc after reading the decision. "Applied knew the appeal was hopeless, so all they wanted out of it was a court blaming Holliday & Bennett for doing something closer to malpractice than just being too chicken to put Tom Dolan on the stand first."

Rhodes was not a terrible lawyer. After reading over the whole of the Dolan transcript, Sullivan considered the man merely mediocre, not incompetent. But he was a mediocrity who had let himself be trapped, and his career was finished.

How am I going to turn this mess into something positive? thought Sullivan. As the Court of Appeal had clearly said, Homer Rhodes' failure to prepare his damages expert for deposition was materially negligent. This meant the only defense Holliday & Bennett had to the malpractice claim was that Applied's case against Dolan hadn't been worth much to begin with. While this had the obvious virtue of being true, it left Sullivan wondering how he could explain away Holliday & Bennett taking Applied's ten million dollars.

Spending that much to chase ghosts had to have involved more than greed and gullibility. Sullivan needed to show that Applied and its single-minded president, Louie Habash, bore some responsibility for what had been done.

But could Holliday & Bennett really get away with blaming Applied for bad judgment? All Sullivan had to make a case were the quarterly status reports Rhodes had given Habash. Those letters, while acknowledging the risk in going after Dolan, had too much cheerleader language for Sullivan's taste. It was going to be too easy for Applied to read Rhodes' most optimistic prose to a jury and then finish up with a description of the Court of Appeal hanging a rose on Holliday & Bennett for sloppy pre-trial work.

Unlike Rhodes, Sullivan knew Applied was a bad case; five years earlier, he'd been caught in another one. He'd gotten so cocky after winning a series of pre-trial motions that he'd refused a half-million-dollar settlement. After the five-million-dollar verdict came in the wrong way, Sullivan went into shock. He'd hired Gerry Frank to bail him out, of course, and Frank had managed to cut a deal at one million. But the client had very nearly sued Sullivan, and as far as Shane was concerned, he'd deserved a malpractice case.

Shane was excitable. And that excitability had painful roots. Shane had completely broken down early in his last semester at Harvard. He'd spent most of that winter on a psych ward out at McLean Hospital in Belmont. At times he was so tranked on Thorazine he'd have been happier being lobotomized. The initial diagnosis was schizophrenia. He'd lost his Army ROTC commission and had to repeat a term the next year.

Somehow, he'd recovered. His delusions—so vivid he could still remember them as well as any of the real events in his life—broke during a group-therapy session. His resident on the training ward soon noticed the change, cut his medication way back, and Shane was out on the street in short order. He was broke, the Wellesley girl he'd been in love with recoiled in horror when he called her on his first day out, and his friends were all about to graduate without him. But for a while the joy he got from ordering breakfast at the local greasy spoon and afternoon trips to the movies made up for all the rest.

The next school year proved so full of painful memories that Sullivan gave up any hopes of Harvard Law. He wound up as far west for law school as his ratty Mustang would take him, at Berkeley's Boalt Hall, where the sun shone all winter long and nobody knew or cared what had happened to him as an undergraduate.

He'd had enough brushes with psychiatry since then to understand what had happened to him. His family tree was loaded with drunks and suicides, portents of bipolar disorder. Unlike schizophrenia, it was something you could nearly recover from. It still left you odd, made you hyper under stress. Robbed you of your judgment just when you needed it most.

Great disease for a trial lawyer, Sullivan often thought. But he believed he had it licked. Some manic-depressives ended up as drunks to compensate for their otherwise unmanageable highs; Shane had quit drinking at thirty. Instead, he beat his demons out in the gym. Still, he'd lost his composure at trial more than once, and every so often a bad result sent him to some shrink's office.

Now he was being forced to handle a case that seemed almost unwinnable. Bondoc loved the short-term cash flow it was generating, and had shown no concern for the fallout a verdict even larger than Frehen would cause Sullivan. What was worse, Rhodes was going to be completely unmanageable as a witness—from their brief introduction, he seemed like he might be the most obnoxious lawyer Sullivan had ever encountered. His sidekick, Tom Martin, was an OK guy, at least—sympathetic, malleable, someone who would do what it took to win, if there was a way to.

Sullivan decided that he'd quit his new firm unless he could truly run this case. But he knew Bondoc would never let that happen—Holliday & Bennett would remain under Gus's ultimate control until the last dime had been wrung out of them. The one pledge he'd extracted from Bondoc was that the older man wouldn't poach the trial work. Unfortunately, that pledge Bondoc might keep, as Applied was so obviously poisonous that Gus wouldn't dream of risking another hit to his professional reputation by trying it.

If he was going to head for the exits, though, where was he going? And more importantly, what was he taking with him? As lousy a case as Applied was, it still might represent a ticket into partnership: cash flow, even short-term cash flow, was the only credential accepted at many of the firms worth joining. But I'm mobile only if I can convince Holliday & Bennett to stick with me when I make a move, Sullivan thought.

He considered where he might land next. The obvious choice was Baum, Baum & Cooper; he'd been referring work to them for years. John Cooper had been Sullivan's own lawyer, and had saved him from a malpractice claim more than once. Cooper's firm was losing lawyers, and rumored to be in trouble because of it. This was good and bad—it made obtaining a partnership easier, but it wasn't clear what that would be worth.

Still, there was no harm in talking. He and John were friends; they had lunch every couple of months. Sullivan assumed Cooper was disturbed by his move over to Bondoc's firm—he'd already told John that Bondoc had cut the Baum firm out of a referral.

So one morning in January he called John and told him he'd like to buy him lunch. They met that same day at Cafe Puccini, a small restaurant with the composer's picture on every wall and a jukebox that played only Italian opera. And after the usual pleasantries were exchanged, Sullivan got to the point.

"I'm having a tough time over here, John."

"I'm not surprised, Shane—I've never been able to figure out why you wanted to go back to Bondoc after all you've told me about your first experience with him. Remember how pissed off you were? It must've taken you five years to cool off."

Sullivan looked over at Cooper. He was as calm as Shane was mercurial.

"Well, it's not complicated—the business was on the rocks, Treister was driving me crazy, and Bondoc was interested in helping me out. Or at least that's what I thought at the time. Now he and Treister have been taking turns screwing with me, and I guess they both think I'm too dumb to know it. But I know whose name is on the door, and I realize I'm just a glorified employee.

"But that's not the problem," Sullivan continued. "It's this case I'm working on." He hesitated, and Cooper stared at him, sensing opportunity. "We've got to be careful here," Sullivan went on. "What I want to talk to you about concerns some heavy-duty work I'm doing for Holliday & Bennett, which is still Bondoc's client for some unfathomable reason. But I'm afraid we might be criticized for even having this conversation."

"Who's on the other side?" asked Cooper, thinking Sullivan was worried about conflicts.

"It's not a conflict problem, John. The other side is some San Diego medical-supply company I'm sure you guys have never heard of. The problem is, I want to make a move out of Bondoc's firm and bring this Holliday & Bennett work with me. And I'm thinking my prize client and I may want to jump over to your firm. But I don't want to keep talking unless you want to keep listening, because this isn't going to make Bondoc happy."

Behind his naturally impassive exterior, Cooper was considering the situation. He knew Sullivan was an effective lawyer, but worrisome. He'd seen the messes Shane could get himself into. On the other hand, Holliday & Bennett was a once-in-a-lifetime client, certainly worth the risk of taking Sullivan on as an employee, maybe even as a partner. And the rumors were right—Cooper's firm was in trouble, losing good people every month. It was getting harder and harder to avoid the kind of unwelcome media attention that would kill the place where he'd spent his career. If there was something he could do to stem the tide, he was certainly prepared to do it, even with someone as problematic as Sullivan. "I'll eat and you talk," he said finally.

So while Cooper had his sandwich, Sullivan explained the Applied case in general terms, emphasizing the cash flow it was generating for the Bondoc Firm and his perception that the case was unwinnable at trial. "I'm being set up as the goat here, John. Gus is going to collect millions in legal fees, and I'll fall on my face because he doesn't have the sense to see past the money. And right now, I have zero say in what the client should do—I've never even met Tom Gilhooly, the Holliday & Bennett chairman, and I'm afraid if I rat Bondoc out to Ed Zbrewski, my direct contact with New York, it'll get back to Bondoc somehow."

Cooper stopped eating. "Why don't you quit? Nobody's making you work there."

"That's exactly what I want to do. But I want to land someplace, and if I've done enough good work for them, maybe I can bring Holliday & Bennett with me wherever I go."

"But it's a lousy case, right?"

"Sure it's a lousy case, but it's a rich lousy case. And I don't mind working it as long as I'm in charge of what happens to it, not Bondoc."

"But Shane, you've only been on this for a few months— why do you think you can pull it if you leave? We both know Bondoc's no slouch when it comes to client control. I mean, it's a miracle he's still got Holliday & Bennett after the Frehen case."

"Well, I'm not leaving tomorrow—that's one thing. There's some motion practice coming up that's going to make Mr. Zbrewski extremely happy with me, if it goes the way I think it's going to go. And the closer we get to trial, the harder it'll be to replace me. But look, what I want to know is, if I can pull this off, do you think they'd want me on board over at your shop?"

Cooper hesitated. This was not a normal situation. Sullivan was suggesting that Baum, Baum & Cooper encourage him to jump ship with Bondoc's client at some indefinite point in the future, after Sullivan had ensured that his own firm was helpless to prevent the theft. The potential for legal liability was obvious. But Sullivan wasn't asking for a contract—just an opinion. And there wasn't any reason this conversation was ever going to come to light.

"The whole plan sounds screwy to me, Shane. I don't think you're going to get to first base trying to take Holliday & Bennett away from Bondoc. Like you said, you don't even know how he's holding on to them now."

"Yeah," interrupted Sullivan, "but spare me your doubts. Answer my question. What if?"

"What if, maybe yes. That's what I think. You know my firm's anxious to get into private-pay malpractice defense and away from the insurance industry. The rates carriers pay are eating us alive. So yeah, maybe I could sell it. But only if Holliday & Bennett is committed, and only if it doesn't look like Bondoc's going to sue us for poaching. Neither of which I think you can deliver. But yeah, I'd say we'd be interested under the right circumstances."

The rest of the lunch passed pleasantly enough.

15

San Francisco
{April 17, 1995}

Edouard Jones had been looking forward to this morning for some time. Armed with a comprehensive dossier on Gus Bondoc's activities over the past six months, right down to his ineffectual attempts to put an end to his affair with Gina Costello, Jones had called Bondoc's office and arranged an appointment. Nothing threatening over the phone, just "I'm with the Haitian consul's office in New York, and have some business I'd like to discuss with you privately." Bondoc had been wary but curious, and had agreed to meet.

When he'd arrived, of course, Bondoc was waiting for him with an associate in tow. It had taken some time to convince Bondoc that what he had to say was sufficiently confidential that his government preferred not to have anyone in the room but the two of them during their discussion. After a careful examination of Jones's consular identification, Bondoc had sent Marcie Schumann packing.

"Well, Mr. Jones," Bondoc said, "what can I do for you?"

"Do you have a Gina Costello working here, Mr. Bondoc?"

Jones replied, grinning inwardly at Bondoc's well-concealed shock.

"Who?" Bondoc asked, stalling. Why would this well-dressed representative of Haitian officialdom walk in here and ask him about Gina? What could Gina possibly have to do with the Haitian government? Jesus Christ, what was this guy really here about?

"Please, Mr. Bondoc—don't insult my intelligence. The Gina Costello you had sex with on Monday afternoon at the Hilton Hotel on Bay Street. Surely you remember?"

A look of disgust mixed with great anger crossed Bondoc's heavily jowled countenance. "You come in here and say that to me?! Who the hell do you think you are, pal? What business is that of yours? What's this all about?" It had to have something to do with Baby Doc. Were they trying to find some way to embarrass him into betraying his client?

"So I take it you do remember Ms. Costello, then? Am I correct?"

The man's insolence was driving Bondoc over the edge. "Fuck you, Mr. Jones," he said. "I don't know what you hope to gain coming in here and parading my dirty laundry around, but in case you didn't know, consensual sex is not against the law in California. You can take your so-called information and shove it up your ass. You have exactly two minutes to explain why I shouldn't have you thrown out of here."

In response, Jones pulled back his suit coat, exposing a large-caliber automatic pistol snug in a shoulder holster. Before Bondoc could dive for the floor, Jones said "I'm not threatening you, Mr. Bondoc—at least I have no intention of killing you right now. I'm merely showing you how vulnerable you are, how easy it would be to cause you injury if I wished to. Now relax. I have some information about Ms.

Costello that you will wish to hear. And then we can talk about alternatives."

Bondoc cursed himself. Why don't we have any security against this kind of thing? After 101 California, how could I be so stupid as to let somebody into my office with a pistol?

"Gina is Haitian, Mr. Bondoc, did you know that?"

Bondoc stared. Gina's features were not African. She was just a dark-skinned girl from New York. Anyway, so what if she was Haitian? What difference did that make to him? Did this asshole think he was a racist, for God's sake?

"Gina is a close friend of Pierre Esclemond, Mr. Bondoc. Perhaps you have heard of him. He is the editor of *Haiti Today*?"

Bondoc was lost. He had some vague awareness there were a number of publications for Haitian émigrés in the United States. He knew these publications were usually very critical of the Duvaliers, but so what? It was a free country.

"I see you're still confused, Mr. Bondoc. Let me simplify the picture for you. Perhaps you remember last summer, when the American press reported that Baby Doc's Swiss accounts had been lightened by sixteen million US dollars. You do remember that, don't you Mr. Bondoc?" Jones grinned into Bondoc's flushed face. "Now how do you think that came to happen? And how do you think Baby Doc would take it if he were to learn that the young woman who made it happen is the mistress of his own trusted California lawyer?"

Bondoc was nauseous. The last time he'd felt this bad was when the Frehen verdict came back, and then at least he'd been safe from physical harm, not locked in a private office with a pistol-toting heavy who might really intend to do him in. My God, Gina, how had this happened? He knew Baby Doc would never accept any protestations of innocence—

he'd been sleeping with the girl, therefore he was in on it. And even if Baby Doc were persuaded that Bondoc wasn't involved, he might kill him just on general principles.

Bondoc fought for control. He stared intently at Jones, not looking scared, just grave. "If I knew whether to believe you, it might make this a lot easier on both of us," he said.

So Jones told him. Told him about Pierre's initial approach to the Haitian Consulate in Manhattan and his pathetic attempt to claim a reward after the sixteen million had been cleared out of Baby Doc's bank accounts, even described in some detail how he'd beaten Pierre within an inch of his life in his Bronx office. Then he went through Kroc Associates' efforts to trace Pierre's contacts with Gina, and explained how Kroc had, at last, made the connection between Gina and Bondoc.

"Not complicated," Jones said, self-satisfied, "not for someone who knows what he's doing." Now it was Jones's turn to stare at Bondoc, waiting to see the older man sag.

Bondoc was convinced by Jones's story. He'd check it out, of course, but he was convinced. And he wasn't just frightened; he was sexually bruised and deeply angered. If he could order Gina shot in her cubicle, he'd gladly do it. But life was never that simple.

"All right—let's say I find your story somewhat believable. But let's also say I expect you to believe I'm not guilty of complicity in whatever Ms. Costello has been getting herself up to with Mr. Duvalier's money. Now I want to know why you're here at all—why does the Haitian Consulate want to expose Ms. Costello to Mr. Duvalier's own lawyer, of all people?"

"I do not come to you on behalf of Haiti, Mr. Bondoc. Helping Haiti is beyond either of us. I've come here to save you from Baby Doc and to make a profit. If you are uninterested in being saved, then I will quietly say good day."

There it was. Blackmail. Nothing complicated. Pay me or I'll turn you in to Baby Doc, who may well kill you. But the hold was too great. Once the first payment was made, there was no reason to think Jones would ever let go of him. And there was the risk that Jones would eventually sell him to Baby Doc anyway.

"What about Gina and this Pierre fellow?" Bondoc said, thinking out loud. "How do you make them go away, make sure they won't attract attention to me? What is it you really have to sell here, Mr. Jones? If things are the way you say they are, Jeanne Claude is bound to figure this out for himself sooner or later."

Jones looked Bondoc straight in the eye. "Better for you if it's later, Mr. Bondoc. Yes, definitely better, I think."

The man had a point, of course, and there was nothing for it but to placate him, if only temporarily. Until he could trap him. And Gina. And Pierre, whoever he was.

"So where do we go from here, Mr. Jones?"

"We don't go anywhere, sir. We just say goodbye for a few days and then I call you and we discuss my profit. And to do that, I'll need to understand your assets." Jones handed Bondoc a scrap of paper with a Bahamian post-office-box number scrawled on it. "Mail me your last year's tax returns later this week, Mr. Bondoc. Then we'll talk. I'll show myself out, don't get up. Don't even think about making a fuss."

After sitting quietly for several minutes, Bondoc checked the recorder sitting on his desk. Gotcha, he thought, knowing he had enough on the recorder to make the US Attorney very interested in Mr. Jones, Gina, and Pierre. All he had to do now was confess to being a fool and put Gina in jail. Messy, though, and it didn't solve the problem he was going to have when Baby Doc found out about things. There probably wasn't a way to solve that one, short of changing his name and taking up residence in the Midwest. The real virtue of confessing was that he'd have the government's help in escaping the long arm of his angry client.

Still, his vanity held him back. Admitting his history with Gina would be humiliating. Once the story was out, he'd be the butt of insider jokes for decades. It was all too much for any quick decisions.

He stared down at the solid-state recording wand. Six inches long and two inches in circumference, it was a voice-activated, state-of-the-art personal note taker; its contents could be downloaded to a PC. The firm had purchased thirty of them earlier in the year. Once he'd discovered the wand's value as a room recorder, he'd told Millie Conroy to download each day's recordings to a series of floppy disks.

He buzzed Millie now, and asked her to show him how to download the recorder himself. It took fifteen minutes to set things up, and her subsequent attempt to explain the process to Bondoc was entirely unenlightening. The one thing he took from it was that he could lose the Jones recording if he wasn't careful.

"It's a little tricky," Millie said. "I hate to admit it, Gus, but the first week I did this for you, I lost about three days' worth of stuff. If this is important, you should keep the recording on the original wand and let me do any backup downloading for you."

He looked at her. She was right, of course. And there was no reason not to trust her—what did she know about any of this? "OK, Millie, but look—I want to keep today's stuff separate from all the rest. Go download the wand to a floppy for me, and make sure you don't erase it. Then put the wand in an envelope with my name on it, and put the envelope in the safe tonight."

Millie promised that it wouldn't be a problem.

John LaBelle had been in the library when Edouard Jones walked by, headed toward Gus Bondoc's office. Black faces were unusual among Bondoc, Treister, Nimmer & Sourwine's clients, especially black faces mounted on white linen suits that covered bulging musculature. An hour later, when LaBelle saw Jones leave without being escorted out by Bondoc, he was sure something unusual was going on. Gus always walked clients to the door. It was firm custom.

At 5:00 p.m., passing Bondoc's office, LaBelle saw Millie download the wand onto her computer and then place it into a large manila envelope. It was an open secret that Bondoc used his personal note taker to record conversations in his office. LaBelle's curiosity suddenly came back to him.

At 6:30, LaBelle called Carla and told her not to hold dinner, he'd eat out. He came back to the office at a quarter to eight, and kept working. By 10, other than the cleaning staff and the skeleton word-processing crew tucked away in its own room, he was alone.

He tucked a floppy into his pocket and approached Millie's cubicle. Within a few minutes, he found today's input from Bondoc's wand on her computer, stored in the same directory as all the others. He glanced carefully around the empty office while he made his own copy of the events of April 17. Then he headed home.

He got to Novato close to midnight. Carla was asleep, and he didn't bother waking her. Instead, he went to his home PC and tried to open the file he'd copied onto the floppy. But he'd never loaded the software for the wand onto his home PC, and there wasn't a thing he could do with it. He carefully put the disk back in his briefcase and went upstairs to sleep.

The next morning, over breakfast, he told Carla what he'd done the night before.

"This is it, John," she said, instantly beginning to harangue him. "I told you not to play detective—this is too important for amateur-hour stuff like that! Why are you getting Claire and me involved in this? Don't you get how dangerous this could be? Someone could show up here with an arrest warrant for what you pulled last night! Or they could just skip the legalities and come after your family! I told you I'd leave you, John, and I wasn't kidding!" She was shouting now, and the baby was crying and throwing food.

LaBelle was caught. He'd had no idea his stunt would make Carla so angry with him, that she'd feel so threatened. But her career had exposed her to the realities of street violence and left her paranoid. Now he wished he'd never known of Bondoc's recording, and he'd certainly lost all appetite to listen to it.

"What should I do, Carla? Just tell me what you want me to do here and I'll do it." She was sobbing now, and Claire's cries had reached a new crescendo.

"Fuck you, John, just get out of here," she screamed at him. Then, calmer, she said "Until I can figure out what I'm going to do to you for getting us into this fix, you and I are separated."

LaBelle couldn't believe what was happening to him. By deferring to Carla in most things, he'd managed to have a quiet marriage. He'd never been thrown out of his own house before—not for missed birthdays and anniversaries, not for all the inevitable consequences of being overworked and underpaid. He took another look around in his kitchen and left.

16

San Francisco
{Morning–Early Afternoon, April 18, 1995}

Gus called John Epimere mid-morning.

"I've got trouble, John," he told the older man. "I've got trouble and I need help." Bondoc and Epimere had been colleagues for nearly twenty years; in all that time, he'd never made such a direct approach.

"OK, Gus. Let's meet over here in an hour."

Epimere was famously security conscious, and typically monosyllabic over the telephone. His office was routinely swept for bugs, and he'd had special windows and insulation installed to thwart any would-be eavesdroppers. His stand-up writing desk, where he often reviewed what he liked to call "sensitive paper," was deliberately positioned to prevent onlookers in other Bush Street buildings from peering into his inner sanctum.

Bondoc retrieved the envelope containing his wand from the office safe and walked over to Epimere's office at the appointed time. On the way over, he thought of his friend, whose energies were so effectively sublimated into his law practice that his sexual encounters could be counted on one hand. After Gus had put such effort into cultivating a personal relationship with him in the late 1970s, one such episode had involved Bondoc. It had been a difficult situation. He knew Epimere could help his career; he also knew that faking an interest in an erotic relationship was not likely to end well. By repressing his own phobias and treating Epimere with dignity, Bondoc had successfully rebuffed the older man's advances while still cementing their business relationship.

Having cleared the heavy security in the building PW&S shared with Union Oil Company, Bondoc took the brass-ornamented elevator still run by a lift operator to Epimere's floor. He was immediately shown into Epimere's private office.

"OK, Gus, this must be pretty heavy—what have you got?" Epimere was genuinely curious. He'd turned several possibilities over in his mind since receiving Gus's call--tax trouble, marriage trouble, even trouble with his children. Something so personal it would really sting. Had to be at least that, he thought.

"Probably best if you just listen to this, John. Then I'll fill in the details." Bondoc took the wand out of its envelope. It took around sixty-five minutes to get through Jones's visit. Epimere listened silently, not looking at Bondoc.

"Where's the young woman?" Epimere asked, finally.

"She's around, she doesn't know anything."

"You're not considering paying this man, are you?"

"I don't think so—that's what I'm here to discuss."

"You can't pay him, Gus. You know that sort of thing never ends well. Plus, it's undoubtedly misprision of a felony."

"What? What felony?"

"Ms. Costello broke into your computer system and stole Mr. Duvalier's information. She may get away with it by claiming she's only a naive do-gooder, but don't think the US Attorney won't try to hang you if you cover this thing up."

"Jesus, John—I can't let this man Jones go blabbing to Duvalier. He'll only understand one thing: I was sleeping with a woman who exposed his bank accounts to the Haitians. I could get hurt here, John—that changes the rules some, doesn't it?"

"Yes and no, Gus. I'm sure you've already thought about going to the government with this recording, and then letting them protect you. After all, you're a victim here; Jones, Ms. Costello and Esclemond are the criminals."

"I have a life, John. I can't abandon everything I've worked for, give up all my standing in the legal community. Not to become a laughingstock and spend the rest of my life looking over my shoulder."

You might have thought about that before you accepted a client like Duvalier, Epimere thought to himself. Bondoc's clients had often been unsavory, but Duvalier was a stretch even for him.

"You're taking a terrible chance with your liberty by not going down to the US Attorney with this recording right now. But I can certainly understand your concern about your safety, and the sacrifice you'd be making."

This was it, thought Bondoc. Epimere was a genius. He'd bailed more large corporations out of impossibly nasty situations than anyone on the West Coast. He looked at his friend expectantly.

"It doesn't solve the misprision issue, but you could try sending Jones a copy of the recording. Offer to meet with him—in New York, if he likes. Explain that if there's any more talk of blackmail, you'll go public with the recording, at which time he'll find himself back in Haiti awaiting trial for treason, or whatever they call this kind of behavior in that godforsaken country. Same result if you find out he's leaked to Duvalier."

Blackmail the blackmailer. It was so cute that Bondoc wished he'd thought of it himself.

"Now look, Gus—you're playing with fire here. This Jones fellow may rush off to Duvalier as soon as he gets this recording and realizes you're going to stonewall him on money. People don't always act rationally. And the longer you wait to approach the US Attorney, the less certain it is that you won't be a target defendant."

It was the rat-train problem. Snitches who boarded the rat train early could typically cut an immunity deal and obtain protection from their co-defendants. Late arrivals wound up as entries in a prosecutor's statistics book. Guilt and innocence were very fluid concepts in the criminal-justice system, especially in the white-collar arena. It was more about public relations and political careers than anything else.

John LaBelle didn't show up that morning until well after Gus had left to see John Epimere. After the morning scene with Carla, he'd checked into a tourist motel on Lombard. Once he'd ascertained that Bondoc was safely out of the office and that Millie hadn't sensed anything amiss with her PC, he retreated to his office to think things over. Once there, with the door closed behind him, he held the floppy disk in his hand and stared at it. The software that would permit him to listen to Bondoc's conversation was on his own PC, but he knew he'd lost all appetite for eavesdropping. He was thinking quite seriously of just erasing the floppy and trying to forget the whole thing. He knew that was what Carla wanted him to do.

Just then, Sullivan walked in without bothering to knock.

"Where've you been, John? I've been looking for you all morning. I need some backup on this summary-adjudication motion in Applied; the opening brief is due tomorrow, for Christ's sake."

Sullivan had been devouring the Applied file over the past months, and had decided to take a shot at dismissing most of the case based on the standard of care. It wasn't clear whether Holliday & Bennett could get away with the argument that its expert's misfortune was so unpredictable that it couldn't form the basis of an independent claim against the firm. And even if Sullivan won his motion, it would leave Holliday & Bennett facing fraud charges for overselling Applied on the case. But accomplishing anything positive would be a major coup, and LaBelle knew Sullivan had put enormous effort into the motion.

Still, he ignored the other man's impatience. "Look, Shane—there's something going on around here, and I think you might be interested in hearing about it."

"Office politics don't interest me, John—you know that. We've got work to do. What's that damn floppy disk you're staring at? Are those the three declarations I asked you for again yesterday?"

Shit, thought LaBelle. He'd never finalized his last assignment.

"Don't get sore, Shane—you know we don't absolutely have to file tomorrow."

"Goddamn it, John—what are you talking about? We've cleared dates with the court and Carpuchi's office—of course we have to file! Can't I count on you for anything?"

Embarrassed, LaBelle pressed ahead. "I have a good hunch this is a lot more than just office politics, Shane. What I've got here is yesterday's voice recording from Gus Bondoc's office. I haven't listened to it, and I'm not going to listen to it. Before you showed up, I was probably going to erase it. It's yours, if you want it."

"Have you gone crazy, John? Why do you have Gus's voice recording? What's he doing recording people in his office anyway? And why should I waste my time listening to his private business?"

"Look, Shane—I'm not going to force-feed you this stuff. It'll play on your PC, OK? If I'm right, and if you care about working here, you'll want to hear what went on between Gus and a guy who came to see him yesterday. At least you'll understand why I've been a little distracted lately."

"OK, John—if you want to play cloak and dagger, give me the floppy and I'll listen to it. But only if you promise me to finish off the last three declarations and then proofread and Shepardize the opening brief. For Christ's sake, this is a law office, all right? We're not the CIA."

17

Shane Sullivan cancelled his hearing date half an hour after listening to LaBelle's floppy disk, buying an extra two weeks by claiming illness. Then he grabbed LaBelle.

"Who the hell is this lady, John?" Sullivan asked. They'd left the office, and were heading toward the Northern waterfront.

"I take it you found the recording interesting?" LaBelle replied, amused by Sullivan's sudden change of attitude.

"Look, don't play games—you know what's on that floppy as well as I do."

"No, I don't, Shane. And I don't want to. I know a few things, but I don't want to talk about them and I don't want to talk about how I found them out. I don't want to get anyone in trouble, especially me."

"If you think anyone's going to come out of this one clean, John, you're kidding yourself. What's on that recording could bring the whole firm down. So why don't you help me figure out what to do here?"

"Why should I care what happens to the firm, Shane? I'm

out of here in a few months whether I like it or not. And to tell you the truth, I like it."

"I know Gus treated you like shit, John. But I hope you don't think I was part of that."

"If I thought that, Shane, I'd never have given you the recording. All I'm trying to do is make sure you don't go down with the ship—that's it. You don't know all the trouble this thing has already caused me. When I told Carla I had the recording this morning, she threw me out of the house. She's convinced Duvalier is going to come after people when this thing breaks, and she doesn't want me involved. I still don't know when she's going to let me come home."

"Look, John, I'm not sure your wife's too far off-base. But I also think Gus might try to save himself by turning this girl over to Baby Doc. How would you like to have that on your conscience? And what about our law licenses? There's been at least one crime committed here, and if we stay quiet about it too long we'll become part of the problem."

"What do you mean there's been a crime, Shane?" Now Sullivan was worrying LaBelle, who was angling for a job in the Solano County District Attorney's Office. Any disciplinary blemish would queer that prospect but good.

"Isn't stealing financial information a crime, John? Even if it's from a creep like Baby Doc, it's still garden-variety theft, and with a big number attached. And Baby Doc is the firm's client—you and I have ethical obligations here."

LaBelle's head was spinning. At least he knew that Sullivan would do something, not just sit on this the way he would have. The trick now was to get the hell out of the way—if Shane went down in flames, LaBelle didn't want go with him.

"I can't be part of this, Shane. I really don't know what's

on that recording, but from what you've said, it sounds like you already know more about this than I do. Can't you do this without me? I'll back you up if it comes to it, but please, I'm begging you—I'll lose my wife and kid if I get out in front on this one. You've got to help me out here."

"Do you think I'm stupid enough to go into this blind, John? Maybe if you start by being honest with me, tell me what you know and how you found it out—maybe then I can keep you out of this. But if you just clam up, I'm not promising you anything. All I'm going to do then is look out for my own self."

It took LaBelle another hour to tell Sullivan how Millie Conroy had picked up on Gus's affair with Gina, how Pierre had been overheard boasting about Baby Doc's money, how Carla had put Pierre's boast into context. He described the man who'd come and gone yesterday, and his own acquisition of Bondoc's recording.

"How am I supposed to believe you've never listened to it, John?" Shane asked once he'd finished.

"Believe what you want, but I couldn't get it to load last night—I didn't have the software for it at home. And after Carla threw me out this morning, I didn't have the heart to listen to anything. If you hadn't come in and reamed me out over those declarations, I'd have erased the goddamned thing. I'm telling you, I don't want to know about this mess—I just want to get out of this firm with a whole skin and an intact marriage. Is that too much to ask, after fifteen years?"

"Do you know this Gina, John?"

"Just to say hello. I've never had a real conversation with her." LaBelle was mister personality with the staff, well-known for his thoughtfulness and affability. Sullivan, on the other hand, had trouble remembering people's names.

"Describe her for me."

"She's nice-looking, about 5'6". Long straight black hair. She could be Italian, just dark-skinned Italian. About twenty-two, maybe twenty-three tops."

"I feel sorry for her," Sullivan said, more to himself than anything. "She's in way over her head. Stealing Baby Doc's money and sleeping with Gus Bondoc. That's some résumé she's building."

"What are you going to do, Shane?"

"I'm going to go to the cops with this, John. It's just a question of when. I'm worried about somebody getting hurt, but I don't want to get in Gus's way if he's going to go to the cops first. I don't like him very much anymore, but I don't want to ruin him either. He deserves some time to do the right thing."

"How's that going to help Gina?"

"That I haven't figured out. I mean, I'd like to warn her she's in trouble, but then she's liable to beat Bondoc to the prosecutors, try to cop a plea early. So my instinct is just to keep an eye on things for a few weeks, hope to God nothing terrible happens."

"What about me, Shane?"

"What about you? I think you're very lucky you told me about this. You're in no shape to handle this situation by yourself. Get things patched up at home—just tell your wife not to worry, I'll take care of it. I'll keep you in the loop, and you keep an eye on Bondoc's secretary, make sure she doesn't get worried something funny's happened to her computer. I can't believe you just went in and lifted that recording, John. Man, that took balls. I'd never do something like that."

It was now nearly 7:00 p.m. Despite the high-sounding platitudes of the afternoon, Sullivan was mostly thinking about how he could turn the recording into a ticket out of Bondoc, Treister, Nimmer & Sourwine LLP, with Holliday & Bennett in tow. He needed at least a minor victory in the Applied case, along with the ability to turn LaBelle's recording into major damage to Bondoc's reputation. Then he could sell Zbrewski on the idea that it was better for all if he left his failing firm, and took the Applied case with him. The summary-adjudication motion should provide the requisite legal dazzle. And Bondoc's predictable attempt to wiggle free of responsibility for the affair with Gina should do the rest. It was just a matter of time.

18

Fisherman's Wharf, San Francisco
{April 21, 1995}

Gina sensed a new tension in Gus. Maybe his wife knows he's still seeing me, she thought to herself. Even if they'd avoided another discovery, Peg had to know she couldn't trust him.

In fact, Peg was aware that her husband had broken his word. But having satisfied herself that he didn't want a divorce, she'd decided to ignore this more circumspect dalliance. Gus's problem was not Peg. Gus's problem was Jean Claude Duvalier. Since he knew what Gina had done to his client, he had to find a way to end his relationship with this viper without panicking her, without sending her to the cops, looking for a deal. If anybody was getting on the rat train first, it was going to be Gus.

They were in the Hilton Hotel again. For a tourist trap, it wasn't bad. Its principal flaw was across the street, in the form of a 1950s public-housing project plopped down in what had subsequently become prime real estate. It wasn't unusual for the sound of gunshots to disturb tourists from Iowa waiting at the Bay Street turnaround for their first cable car ride.

It was around 1:00 p.m. They'd gone up to the room

a little after noon, and Gus had had her twice in quick succession. She thought he must be taking that new drug, he was so horny. She needed to shower and get back to work, but he stopped her before she could get into the bathroom.

"We need to talk."

"Gus, if I get back late again, I might as well wear a sign that says 'Been Screwing the Boss.' I'm sure Millie knows there's something going on—don't you see the way she looks at me? Do you want this out in the open?"

"That's what we need to talk about, Gina—we need to talk about ending this. I don't think Millie's the problem; Peg's the problem. She knows I haven't stopped this. She's not saying anything, but she knows. And I don't want to be forced into a divorce."

"So why don't we stop, Gus? It's not me who's pushing this thing. You're the one who keeps pressing sex on me. I don't know why I go along. I mean," she grimaced inwardly, groping for the right words, "I mean, you're nice and all, but you're a lot older than I am. I never meant for this to go so far."

That's probably true, thought Bondoc. I'm sure you never thought you'd have to do anything more than just fuck *with* me, you cunt. What he really wanted to do was take her into the toilet and drown her. You have no idea what you've done here, Gina, he thought.

"Half the time I don't know what I'm doing anymore, Gina. This business has really confused me. But I don't want a divorce, and if this keeps going that's what I'm headed toward."

You didn't act confused when you had me spread-eagled, she thought. Why, look—the son of a bitch still has an erection.

"Look, Gus, I do understand. And it's probably for the best. Do you want me to quit and sign a release or something? Is that it?"

Under normal circumstances, he would have jumped at this. But he didn't want her to leave; he wanted her around and unsuspicious.

"Look," he said. "You know how badly I'm exposed here, sleeping with someone from the office like this. Especially someone as young as you. If you want to quit, just sign the standard office release, it picks up this kind of stuff, and I'll help you out privately with money, a job recommendation, you name it. But what I'd really like is if we could just go on as usual at work for a while, let things simmer down, and then deal with the future. You think about it."

"OK, Gus. I'll do that. But now I have to shower and get back to my job. And you should get over to the Bay Club." By passing through the Bay Club before returning to work, Bondoc came back from a different direction. So far, it had spared them any obvious embarrassment.

Later that afternoon, pounding out Shane Sullivan's dictation of the Applied summary-adjudication motion, Gina considered her position. All thoughts of further exposing Baby Doc's finances were long past. Disgusted by her experience with Gus Bondoc, she was weak with relief at the thought of breaking off the liaison. Escaping California was now her first priority.

Pierre would be a problem, though. He was continually threatening to visit, coming up with one fantastic scheme after another to flush out new information. She realized that his desperation for fresh financial data was likely motivated by some hope of reward. As soon as she left Bondoc, Pierre would know none was ever coming. What might happen then really frightened her. Would Pierre give her identity away?

And there was something else. Millie Conroy had gossiped to her about a government man from Haiti who'd come to see Bondoc and ended up upsetting him to no end, a man who looked like a thug.

With all that was going on, Gina decided to wait. The Bronx would always be there.

19

San Francisco
{April 24–27, 1995}

John Epimere's secretary patiently transcribed the Jones interview on an old-fashioned Underwood typewriter. Using carbon paper, she made a single copy for Bondoc. Epimere locked both the original transcript and the wand itself in his wall safe. The carbon paper was shredded.

Bondoc took his copy, stuffed it into an envelope, and sent it by DHL to the address in the Bahamas Jones had given him. He attached a short typewritten note: "Suggest we discuss the original of this before you act."

Two days later, Jones called. He clearly assumed Bondoc was taping his call, and said only that he would meet him the next afternoon, at 4:00 p.m., outside the main entrance to the United Nations building in Manhattan. Bondoc called Epimere as soon as Jones hung up. An hour later, the two men were once again sitting opposite each other across Epimere's stacked-up desk.

"This is a dangerous adventure you're embarking on, Gus. This man carries a weapon, he's a brute, and you've stung him badly. You have to assume he'll attempt to record anything that passes between you. What you should really do is turn him in to the authorities—let them treat this as a sting."

"I know you're right, John, but I just can't. It's too disruptive. So the question is, how do I get through this without making a complete hash of it?"

"You don't. You use a professional."

Bondoc knew immediately who Epimere was referring to. David Israel had been around the San Francisco scene for decades. A disciple of the late Hal Lipset, Israel ran his all-but-invisible private-investigation agency out of a Nob Hill apartment. You never asked him how he did the things he did; you just told him what you needed, and invariably he got it for you. It was just a matter of how much you wanted to pay.

"Jesus, John. I'm as big a fan of David's as anyone, but bringing somebody else in on this? I mean, come on. And how could we get him on such short notice anyway?"

"I've got him waiting upstairs in my conference room—I asked him to come over here right after you telephoned me. David owes me a few favors."

Bondoc looked across the desk at Epimere. You've got to trust somebody in this thing, he thought, remembering how Epimere had laughed when he'd blanched at having the older man's secretary transcribe the wand. David Israel was a pro. He wouldn't blab. His reputation depended on his discretion, and when John Epimere said David Israel owed him some favors, Bondoc understood just how pregnant a statement that was. Anyway, almost anything seemed better than confronting Jones on his own again.

"OK, John—the doctor knows best. Why don't you bring David down and let's talk this over with him."

A few minutes later, David Israel was shown in by the secretary, the door was closed, and Epimere began briefing the man on Bondoc's problem.

"It seems our friend Gus here has gotten himself involved with a rather unusual young woman, David," Epimere began.

Israel was surprised. Not that Bondoc—or any successful middle-aged man, for that matter—had woman trouble, but that John Epimere would have him come down on half an hour's notice for something so trivial.

Epimere went on. "Gus represents Jean Claude Duvalier. The young woman in question took a job at Gus's office and used her position of trust to steal information that cost Mr. Duvalier sixteen million dollars. Then she tricked Gus into having an affair with her—probably thought she could get more information from him. Gus found out about all this a week ago from a Haitian government official who's been tracking this young woman's activities. Now, if you can believe it, this man wants to blackmail Gus. He's betting Gus doesn't want his client to find out what's happened on Gus's watch."

Israel felt his interest warming. Gus Bondoc was way up shit creek, the investigator thought. Jean Claude Duvalier must be a peach of a client, very forgiving when an error of personal judgment costs him money. And sleeping with the perp. If he had any sense, Bondoc would be over at the US Attorney's office. Volunteering for the witness protection program. Or maybe the French Foreign Legion. But what these two corporate types thought he could do, he didn't have a clue. While his mind was busy, Israel looked placidly over at Epimere, waiting to see what he had in mind.

"Gus is supposed to meet this man tomorrow, at the

U.N. building in New York. Gus recorded the blackmail attempt, and has sent the man a transcript of the interview. Somebody has to make this fellow understand that it is not in his interest to draw attention to Gus's problem, and I don't want that person to be Gus. He's not a pro at this kind of thing, David. You are. Both Gus and I hold you in the highest regard. Always have."

At this point, Epimere went to his wall safe, carefully twirled the combination out of sight of his guests, and brought the original transcript over to Israel.

Once he'd read it, Israel understood it represented a clear ticket out of the US—and probably into a Haitian jail—for Jones, and that Epimere wanted him to use it to bluff his man's way out. Make the blackmailer believe he'd suffer more than the victim would. Might work, but it wasn't a long-term solution for Gus Bondoc's problem.

Still, John Epimere wasn't the kind of person you said was full of shit, at least not to his face. He wanted a technician, somebody who could make contact with Jones, explain the facts of life to him in a credible fashion, and get away without leaving any trace of the conversation. David could do all that with some ease. He'd have to be sure Jones wasn't bugged, and assure Jones that he wasn't bugged either. Have some backup in case Jones played rough, but the location made violence unlikely—the U.N. Plaza was alive with cops of every stripe. No sensible person would so much as spit on a pigeon there.

"Do we have a photograph?" he asked Epimere.

"Unfortunately not, David. Gus could point him out to you, of course, but I'd rather Gus never left California."

"Give me a description, Mr. Bondoc," David said, feigning a respect he no longer had for him.

"Coal black, brown eyes, close-cropped kinky black hair.

He's about 6'2", body-builder type, very flat nose, broad forehead, pockmarks on his face. Wore this Sidney Greenstreet-style white linen suit with a white shirt, green silk tie. No hat. He had a shoulder holster with a very realistic-looking automatic pistol in it. Just showed it to me, didn't go for it. Scared the hell out of me."

"If you want him to stay back here, John, you're taking a chance. There are a lot of people who meet that description in New York, and there's no guarantee this guy will show up dressed like Tom Wolfe again."

Epimere looked over at Bondoc and made a decision. "There's no way he's going, David. I don't want to put him forward in this situation. You'll just have to work with his description."

"All right—whatever you say. Just want you to realize I'm not Superman. I could wind up missing this guy, that's all."

That morning, after Gus left his office, Millie asked Gina to join her for lunch. She told her she had information Gina needed to hear directly from her. It was enough to make Gina move her lunch hour up, and she met Millie at the Waterfront Restaurant.

The two women had beaten the rush by half an hour, and they had their section more or less to themselves. Millie looked both flustered and conspiratorial.

"Gina, I want to tell you some things, and I want to do it before this place fills up."

"OK," Gina said. "Relax, Millie—I don't know what's got you so bothered, but whatever it is it can't be that bad."

"First, we never had this lunch. You have to promise me, honey—I mean, you just have to swear to God you're never going to tell anyone where you found out the things I'm going to tell you."

Gina had a sinking feeling. Obviously, Millie knew about her affair with Gus. But that couldn't have put her in this state—what was her problem? She looked over at her obviously well-meaning companion. "I'll give you my word, Millie. You can trust me."

"Gina, Gus knows you were involved in stealing money from his client."

Gina was so startled she spilled her water in her lap, thoroughly soaking herself. The waiter saw the glass tip, and began to come over.

"I'm fine," Gina said, warning him off. She put her napkin over her thighs, and her face flushed bright red. She wanted to scream, but she bit her lips instead. She'd never been so frightened in her life. Oh my God, she thought, that horrible man, he knows and he's been keeping me on a string. What's he going to do to me? What will Baby Doc do to me? I'm only twenty-one, how did I ever get in such a world-class mess at twenty-one?

Millie could see Gina was losing it. Still, she felt she had to press on. "Look, I've known about you and Gus for months and months. I've felt badly for you, like I should say something, but people your age never listen. So I kept my nose out of things that didn't concern me. I overheard your friend Pierre that night he came over and bragged about catching sixteen million dollars, though; I just never knew what it meant. Then this other fellow, this Haitian man, came in to see Gus last week, and when he left, like I told you, Gus was really shook."

"Is he the one who told Gus, Millie?"

"Yeah—that's what happened. Gus recorded him, and I've got the recording stored on my hard drive. I finally decided to listen to it and Jesus, Gina—this guy's blackmailing Gus, threatening to expose his relationship with you to Baby Doc. He even showed a pistol, right in Gus's office. And now Gus is over at John Epimere's—I know those two will try to find some dirty way to keep Gus from getting in any trouble. That means big problems for you, though—jail or something worse. I hate to frighten you, but this Jones man is obviously violent. That's why I couldn't let this go on any longer without warning you."

Gina looked at Millie gratefully. "I won't forget this, Millie. I know how hard it must have been for you, telling me all this. You've been a real friend ever since I got to the firm; I've just been too wrapped up in my own problems to see it."

"What are you going to do, Gina?"

"Better for you if I don't say too much. But I'm not going to stick around the Bay Area anymore, that's for sure. I don't even think I'll go back to work today—I'm just going to clear out. And it would be best for both of us if you didn't mention anything about me being gone. Let Gus and the rest of the office figure it out for themselves. I'll be out of my apartment by the time you get home tonight."

"But how will I know you're safe, Gina?"

"I'll be OK—I just need to go somewhere else. I'm sure this will all blow over eventually."

"I hope you're right—but I'll worry about you, so if you can find some way to let me know you're fine—"

"I'll try Millie, but I'm not promising. You might try calling my Mom in New York; she's in The Bronx phone book under Eugenia Costello, same as me. I'm sure I'll stay in touch with her, and I'll tell her to expect to hear from you. Just don't call her too often—I don't want her getting dragged into the mess I've made here."

With that, Gina asked the waiter for a fresh cloth napkin. She rubbed it back and forth on her skirt, drying it out as much as she could. Then she got up, put her sweater on, and left the restaurant, leaving Millie to order lunch alone.

20

New York City
{April 28, 1995}

Gina took the PATH train into Manhattan, then rode the IRT up to her mother's apartment in The Bronx. She'd called her from a pay phone in the subway, and Eugenia was waiting up when she arrived, well after midnight.

She'd only packed a single suitcase. Her rent was due in a few days; it wouldn't take long for the landlord to clear the rest of her stuff out and start looking for a new tenant. Gina didn't intend to stay here, but she felt safer as soon as she walked in the door.

"What's going on?" her mother asked. "First you take off for California. You're gone for a year. I hear from you three, maybe four times. No details. Then, again with no warning, you're back here with one suitcase in the middle of the night? It has to be a man, Gina—I'm not stupid. But how serious is this? Are you pregnant? Did he hurt you?"

"No, no—I'm just in over my head. It's an older man, a married man. At work. And now I'm through with him. I'm not pregnant, that's not it. But I need to go somewhere and start over, and I need this creep to stay out of my life and not find me. He's rich, Mom, and I think he may start looking for me when he realizes I've left him. So I'm going to need some help—some money, for one thing. I shouldn't tell you too much—you wouldn't believe what a creep this guy is."

Eugenia was furious—how could some married man make her daughter so upset? Ruin her young life, make her feel she had to go into hiding to protect herself? Gina should be in college, studying computer science, getting ready to become an independent person with a good job.

Gina could see how upset she'd made her mother. "Calm down, Mom—it's my fault, all of this, and I'm going to have to work it out in my own way. I don't want you interfering. That won't help me. You want to help me, don't you?"

"Of course I do, darling—you know I do. But shouldn't we go to a lawyer, get a harassment order so you don't have to worry anymore? I hate to see you in this state, I really do."

"This man is a lawyer, Mom—he won't care what kind of paper we get. The only way to deal with him is to stay away until he forgets all about me. Please believe me, I know what I'm talking about."

"Maybe we should talk to Pierre, honey. You know he's someone I rely on when I'm confused about things. And I know how much he cares about you."

How could her mother be so blind? Gina thought. Not to know Pierre wasn't what he appeared, that he'd been pushing her on Bondoc, that he saw her as an easy way to save his failing newspaper. To Eugenia, Pierre was still a hero.

"Mom, I don't want to drag him into this—I don't want to drag anyone into this. Please let this just be between you and me. If anyone else gets involved, it could make things very bad for me—you've got to believe that. Just help me out with a place to stay tonight and some money in the morning, before I go."

"Will you call me?"

"Of course I'll call you. At least once a week. And you may get a call from a woman named Millie Conroy—she's been a good friend to me. She'll want to know I'm OK, and you can keep her posted. But don't talk to anyone else, Mom. I mean no one."

Meanwhile, David Israel took a cab from JFK into Manhattan. He was booked into the old Tudor Hotel at East Forty-second and Second, within easy walking distance of the U.N. Building. Eric, his local contact, was waiting for him in the hotel bar, and the two men moved to Israel's room.

"This is just a meet and greet," David told him. "Nothing fancy. I have a message, I deliver it, and I leave. You're along in case the fellow doesn't like what he hears."

Eric was 6' 4", a former Navy Seal. David had asked for someone able to make trouble go away easily. "What about wires? Are you recording?"

"No."

"What about the opposition?"

"I'm going to take him through the metal detector on the way into the building, before I start talking—that should flush him out. If he won't go, then I'm going to walk away. That's where you might come in."

"It's not foolproof."

"Life is short," David said. "This whole assignment is a rush, and I'm going to have to take some chances to get things done. What I have to say is relatively innocuous anyway."

"Photos?"

"Yes. I'd like shots of my approach outside the building. But don't risk disrupting my contact. If there's any sign you're making him suspicious, sacrifice the photos. And don't come in behind me—once we've cleared security, wait for me outside. Then tail the opposition home and file your report. I assume someone else will be making sure I'm not tailed back here?"

"Right," said Eric. He left. Israel watched an in-room movie for an hour and then went to sleep.

The next day, the private detective got up shortly after 11 a.m. He had breakfast in his room and settled down to reading one of Dashiel Hammett's lesser-known works, *The Big Knockover*. By 3 p.m., he was dressed and on his way over to the U.N. Building. By 3:30, he was standing in front of the main structure, admiring the 189 different flags flapping in the breeze. He didn't see Eric, which was just as it should be.

Jones showed up at ten minutes past four. He was looking around, obviously greatly disturbed not to see Bondoc. Israel could see he was an amateur at first glance. He wondered at his claim to diplomatic status—with countries like Haiti and Liberia, anything was possible. Somebody important's nephew, no doubt.

Israel walked over. Bondoc's description was quite accurate: Jones was a large, very muscular man, and he'd kept the white linen suit.

David Israel was 5' 5", and not in particularly good shape. His shtick was to seem friendly, which he could do without difficulty. He smiled at Jones, who glowered suspiciously back. "I'm here on Gus Bondoc's behalf, Mr. Jones. I'd like to speak with you."

This was the crucial moment—Jones might walk away once he understood Bondoc had refused his request for a private meeting. What made Israel optimistic was how confused Jones looked. The man was frightened, that was clear.

Before Jones could act, David spoke again. "I'm not wired, Mr. Jones, and I assume you aren't, either. So let's just both make sure we can trust each other by going through the metal detectors inside. We can resume our conversation in the photo gallery on the main floor."

By now David had spotted Eric, dressed in what appeared to be a limousine driver's uniform, snapping pictures of tourists. Nice touch, he thought, reminding himself to compliment Eric's employers on their agent's creativity.

Without saying anything, Jones allowed himself to be led into the security area outside the building's main entrance.

"Please don't try to use any diplomatic I.D. to walk around security, Mr. Jones. If I'm going through, so are you."

They both passed through without incident. Israel walked ahead, into the fifties-style modern architecture of the main lobby. They planted themselves by a window overlooking the East River, and David began speaking.

"Mr. Bondoc has friends, Mr. Jones. Important friends. If he is embarrassed further, if Mr. Duvalier is brought into this affair in any way, Mr. Bondoc's friends will see to it that your role in this business is fully exposed to your own government, and to Mr. Duvalier. Mr. Bondoc recognizes there is danger in this for him, but he wants you to know he is willing to accept that danger, and that no matter what else may happen he will see to it that you will get no benefit from your involvement in this."

"Mr. Bondoc is a brave man," said Jones, sneering.

"He has reason to be brave because of who he is. Who are you, Mr. Jones? No one important, I believe. Think before you act. That's all I came here to convey. If you behave with caution, then perhaps Mr. Bondoc will also be cautious. And everyone can forget this incident ever happened."

Without waiting for a reply, Israel walked away. Jones started after him, but caught himself—he decided he needed time to do some thinking. This affair was not turning out at all the way he'd wished. Blackmailing Bondoc wasn't going be simple, and the idea of approaching Baby Doc truly frightened him.

After a few minutes, Jones headed west on Forty-sixth Street. By this time, he'd been photographed repeatedly by Eric, who'd slipped out of his chauffeur's jacket and into a leather coat. Eric trailed Jones back to the Haitian Consulate on Madison, where he watched him flash his I.D. and proceed past the security desk, into the restricted area of the consulate. Then he headed back to drop off his film.

21

San Francisco; New York City; and The Bronx
{May 1995}

Pierre became frantic about Gina's safety soon after telephoning Bondoc, Treister, Nimmer & Sourwine. Someone there told him she hadn't been seen at work for more than a week. He tried pumping Eugenia for information, but she insisted she hadn't heard from Gina in several weeks. Jones had tracked her down, Pierre believed, and now she was in the hands of Baby Doc. And it was all his fault.

Gus was quite concerned himself. He assumed Gina had found out that her role in the exposure of Baby Doc's banking information had come to light. But what really bothered him was that someone must have tipped her off. As far as he knew, only he, Epimere, Pierre, and Jones were aware of what Gina had done.

There was no obvious reason for Jones to tip Gina off. But she'd disappeared the same day he'd had Israel tell the Haitian to stop his blackmail threats—was it revenge? There was even a chance that Jones had brought Baby Doc into things, but the timing was too immediate to make that scenario very likely. Israel had said Jones looked like a man who wanted to think things through, not like someone about to run headlong into traffic.

Epimere's lack of direct involvement with Gina was beyond question. And Pierre Esclemond had no way of knowing what Gus knew, so it didn't make sense to blame him either. It almost had to be someone else, someone in the office, and that someone else was almost certainly his secretary Millie. She'd been near enough to realize something was up. And she'd had access to the wand.

It seemed incredible to Bondoc that his mousy secretary, who'd been living off the crumbs of his largely pretended affection for decades, would suddenly take it upon herself to start interfering in his life. Under almost any other circumstances, he'd have questioned the integrity of Epimere's maidenly secretary Mary Bennett, who'd transcribed the wand on her Underwood, before doubting Millie's loyalty. But Gina was gone. And there had to be a reason.

Pierre was the first to act. He flew to California the second week of May, checked Gina's apartment complex, and found her personal property had already been removed and stored by her landlord. That same day, he marched into Bondoc, Treister, Nimmer & Sourwine and confirmed with the head of personnel that Gina had not shown up for work since late April. Then, at both the San Francisco and Contra Costa police departments, he filed missing-person reports. He went to a great deal of trouble to impress the suddenness of Gina's disappearance on the detectives with whom he spoke.

"It's like she's vanished into thin air," he said. "She's never out of telephone touch with her mother and me for more than a few days at a time, and she's the most reliable employee you can imagine. But now she's gone from work with no excuse. and she's out of telephone contact—all for no reason. You gentlemen should take this case seriously. This is no runaway teenager—she's a highly responsible young adult, and I'm afraid something may have happened to her."

He lied through his teeth about specifics, of course, made no mention of Baby Doc or even Jones. Bondoc he referred to only as Gina's employer, never letting on that he knew anything about an affair between his young protége and her boss. Then he went home, his conscience at least somewhat relieved.

Several weeks later, the police made their first inquiry at Bondoc's firm. A police detective stopped by around 11 a.m., asked to speak to the managing partner, and was shown into Kelly Nimmer's office. The detective, a portly man named Sean Hennessey, was in his late forties; he had the distracting habit of sucking breath between his teeth to punctuate his sentences.

"This is just a routine follow-up to a missing-person report on one of your employees, Mr. Nimmer," the detective began. "Female, name Gina Costello, twenty-one, born in Haiti but lived most of her life in The Bronx before coming to the Bay Area and going to work at this firm. Hasn't been seen since April 28, when she left her apartment in the early evening and disappeared. If you ask me, probably just got sick of her job and went home, but the mother in New York denies any contact. So here we are, need to interview anybody in the office who was friendly with her, who might shed a little light on where she's gone, just to make sure she hasn't gotten herself into any trouble." Each pause was accompanied by a distinctive slurping noise.

Nimmer looked blankly at Hennessey. Gina's sudden departure had caused quite a stir in word processing, leaving the other operators with more than they could handle workwise. He'd had to hire two temps to replace her, and still hadn't managed to get production up to what the firm needed. Other than that inconvenience, however, Kelly hadn't given Gina's absence a second thought. The idea that she'd been characterized a missing person immediately set him to wondering what liability the firm might have.

Kelly referred the detective to Gina's supervisor in word processing, Madeline Crow, a largish woman in her late forties. While theoretically supervisor of the word-processing pool, Madeline was really just its longest-running employee. She made no effort to get to know, let alone supervise, any of her fellow word processors, and she told Detective Hennessey she'd rarely spoken to Gina, usually worked different shifts than the young woman, and hadn't realized she was missing. One of the other word processors, however, mentioned that Gina had been living in the same Richmond apartment complex as Millie Conroy, and that she believed Gina and Millie were friendly.

By the time Hennessey got to Millie Conroy's desk, Kelly Nimmer had already been in to see Gus Bondoc about the detective's visit.

"There's a cop on the premises, Gus. Seems somebody's filed a missing-persons report on one of the word processors, Gina Costello. Disappeared about two and a half weeks ago, just took off—no forwarding address. I don't see how we can be held responsible for her, but I wanted to tell you what's going on. Oh, and by the way, the cop says she was Haitian— what do you think about that?"

Bondoc looked at Nimmer. Kelly still didn't have a clue. Amazing. But he knew Millie suspected something; Gina had told him as much. And cops—Jesus, he hadn't expected that. He thanked Kelly, told him not to worry about it, and let the managing partner go.

Should he confide in Millie, or take a chance on her blabbing something to the police? It was a hell of a question. If he told her anything, anything at all, she'd be a threat to him. But if he didn't tell her to keep quiet, who knew what she might say? If only he could be sure she'd keep her suspicions to herself without having to tell her to shut up.

He buzzed Millie and asked her to come in. She apologized, saying a Detective Hennessey was questioning her about Gina Costello, and could he wait a few minutes until she was finished with the police officer? Shit, thought Bondoc. I should have walked out to check on her. Now all I've done is make her nervous and draw attention to myself. He decided to call Epimere.

"John," he said urgently, "I've got a policeman outside my office interviewing my secretary about Gina Costello's disappearance. I'm desperate. What do I do?"

"It's noon, Gus. Why don't you and I have lunch at the Pacific Union Club? Time you were on your way, don't you think?" Epimere hung up, and Bondoc realized it was a command performance. The older man had told him to get out of the office by any means necessary.

Bondoc got his coat on and went through his office door, right past Millie and Hennessey, giving neither of them time to look up. He made it to reception without being importuned, and soon Bondoc was on his way up Nob Hill, past the Fairmont and the Mark to the grand old Flood Mansion—where the stuffiest men's club left in San Francisco had its headquarters.

The average age inside was at least seventy-five. Many of those present had arrived before 10 a.m., gone promptly to chairs in the spacious library, and not moved since.

Over the club's long history, various important personages

thought to have fallen asleep during the day or early evening were later discovered to be stone dead. Under current policy, members who sat inert for too long were gently shaken by an attendant. As a result of this still-controversial directive, and despite an ever-aging membership, no deaths had gone unnoticed in almost three years.

Lunchtime always brought new blood—the median age in the three-story atrium where that meal was served often sank as low as the mid-sixties. When Gus walked in, Epimire was seated by a twenty-foot window, the sun shining gloriously in on him. He was already slurping the red tomato soup that was the club staple.

"Welcome, Gus," the older man said gently, looking nonchalant but somewhat concerned. "No trouble getting away, I hope."

Bondoc sat down opposite Epimere. "You saved my life, John. Another twenty minutes and I'd have had that cop sitting in my office. Just walking out, it was the obvious thing, but I'm helpless now. I had to hear it from you to know to do it."

Epimere stared at Bondoc. Was the younger lawyer enjoying this self-abasement? Was it a breakdown?

To get through what was coming there was no room for either panic or cowardice on his friend's part. Bondoc's great cunning had always been reinforced by a steady nerve; if that nerve was gone, Bondoc was finished. And Epimere had no patience for lost causes.

Epimere ignored his doubts and plunged ahead. "Ways and means, Gus; ways and means. The girl is gone, and the police are making a search for her. Is your secretary a threat here?"

Bondoc hated admitting that he didn't know what Millie

knew, or what she might say. But pride gave way to fear, and he told Epimere that Millie probably knew he'd been sleeping with Gina, if not more. Just from being around the two of them, she must have guessed that.

Anything else, anything serious, like the money and its connection to that thug from the Haitian consulate—Gus couldn't believe Millie knew that. Didn't want to think about it. It meant that Millie could be ruining him right now, that the cops could be on their way here, to the club. Gus actually looked over his shoulder at the gigantic wooden doors spread wide open in welcome to the P.U. lunchers meandering into the round room.

Epimere saw the loss of balance in Gus's face. He put on his most officiously calming air, the one he used only in extremis, for CEOs facing indictments that were sure to doom them.

"What's done is done there, Gus—your girl's no doubt finished giving her statement, and I don't hear any squad car sirens, do you? We're dealing with, what, a local police sergeant? Why, if you call in sick from here, he'll wait a week before coming back—and then only if his lieutenant makes him. Please, no melodrama. We have plenty of time to fix this. Have some soup."

Gus declined the soup; it was always terrible. But he managed to get through lunch, and a hushed library conversation with Epimere afterward. A plan was formulated: David Israel would find Gina; Gus would not question Millie about her interview; he'd go back to the office now, leave early, and then take off for Sonoma for a week, no explanations given. And through it all, Gus would not give in to emotion; his friend, John Epimere, was on top of this.

22

Far Rockaway, Queens; New York City
{Morning, Afternoon, Evening, May 1, 1995}

Her second morning home, Gina had repacked her bags and walked with her mother to the Dime Savings Bank off Fordham Road. Together, they withdrew a thousand dollars in cash. After Gina had faked a menstrual emergency, allowing the two women to lock themselves into the employees' rest room, mother and daughter had wound duct tape around Gina's middle, fixing the banded stack of ten one-hundred-dollar bills onto the small of Gina's back. Gina then left the bank alone, and descended into the IRT station on the Grand Concourse. Hours later, after many subway transfers, she emerged from an IND terminus located in Far Rockaway, Queens, at the base of the Rockaway Peninsula.

There were Haitians living in the Far Rock. Many of them had jobs, and thus something to steal, so they were the ones who got robbed and beaten out here, among the housing projects that dominated the landscape along with a few tin-roofed bodegas proffering everything from untaxed cigarettes to no-condom-necessary acts of fellatio from what only appeared at first glance to be young women.

Gina had gotten a name while she was on the train—somebody who was in the hospital, who might die he'd been beaten so badly. Somebody who had an apartment in the Far Rock Projects. There was no family. The neighbor had a key. No one would know where she was.

The Far Rock was too frightening for anyone to think someone not condemned to live there would go for any reason. By the time she got inside her new apartment, Gina felt she was safe from the men in suits she feared much more than the crackheads and criminal types who were now her neighbors. With the thousand dollars she'd gotten that morning, she could live for six months without talking to a single soul who knew her.

23

San Francisco
{Afternoon and Evening, May 23, 1995}

John Epimere called David Israel at four, after getting back from lunch with the much-reduced Gus Bondoc at three. He had spent an hour with his feet elevated on an ottoman and his eyes staring blankly up at the ceiling. This fall from grace had played out many times for people he liked, people he drank and played bridge with. Some frailty would surface and down they would go, leaving hardly a ripple.

But this—this was a true surprise. That sex would prove Bondoc's undoing.

When he first met Gus, the younger man's cunning was an erotic thing to Epimere. And Epimere remembered well Gus's reaction to an unmistakable bulge in Epimere's pants when the two men were alone one evening early on in their acquaintance.

Despite Gus's best efforts, Epimere saw his repulsion, and his ambition, and, ultimately, his willingness. But then Epimere had let the whole prospect go by the board. Bondoc was sexless, Epimere had judged, and not worth the fuss it would take to pursue him.

Yet now, after so many years, this young girl had stolen money from Gus's most dangerous client, slept with Gus himself, fucked him over and over, and then she'd disappeared to God only knew where, turning Gus upside down in the process.

David was out, and Epimere didn't hear from him until well after nine that night, once he'd returned home.

"We don't know why, and we can only assume the worst, but Gus's girlfriend has disappeared, David, and today the SFPD came looking for her. They nearly put Gus under an unsupervised interrogation."

David Israel was, in fact, much smarter than most of the lawyers who used him. But David particularly respected John Epimere, so he stayed quiet and waited to see if John had anything to add, some theory as to where all this was leading. Right now, it all sounded pretty lousy for Gus Bondoc's ex-girlfriend—she was likely either dead or locked up someplace medieval. Either way, it was bad news for Gus Bondoc that she was gone.

Why would anybody sane represent Baby Doc Duvalier? This need for a big swinging-dick book of business—it had to stop somewhere, didn't it? Duvalier was a stone killer, and somebody had just reached in and taken that man's money. What was happening now was the only natural outcome, David thought.

The silence went on and on, and then Epimere spoke again.

"Maybe she's in trouble, maybe she's not. We have no clue about anything Duvalier may be doing. The shells are simply coming in from too many directions to tell us anything sensible, David. This is a complete clusterfuck."

Israel realized he hadn't heard Epimere use the word fuck

before, not even once; not in the whole time he'd known the man. Twenty-five years.

"David, I don't want you to analyze a bloody thing for us here. What I want is more mechanical. This young woman must have given Gus a written resume of some kind to get a job last year. Some of it may even be true. Use it to try and trace her now. Be discrete, and keep me out of it, but do anything else you like. I'll buy you FBI badges if you want them, and pay for your defense counsel if you're caught.

"Once you find her, put her under a comprehensive surveillance. Keep her safe at all costs, and spare no expense in doing so. I repeat, spare no expense to keep her safe from any harm. You get me a secure cell phone and I'll be available to you at all times. Do not approach her without my say-so. I will not forget what you do for me here, David, and you will not regret the investment of your time or any legal risk you take on my behalf."

David Israel had to stifle a laugh, so sonorous had the old man become at the end. After a moment, he managed to choke out an appropriate rejoinder. "John," he said, "I appreciate your faith in me, and I'll certainly do my best to accomplish everything you ask."

Left to his own devices, and rather than diving into this rat's nest, David would stay in San Francisco for the next six months with the phone shut off. He could live on his considerable personal savings, kept all in cash and safe-deposit boxes, and re-read his entire collection of Dashiel Hammet first editions, sitting comfortably in the cold sunshine of Mission Dolores Park.

Really, anything would be better than trying to hunt down some poor twenty-one-year-old Haitian girl in order to "save" her for Epimere (and Christ only knew what that meant—probably something akin to "saving" a turkey for Thanksgiving dinner), even assuming she was still walking around alive and free, which David very much doubted.

As he called his contact in New York again, this time to set up a semi-permanent base of operations in Manhattan, he found himself wishing Gus would moot this assignment by taking an accelerated ride into the toilet, maybe even literally. David remembered, almost fondly, a long-gone Las Vegas criminal-defense lawyer who'd been autopsied as "drowned, with traces of urine and feces present in lungs." But no such luck here, he thought. People like Gus clung. Such a nice guy. Such a nice situation.

Sergeant Hennessey's interview with Millie Conroy, the cause of Bondoc's latest worries, was in fact rather unproductive. Millie told him that she and Gina were neighbors, that Gina's leaving town had been quite unexpected, and nothing more. When she asked him why anyone would be investigating such a commonplace occurrence as a word processor walking off the job, Hennessey looked at his notes and volunteered that a black man from the East Coast had flown all the way out from New York and raised a big stink, claiming that Gina was in some kind of danger. "Seemed like a nutjob to my lieutenant," Hennessey said, "but you never know. We checked it out, and you guys do represent some pretty shady people, though I never heard about law firms going after typists before."

Just as Hennessey was asking to see "the man," Bondoc had come steamrolling past the two of them, headed for the P.U. Club on Epimere's orders. Millie could see that Hennessey didn't like it. But Hennessey wasn't used to pushing big people around, especially not on the basis of information from nutjobs. He'd given up on promotion, but wasn't looking for any opportunities for demotion either. Observe and report, that was his motto.

Hennessey poked around the law firm for another hour, but at 2:30, with Bondoc still gone, he left his gold-badge-embossed business card for Kelly Nimmer and departed the premises. By 3, Millie had fled to the ladies' room, where she vomited until her stomach ached so intensely that her prior experiences of food poisoning seemed like nothing at all.

Gina was dead. Or worse. It was obvious. And somebody was trying to help her by going to the cops. But the cops were so stupid. And only local cops, at that. She'd dated lots of cops like Hennessey. Drunks. Grabbers. Fuck you in the ass if they could. They all wanted to do that. First the pussy, then the mouth. Then, just before they dumped you, always they wanted to do you in the ass. Something about the sheer Catholic sinfulness of it must be what drove them.

But mainly, the cops she knew were stupid, violent men, no match at all for her boss and that evil fuck Epimere. Those two wanted Gina out of the way, to save Bondoc from Baby Doc. She wasn't sure if Adolph Hitler and Josef Stalin could stop Bondoc and Epimere, but she knew that San Francisco cops certainly weren't up to the job.

When Millie was helped out of the toilet by several worried-looking coworkers around 4, she discovered that Bondoc had already come and gone. Emboldened, she staggered down the hall to John LaBelle's new associate-sized office. One look at Millie was enough for him.

"Not here," he said as soon as Millie closed his door behind her. "I've been thrown out of my house, and I'm over at the Harbor Hotel in Room 654. Here's my key. Pretend you're going home and meet me there in an hour. I'll try to bring Shane. I know it sounds stupid, but please try to be sure you're not followed. I'm about ready to jump out of my skin, and I know if I screw up, Carla will never let me see my baby Claire again."

At the thought of that happening, Millie broke down. She sat quietly crying for nearly ten minutes while LaBelle watched her warily. Then, finally, she composed herself and left.

LaBelle waited for almost half an hour before buzzing Sullivan. He began matter-of-factly: "Shane, I assume you know there was a cop here looking for Gina today?" Typically, however, Sullivan was clueless. He'd been at the Hastings law library, writing an involved motion trying to limit damages in the Applied case—something most lawyers of his seniority left to underlings.

"Look, Shane, Gina might be dead, OK? Dead. Now Millie and I are going to act, with you or without you. But we want your counsel. Just walk out of work with me tonight and I'll take you to a meeting with Millie. We'll all decide together what to do—together. I'll listen to the goddamn tape so I'm in it all the way up to my neck too."

At 4:50 p.m., Sullivan and LaBelle left early, supposedly to have a drink and talk over the motion Shane had been working up at Hastings. The junior lawyers he'd been with all day at the library were told they weren't invited.

The 1989 Loma Prieta earthquake knocked down the Embarcadero Freeway, San Francisco's even uglier version of the West Side Highway. Nothing else short of an act of a capital "G" god—in as godless a City as has existed since, dare one say it, ancient Sodom—would ever have opened up the long blockaded waterfront otherwise. With the collapse of the freeway, the old Army-Navy YMCA became waterfront property. It was allowed to sell some of its ownership rights and consolidate its own operations on the lower floors. A hotel operator took the top floors, renamed them the Harbor Hotel, and modestly refurbished the pre-WWI, YMCA-dimensioned rooms, many of them now with views that few other spots in the city could rival.

John LaBelle had a rear room, however; it looked out over an air vent. It was cheap, rented by the month, and smelled like the Y room it always had been. When he and Sullivan knocked, Millie immediately sprang up from the lone metal chair—other than a heavy wood chest as old as the Y and a lumpy double bed, it was the room's only furniture. She opened the door to them without even asking who was there. LaBelle couldn't be sure, but he thought she'd been heaving again.

Maybe Sullivan didn't drink, and maybe Millie shouldn't, but Labelle had bought a sixer of Beck's and some ice on the way over. He took the top off one and put the others in the tub after Millie waved him off with a wan look.

Sullivan watched LaBelle drink his beer. This effete shmuck and Bondoc's ragamuffin secretary were panicked about some lowlife cop who had shown up at the office after taking the day off from directing tourists at Pier 39. And they were forcing him to act prematurely in a very delicate situation. There was money on the table. Money he'd put on the table, he reminded himself, by pushing Bob Treister into a very-bad-for-the-Sullivan-family merger and losing Treister as his patron saint in the bargain.

Shane thought of his own family at that point. The wife he'd met at Berkeley, who'd seen him through all his emotional ups and downs. His six rambunctious kids, among them the oldest, his favorite, a girl, Grace, just two years younger than Gina. A freshman at Princeton. Grace was too delicate, too creative for Shane's alma mater, Harvard. People self-destructed right before your eyes at the Big H, which was like the Marine Corps, always proudest when it got the most guys killed fighting side by side with the other services.

Grace was blond, Gina was dark. Grace was highly privileged, emotionally pampered, and safe behind high walls, while Gina was poor, unprotected, and now thrust stupidly into extreme danger. Suddenly Shane became choked with worry about both of them.

Sullivan was a pure alpha, and that was how he liked it, the only way he liked it. He was also a deeply intuitive alpha, and he had decided Gina was in trouble the moment he had emotionally identified Gina with his own dear Gracie. Thus, Gus Bondoc, with all of his other problems, had inadvertently tripped yet another detonator in Sullivan's multi-booby-trapped-personality, right there in Room 654 of the small dingy Harbor Hotel, this time through absolutely no fault of his own.

While Sullivan was thinking matters through, LaBelle's attention had never left his Beck's. Sullivan's angst was invisible to him. Millie Conroy could see the turmoil in Shane's face, but she knew nothing of Shane other than his well-earned reputation for outrageous sarcasm to staff. So she said nothing, just dropped her eyes to the floor and waited for someone else to begin speaking.

LaBelle was halfway to the tub to get another Beck's when Sullivan brought him up short. "Listen, you sorry little dick—I didn't come here to watch you get off on beer. Drink the rest of that shit when Millie and I are gone, and then you can pull your pud too, for good measure. We have some serious things to deal with tonight."

Rather than making him angry, Sullivan's words relaxed

LaBelle. Bondoc was vicious, and only someone just as vicious was going to be a meaningful ally here. Sullivan was the right man. And one thing LaBelle knew how to do, and do well, was play lapdog to the King.

Millie, on the other hand, was horrified by the exchange. She nearly left the hotel room, but instead she dashed to the toilet, retching again. Macho games, macho games about who gets to drink an extra bottle of beer, she thought, when my poor girl may be dead or in pain. Men are such pigs and wasters, and here I am asking these two selfish bastards for help.

When she emerged from the small dismal bathroom, she was shocked to see Sullivan and LaBelle engaged in a cordial, relaxed conversation. The ice was melting in the tub, and LaBelle's beer was getting warm. Sullivan, from memory, had just finished giving LaBelle a more or less verbatim rendition of the contents of the recorded conversation between Bondoc and Jones, and LaBelle was shaking his head with wonder. They both turned to face Millie.

By the time the meeting was over, a plan of action had been established. Shane Sullivan would act for the group. As John LaBelle and Millie Conroy were petrified, this point had been quickly agreed upon. Shane thought it best to approach the United States Attorney's Office for the Southern District of New York, the largest and most prestigious federal prosecutor's office in the country, and urge that office to initiate a meaningful search for Gina and an investigation of any possible link between Bondoc and Gina's disappearance. "It's the nuclear approach," Shane told his colleagues. "My favorite." No one said no, and that was always enough for Shane.

24

New York City; The Bronx
{June, 1995}

Practically speaking, no one got the attention of Mary Jo White's staff without an in of some kind. Even with a tape as hot as the one he had tucked in his briefcase, Sullivan knew he needed someone influential to provide an entrée.

Fortunately, Sullivan's wife's high-toned Seacliff social circle included a political lawyer, a semi-retiree who'd once served as the United States Attorney for the Northern District of California. When asked for help, this man had not asked Sullivan many questions, just ascertained it was a serious matter for Shane and then called his old pal Rudy. An in-person interview with a mid-level lifer in the Southern District of New York hierarchy, somebody who could run with the ball if there was something good to run with, was quickly arranged.

"Just never forget where you'd be without friends, Shane," the fixer said, winking at the younger man. For Shane, who'd never taken the jocular older man at all seriously, this was almost a life lesson—for, while Shane couldn't pound a nail, change a tire, or even credibly drive a car, in litigating big civil cases Shane always took Daniel Boone's approach to entering bloody Kentucky for the first time in 1769. He brought his own arms, lived by his wits, and expected help from no one who wasn't on the payroll. Friends just weren't in his operating vocabulary. But then, rescuing Haitian damsels obviously required a new approach.

Shane arrived at the West Side Vista Hotel, within the World Trade Center complex, after 4 a.m. His meeting with Greg Wardling was set for 10 a.m. He slept like shit, and despite his well-tailored clothes he looked the same way when he struggled through Foley Square and into AUSA Wardling's spartan private office the next morning, a full ten minutes early—he'd been cleared through the federal prosecutor's office's extensive security apparatus with a pat-down.

Shane knew next to nothing about New York; he'd visited maybe six times in his life. He'd come to Harvard from a small town in Illinois, where his chemist father Marcus Sullivan preferred life for himself and his family, far away from the numerous skeletons in the Sullivan family closet. Then Shane had gone from Cambridge to Berkeley. And from Berkeley to San Francisco. Just small town stuff really, he thought, feeling the rawness of the power at work in Foley Square that spring day.

A power far more intoxicating than the merely omnipresent power of ideas in Cambridge and Berkeley. Here power was some concupiscent mix of big ideas, big money, and, most directly, an arbitrary control over personal liberty in service to the first two, all of which created a real hum in the air. A good place to stay away from, the erstwhile Daniel Boone decided instantly. He reminded himself to be extremely polite to Mr. Wardling.

Greg Wardling was New York City from the tips of his

toes to the top of his curly black hair. Born in Washington
Heights. German Catholic. Regis High School. Fordham
College. Columbia Law. Right into the DOJ out of law
school. Not elite enough to be immediately hired as an
AUSA in the Southern District, where only Yale or Harvard
plus a federal clerkship would normally do, and, where, by
tradition, the AUSAs only stayed on for a few years before
heading to greener pastures outside government. Instead,
he'd been hired on at Main Justice in DC and then shipped
around from one remote federal province to another until,
finally, his competence and tenure had won him a place back
in the homeland. Where he firmly intended to stay until
elevated to his dream job: the federal bench.

He knew the man in front of him had used some mild juice
to get an interview. Just something social that had wound its
way down to him. "See him, Greg. Make nice. He's nice, you
be nice. He's not nice, you don't be nice. Probably nothing.
If it's something, then put it on the list."

If people only knew, he thought, how bureaucratized law
enforcement is. How unimaginative and afraid of being fired
everyone in government is, no matter how secure their silly
jobs really are. How do we ever catch anyone? he wondered.
Criminals are creative and unafraid—that's why crime
attracts them. And they're up against such dullards.

To get through Columbia Law, Wardling had swallowed
his conscience and worked nights in Harlem for GM,
repossessing cars. Mainly he'd worked with moonlighting
New York homicide cops. He'd go into the ghetto before dark
each day, posing as a Vista volunteer, and get information on
his targets for that night's attack.

In contrast, the homicide dicks did no investigations;
they carried their guns around with them while driving

aimlessly through the Harlem nights with their windows rolled up, living in fear that their unmarked GM fleet cars would somehow be spotted and set ablaze by the niggers, coons, spear-chuckers and other charming sobriquets that even the black cops among them used to describe the GM customers whom they were hunting.

Greg made big bonuses and saved his money. The homicide cops mostly made minimum wage, which they usually drank up at the end of each night's work, all before hitting the street for their day shift looking for real criminals. Greg knew that the so-called "Order" scenes in *Law & Order* were the biggest frauds on television. All those NYPD cops were too dumb, drunk, and asleep to catch a cold.

Sullivan was uncomfortable as hell. He understood next to nothing about criminal law, and he had a tape of a private conversation the very possession of which might be some kind of a crime. For the first time in a long while, the idea of causing a "nuclear solution" to every problem didn't seem nearly so droll. In the face of the impassive appraisal coming his way from Wardling's side of the desk, only the emotional link he'd forged between Grace and Gina really pushed him beyond his own instinct for self-preservation.

"Last April a guy in my office brought me a recording. I've got it with me. I don't know how it was made, but I can guess. Now, before I tell you about it, which I'm going to do no matter what you tell me, I just want to know what happens to me here." Sullivan cursed himself for sounding like a guilty fool, but he had to say something before he just spilled his guts, get some kind of a reaction from this smug government cipher.

"Mr. Sullivan," said Wardling, "from what I know, you're an upstanding lawyer, and you're here voluntarily in order to help the government. So, even if you have somehow been, let's say, remiss, in what you are about to tell me, unless your conduct is much the worst of the tale, I wouldn't worry. No promises, of course, but don't worry."

You complete chump, thought Wardling, who, though he meant every word of his platitudinous reassurances to Sullivan, knew that no Manhattan criminal defense lawyer worth his salt would have ever accepted such vague assurances from him before allowing Sullivan to utter another word.

"It's Baby Doc Duvalier," blurted out Sullivan. And if Wardling had been a Doberman, his ears would have stood straight up at the mention of that name.

"My boss is his lawyer. And this young girl, she's from The Bronx and she's Haitian, or she's half-Haitian, or she's something Haitian, she got a job at the office and she figured out where some of Baby Doc's money was. A lot of Baby Doc's money. Then the boss started sleeping with her, or maybe even before, I mean who knows."

Sullivan paused for breath. Wardling impatiently motioned for him to continue, staring intently. "So last April, in comes this guy who says he's from the Haitian Consulate at the U.N., good credentials, the whole deal, only he's really a con man. And he's got a gun, which he shows to Gus Bondoc—that's my boss's name. He wants money. There's a recording of the whole attempted extortion that I've got with me right here. And now the girl's gone, SFPD is looking for her, and I think Baby Doc may have her. Bondoc might even have done something with her— he's desperate to hush this thing up, he's scared so shitless of Baby Doc. I have a daughter almost the same age as the girl, man, and I just can't live with this on my conscience. I'm so sorry I've been sitting on this—it's just been so unclear to me what I should do. Until cops started showing up, I just never thought anyone could be getting hurt here."

Wardling was bored to tears by his job. And here, laid out right in front of him, was the great black defendant—Baby Doc Duvalier himself, murderer of Bronx innocence, international fugitive in exotic ports of call, killer by remote control. Maybe in cooperation with this scumbag lawyer Bondoc.

Or even with this guy Sullivan, who was just trying to come in first, all teary-eyed and all. Though, glancing at the man, the prosecutor checked his more aggressive instincts. If this wimp was a perp, he'd eat his hat. A schemer of some kind, definitely. But a perp, no.

"What is the nature of the forensic material you have with you, Mr. Sullivan?" Wardling asked coldly, trying to conceal his excitement. He really wanted to hug Sullivan and go buy him a stiff drink, though it was barely 10:30 a.m.

"It's an electronic recording of an extortion attempt, like I said," Sullivan replied.

"How is it stored?"

"On a 3 ½" floppy."

""Give it here," said Wardling, opening a clear plastic evidence bag, careful to avoid touching the floppy himself. "I'll have the lab take a look and a listen right away. In the meantime, I'd like to have you wait in our reception area while I discuss what you've already told me with my superiors. You may be in our offices for some time, perhaps a few days even. I hope that won't inconvenience you. You're not in any difficulty, I assure you, and we're most grateful for any help you'll give us."

None of this phony reassurance was public record, so it was deniable and ultimately meant nothing. But Wardling was sure Sullivan really wouldn't wind up in the office's gunsights, so he was playing fast and loose in his excitement. If the man took a fall later on, why didn't the guy know he should have had a lawyer before walking into the lion's den?

For Christ's sake, Greg thought, mentally shaking his head as he ushered Sullivan into reception, he wasn't Sullivan's lawyer, or his psychiatrist, or his goddamn social worker either. He was a mean motherfucking federal prosecutor who'd just had a piece of red meat crammed in his mouth.

It wasn't until two and a half days later that Sullivan was finally released by Wardling and an ever-increasing flock of federal prosecutors and assorted feebees. He slept at the Vista every night, getting back there by 8:00 p.m. and having dinner in his room. Careful lies were told to the office about a sudden flu, with appropriate backup obtained from a cooperative New York doctor in case the story was checked.

As he emerged from the prosecutor's office at last, beaten down and worried, Shane Sullivan looked out across Foley Square at the amalgam of civic buildings staring back at him. Wardling was hooked, no doubt about that. The feds would find Gina if they could, and if Baby Doc or Bondoc had harmed her, it was going to get worse for them.

Sullivan had figured out by about 2:00 p.m. of the first day that Wardling was playing him with all his phony reassurances. A call to a professor friend at NYU had quickly produced, within about an hour, Joseph H. Abrahams— one very aggressive, very expensive New York criminal-defense attorney. A man who made up for Sullivan's naiveté by documenting a formal proffer-based immunity deal for him, Millie Conroy, and John LaBelle, with accompanying screams of outrage directed at Wardling, screams that left the prosecutor chuckling at his prominent adversary's notoriously high energy level.

"Joey, Joey—what do you take every morning to get yourself so excited?" Wardling said to Sullivan's new counsel as the paperwork was prepared.

"Fuck you, Greg. My guy is a shmuck, you know it. So you pull his pants down. Then you stick it in. It feels good. You rub it around. Then you tell me I'm excited when I tell you wear a condom, you may give him a disease. He's a nice boy, from you he doesn't need to get AIDS. And from you, believe me, anybody could get AIDS."

"Joey, I am not homosexual—I'm a good, churchgoing RC who firmly believes sex is only for procreation. All Mr. Sullivan here would ever get from me is the clap, and the clap isn't so bad. He's going to pay you way more for this paperwork than he'd ever pay to cure any V.D."

Sullivan watched the two men joke about the mistake he'd made in trusting Wardling, a mistake that might have cost him and Labelle their law licenses and all three of his group their liberty, whatever Wardling might now say. Fucking selfish asshole. But what'd you expect? he thought. It's not a nice world, and it's not a helping profession.

Before he left New York, Sullivan had two more stops. First to NYU Law's Vanderbilt Hall, on the south side of Washington Square Park in Greenwich Village, where he wanted to thank Professor Pete Brad in person for rescuing him from Mr. Wardling, and then get some practical advice on how to deal with the storm clouds brewing over Applied. Then it would be off to Princeton to see Grace, to make sure she was normal and untroubled in what otherwise seemed a pretty upside-down world.

Brad was in his early thirties. Appointed to the NYU law faculty straight from a Supreme Court clerkship, he had a fascination with corporate governance and legal ethics, and had published the leading textbooks in both subjects within just a few years of his initial appointment. Got tenure last year, itself an unheard-of honor for someone so young, and an honor only extended because of fear that Harvard would beat NYU to the punch if the NYU administration hesitated in any way. Yet the man remained entirely open and approachable, and he'd been a boon companion to Shane all through the thicket of the Applied case.

When he got into see Professor Brad, after first waiting out a student-teacher conference involving a very long-winded student, it took Sullivan about twenty minutes to summarize Gus Bondoc's misfortunes and his own very considerable involvement in worsening them over the past few days. Brad appeared genuinely shocked by what he heard.

"My God, Shane," he said, "I had no idea your firm had such clients. Multi-nationals are bad enough, believe me, I know. But that young Duvalier—he's a gangster, a real serial killer. If there were any effective international justice system in this world, he'd be hanging at the end of a rope somewhere right now."

"Well, Pete, we can't off Duvalier. What I need to figure is what to tell Ed Zbrewski about all this, if anything. I mean, Bondoc's not really involved in Applied, but if the firm blows up—which it easily could—that would hurt Holliday & Bennett, especially if it came close to trial. And the government has sworn me to secrecy, but I don't think they can make that stick—it's just more of that pushy Wardling throwing his weight around. The main thing, though, the reason I stuck my neck out and came East, is I don't want this girl hurt. I can't see how warning Zbrewski is going to do that unless he tells Bondoc what I tell him."

Shane's desire to hijack Applied was obvious to the

professor, who had made a study of the rationalizations used by the highly educated to achieve base goals. He'd acted somewhat unselfishly in ratting Bondoc out to the United States Attorney—he had a heart—but now that he'd done what he could for the girl, Shane wanted Bondoc's book of business. As Pete Brad analyzed it, Shane was even considering taking marginal chances with the girl's safety to get it.

Nothing for it but to bell the cat, he thought. "Look, Shane—we don't know each other well, and this may sound harsh. Anything you tell Zbrewski is in the open. Maybe you have to tell him; maybe you can convince yourself you have to tell him, anyway, because it suits you to believe that. But if Bondoc has the girl, it affects the girl. Simple as that. It's Bondoc's book versus the girl, if that's the way it plays. And you don't want that.

"You're one of the most talented people I know. Not normal, but talented. You don't need this. Play it straighter than you've ever played anything in your life. Take no chances and do nothing to hurt anyone. I know something of this man Wardling you mentioned. This thing is in his world now—that's not your world and it's not my world."

Shane's visit to the dreaming spires of Princeton went roughly the same way. When he told Grace the story, she recoiled. She'd always been brutalized by what he did, shocked at how he used his intellect to dismember people and then strip them of their belongings. As she'd grown older, she'd become reluctant to accept money earned in such a ghastly way. They were gradually becoming estranged, and he greatly feared for their future together. Only the thought that he'd risked himself for a stranger seemed to please her, and she practically cheered at every word of Professor Brad's that he repeated.

Flying home the next morning out of Newark, Sullivan concluded law professors and college freshmen sure thought they knew a lot about life. But they didn't have to make a living.

He wasn't going to murder anybody, and he wasn't going to help murder anybody. But he wasn't going to be a sucker, either. When the moment is right, he thought, I'm going to bite that fucking Gus Bondoc's neck so hard they'll have to use a triple dose of embalming fluid just to pump him back up to normal size for his funeral. Then he settled back in his first-class seat to observe Forrest Gump proclaim that even stupid people know what love is.

Wardling had two feebees assigned full time to the Duvalier investigation. A copy of the SFPD's missing-person file on Gina Costello was obtained through the FBI office in San Francisco; it disclosed Pierre Esclemond, of 14256 East Tremont Avenue, Bronx, New York, as the complaining party. Even the feebees couldn't blow this one, thought Wardling, as he dispatched the pair to pick up Esclemond and bring the Haitian editor back to their Federal Plaza headquarters to sweat him.

Pierre didn't break as much as gush. Gina's disappearance and the lack of any concrete response to his complaints and follow-up telephone calls to various Bay Area police departments had practically driven him to distraction. Gina's mother's insistence that Gina was out of touch with her as well convinced him she was the victim of foul play, probably by Jones, maybe even by Duvalier himself. He'd waived his rights, and was in Wardling's office giving a full statement an hour after he was first picked up in The Bronx. A court reporter was present and pecking away.

As he listened to Esclemond answer questions posed by

one of the more junior AUSA's working up the case with him, it was obvious to Wardling that no jury on earth would ever convict Esclemond for passing stolen information to Jones. No sensible prosecutor would even think of charging him. Robbing serial killers of their financial spoils for no reward didn't qualify one for a traffic ticket, let alone a major felony count.

Jones would have to go home, of course. Beating up one citizen and blackmailing another. And someone at State might want to slip that recording to someone in Haiti, just so they could see what he'd been doing here, and thereby countering any hard feelings about Jones's deportation.

The real issue here was the girl. Maybe they'd eventually have to prosecute her, but first they needed to find her and keep her safe. Based on Pierre's information, they had Gina's mother Eugenia in protective custody by 9:00 p.m. that same night.

She, however, wouldn't talk. Instead, she demanded a federal public defender, and a considerable stink was then raised about who exactly was being protected from what. Wardling was barely able to hold Eugenia in the temporary lockup at Federal Plaza overnight, and the next morning he was facing a very angry-looking federal magistrate who immediately started asking the same questions the public defender had raised the night before.

"Your Honor," Wardling said, "if we can close the courtroom and proceed with a sealed transcript, I believe I can make the government's position clear and satisfy my esteemed colleague, the federal public defender." Wardling actually hated the little pinko who'd drawn the case off the wheel—the man always made his life a misery for exercise. But he was after the great black defendant now, and Sid

Lorand was about to get the most respectful treatment of his life from Greg Wardling. Lorand, a mere Brooklyn Law graduate who was indeed a red-diaper baby, looked over at Wardling like he was trying to catch the joke. The magistrate, however, was all business.

"No objection? Granted. Courtroom ordered cleared. Recess. Back in five. Mr. Wardling, this had better be good."

When the court was back in session, Wardling said nothing—just ran the recording while the court reporter transcribed its contents, under seal, in full. Then, as the impact of what had been heard sunk in, he said:

"The young woman Mr. Bondoc was said to be sleeping with is the daughter of the witness taken into protective custody last evening, Your Honor. That young woman, Gina Costello, has disappeared since this recording was made, and the government is concerned about foul play coming from any one of several directions, not the least of which is the notorious victim of her embezzlement: Jean Claude Duvalier, sometimes known as Baby Doc Duvalier. If the Court will now order Mr. Lorand not to discuss the contents of this morning's hearing with anyone but his client, and order Mrs. Costello not to discuss what she hears of this morning's hearing from Mr. Lorand with anyone but him, then perhaps everyone can join hands with the government for the sake of this unfortunate and endangered young woman, and we can still save her life."

Lorand was dumbstruck.

"So ordered," said the no-longer-angry federal magistrate, who then immediately left the bench.

Wardling then turned to his public-defender doppelganger. "Look, Sid," he said, "the mother can't possibly know what

Gina's gotten herself involved in. If she knows something, anything, we're the ones to tell. We're not going to kill Gina. Sure, we might prosecute her, but how likely is that, even? I mean, stealing from Baby Doc, they'll probably vote to give her a medal. At this point, if she's breathing, I want her to stay that way, that's all. Don't let the fact you think I'm a prick and I know you're a prick get in the way. This is one time we're really on the same side, boychick. So help me. I'll owe you."

Sid Lorand spit on the ground right in front of Wardling. Wardling didn't react.

Lorand looked disappointed. Wardling held his stare. A moment more passed. Then Lorand shrugged. "Okay, okay—I'll talk to the mom. If your goons let me, I'll try and have her in your office in an hour. You could even act like a human being when you see her—I know you're a Nazi at heart, but you should try this one time to pretend you're a human being. This woman is innocent of anything, and she's afraid for her child already, without even knowing any of this heavy shit you're putting out."

Eugenia Costello arrived in Greg Wardling's conference room with her lawyer in tow at 2 p.m. Wardling had a court reporter, his two assigned FBI agents, and a junior AUSA sitting around the cheap metal conference table that must have come with the building. Lorand had clearly told Eugenia about the recording, but the fight hadn't gone out of her. She looked at Wardling defiantly. "You don't care nothing for no one" she sputtered. "You don't fool me, government man—you're all the same. Haiti, the US, all the same. I've been dealing with the INS for twenty, going on twenty-five years now—I know a dirt bag like you. I smell you all the way from my jail cell." Even Wardling was stopped cold by Eugenia's hateful vitriol.

He was mainly a white collar prosecutor now. Some Mafia, sure, but for them violence was just business. This kind of raw contact with the street took him back to his own beginnings, back to when he'd been all on his own—with both parents dead before he'd turned 21—and reduced to jumping in hot cars for GM for a living.

It was virtually his first day on that job when a senile homicide cop spotted a yellow sports car and wrote down the VIN number. The next night, the car was there again, and, naturally, the VIN number checked against the one he'd previously written down in his little black book. So the cop towed the car. Wardling had been along both nights, but he'd been too green to understand how crazed the old cop was. What it all meant was that GM stole some black guy's car.

The old cop went off to get drunk and left Wardling to do the paperwork. When Wardling got the car to the yard and figured out the mess, he called the man who was to become his desk boss for the next two and half years. He could hear a baby crying in the background. "George," he said, "we got this big problem." By the time he was finished, George was actually crying—it might've been the baby, but it sure sounded like George. He kept saying that everyone at 10 Columbus Circle would be fired, just like the last time this happened, and then he wanted to know if that goddamn Johnson, the senile cop, was already drunk when he pulled the car.

Johnson wasn't drunk, Wardling explained—just over the hill. Anyway, he said, let's put the car back, for Pete's sake. So they did, with a caravan of tow trucks from White Plains, three of them, carrying about twelve big mean white guys, all with shotguns. It was late at night, and they were going into a very, very bad part of Harlem—no Vista volunteer story was going to fool anybody at that hour, not the way they looked.

The parking space where Johnson had first sinned was already taken. So Wardling insisted they park the poor mope's car down the street, this time quite illegally. That probably got the pretty little yellow car towed by the City, but nobody ever figured out anything; certainly, nobody at GM ever got fired.

So George was forevermore Greg's great, good friend, and he always watched out for him. Got him the good gigs, where the bonus money was big. Kept him out of trouble. But then there was the Black Panther, the one who had the shitty Firebird and the cheap handgun. The moonlighting cops were useless. He was wanted for crimes in three states, and they couldn't get near the guy even on their day jobs. But the GM computer inexorably required that either the Firebird be paid for or the Firebird be pulled, and the same GM computer wrote George's paycheck. George lived in real fear of that GM computer.

So George was caught. He loved Greg, and he wanted to keep him from harm. But he also loved his job, or at least, after graduating at the bottom of his class at Iona College, he clung to it. George therefore introduced Greg to the possibility of compromise with that nothing-left-to-lose part of the proletariat he would come into much more frequent contact with as part of his later government service.

At George's suggestion, once a month, Greg would meet Mufta Ali in an open field in The Bronx. Greg would be in his GM car; Mufta would be in his long-hunted Firebird. The cheap handgun would not be visible. A bad check drawn on a long-closed account in an ever-increasing amount would be handed over to Greg, and pleasantries would be exchanged. Nothing untoward involving Mufta or his Firebird took place while Greg worked for George. The GM computer was fed and stupidly accepted those checks for nearly two years, until an audit determined that Mufta's checking account had been closed for the last six. Greg was soon fired over his implacable unwillingness to pursue Mufta, or anything associated with or belonging to him, on any basis whatsoever. His replacement, an armed moonlighting member of the NYPD, was shot in the groin during his stupid, but heroic effort to repossess the shitty Firebird.

So now he had another stupid, reckless prole, Eugenia Costello, to deal with. And like that long-ago Black Panther there was no real reasoning with her. How could he possibly get her to focus on the girl, her own daughter? She might, and probably did, know something that would help him find Gina, or at least figure out what had happened to Gina. But if he pushed her, Eugenia would just as soon shoot him in the groin as well.

No help for it, he thought. Try it tough. Be just as big a Nazi as Sid had no doubt advertised he would be.

"Dead, Mrs. Costello—that's what your little girl Gina is. Dead as a doornail. And, if she's not dead, why they've got her tied up to a wall somewhere, and they're hooking up the wires to her labia right now. So you go ahead and tell me all about it. You go on, tell me some more how mean the INS is, as if I gave a shit."

The junior AUSA—out of Harvard Law by way of Radcliffe College, with a stop at the Second Circuit Court of Appeal before arriving at her present position—visibly blanched at this. But one look at Wardling's face convinced her that any dissent would be the end of her career in that office.

Sid Lorand stepped in front of his client and pushed his face right up against Wardling's. "You're a pig, Wardling—a real pig. Even for you, this is a new low."

Before the two men could fall to blows, Eugenia collapsed into a chair. Then she began weeping, letting low moans escape her, cries of real agony. That stopped the macho shit. Finally, ten, maybe twenty minutes later, she began speaking.

"I don't really know nothing. She came home, I don't know, late last April, the 28th, I think. Two days later she gone again. I gave her a thousand in cash. She put it around her waist, poor baby. With tape, so no one robs her. Maybe May 1st. The bank can tell you. Dime up on the Concourse. Half the money I got in the world, but she could have it all if she asked me. Boom, she leaves the bank. Where she went I don't know, she doesn't say. In a cab, on the train, who knows? To where, who knows? Had her bag with her.

Later on I get a post card mailed from California. It says she's ok, but not in her writing. I've got the card in my purse, I'll give it to you. Nothing after that. Nothing. I'm going crazy. I lie to Pierre because she says lie. Now I guess I know why, he get her in this trouble, try to make money on her. Him I will kill, then you can have some crime to prosecute, big government man, that I promise, you write this down right now, you hear. Pierre, he's going to be dead, anything happen to my Gina."

By the end of June, thanks to Wardling, Jones was back in Haiti. A copy of the Jones/Bondoc recording was in the hands of the Haitian Good Government Commission, with a copy no doubt headed in the direction of one Col. Francois Jones, Edouard's father and prominent member of the Haitian military police, as well.

At around the same time, David Israel was having a hurried meeting on a Central Park bench with a high-level employee of the FBI's New York office. The man had used

David as a source for years, and he owed David numerous favors—the information Israel had given him had earned him several promotions.

This was their third meeting. David had already explained who Gina was and what he wanted by way of cooperation if the bureau had somehow developed an interest in the case. Now his contact was prepared to tell him what he could and couldn't do.

"Look, David," the man said, "I don't know who brought it to him or why, but there's a running case on Gina, and the guy who caught it, this Wardling character, he's a real prick. He hates the bureau. There are two young guys assigned to him on this thing, and he's put the fear of God into them. They talk to anyone, me, anyone, they're gone. I'm reported, I'm gone. I only know what I'm about to tell you because there's this AUSA is so outraged by Wardling's language she's complained to the federal ombudsman, for God's sake—something about Wardling threatening to wire Gina's labia or some other crazy shit—and the ombudsman has to report to me.

"So I come to learn Wardling has interviewed two people while looking for your girl—a guy named Pierre Esclemond, and a woman named Eugenia Costello. These are their addresses. No idea what the witnesses told Greg. Everyone is very hush hush about that, including little miss color-me-offended.

"Last thing I can tell you is the two newbies Wardling has assigned to him can't find dick. All they do off-shift is complain that Wardling's all over them, making their life a living hell every day, screaming for action, and still they can't find dick. Girl must be a goner, if you ask me."

Israel knew all about Pierre and Eugenia's brush with

Wardling. He'd picked up Pierre's trail the same way Wardling had, from the SFPD's missing-person file on Gina. He'd gotten to New York ten days ahead of Shane Sullivan and immediately set up round-the-clock surveillance on Pierre. He'd even allowed his local guy to wiretap, something he was normally loath to do.

That led right to Eugenia, whom Pierre called almost daily to see if Gina had called in. When the feebees had arrived, David's people had tracked Pierre, and then Eugenia, all the way to the steps of Federal Plaza. Into that particular red anthill, however, David's local agents dared not go. Instead, David had called his mole.

The problem with all of it, David reflected, nibbling a hot dog in the late June sunshine once his contact had hurriedly departed, is we're hardly any closer to the girl. Sure, the two young FBI agents had eliminated many stupid possibilities, like air travel or passage on the Queen Elizabeth to Southampton. Likely Gina was somewhere in the five boroughs.

But with a thousand in cash and a desire to go to ground, she'd be hard to find. And that was if she was just hiding—if Baby Doc had killed her, or even just had her, then she was gone, period.

If she was hiding, then he still had a chance. And if he found her, well, he'd promptly give her to Wardling. That was the obvious fix, and fuck old John Epimere. Fuck old Gussy Bondoc too, David thought happily. I don't know or care what their game was before, but now that Wardling is in this thing they're shit out of luck. Because Wardling would keep her safe. David knew that and that was what mattered.

He thought for a moment about how happy it would make his FBI contact if Gina's whereabouts were suddenly whispered in his ear at around the same time David's report was being made to John Epimere. Nobody, but nobody, was getting hurt on his watch, he thought—at least not by him, not if they didn't deserve it.

Now he was going to run down and thoroughly interview every human being Gina Costello had ever known in the City of New York between grade school and college, from *Haiti Today* to every Catholic charity affiliate she'd ever helped out. He was going to hire fifty Haitians to help him, if he had to. And he was going to send Epimere some very large bills for the privilege of having him do so.

By the end of June, John Epimere and Gus Bondoc were back having lunch at the P.U. Club. Epimere had just told Bondoc the bad news about the United States Attorney's interest in Gina's disappearance and David's present inability to locate the girl ahead of the FBI. He watched Bondoc's face for the signs of the breakdown he sensed was surely coming. To his surprise, however, Bondoc maintained an outward composure.

"Doesn't prove much, really, does it, John?" Bondoc said. "I mean, it could just be Pierre phoning it in, stirring it up. David said nothing about the Jones recording somehow surfacing, did he?"

"Didn't say he knew either way, but I'm sure that means he doesn't know. And if he doesn't know, that's a very good reason to think you're right—they don't have it."

"So," said Bondoc, "it's not good—but the FBI, so what? They're no match for David. Just pay his bills on a same-day basis and we'll all live in hope. And no, John, goddamnit, no soup for me. Just a cheese sandwich and an iced tea."

25

San Francisco; New York City
{July, 1995}

At the end of the first week in July, Sullivan sent Zbrewski his draft Motion in Limine Number One. The motion focused on Ben Carpuchi's entirely amateurish and speculative presentation of expert testimony establishing Applied's actual damages in its underlying case against Dr. Tom Dolan. It also cited, for the first time, the impressive counter-expert Sullivan had located, whose testimony devastated Carpuchi's man. Not coincidentally, the two experts were rival professors at the same graduate school of business. Carpuchi's professor, however, was an administrator and fundraiser; his real expertise was on the dinner circuit. Sullivan's guy was analytical cold steel.

The motion was far from a no-hoper. If accepted, it would reduce the Applied case to what it really was: a legitimate beef about an inflated legal bill, where the client's own greed and animus toward the defendant would be the biggest part of the defense. An opening statement pointing out Louie Habash's personality defects in that regard could be made with a straight face. What was most appealing about the whole thing was that a mere ten-million-dollar upside just wasn't enough to get that man-eater Carpuchi very excited at this point in his career, which meant winning this one pre-trial motion would give Holiday & Bennett a real chance of settling short of trial.

Sullivan knew Zbrewski was going to love this, and he deliberately sent it blind to the Holliday & Bennett general counsel without even discussing it first with Bondoc. He had another surprise coming for Gus as soon as Mr. Zbrewski called him to express his delight with Sullivan's legal work.

Which didn't take very long. Ed Zbrewski was on the phone to Shane Sullivan two days after the FedEx package containing the draft limine motion left Bondoc, Treister, Nimmer & Sourwine. He was excited and more than complimentary; Shane reacted by downplaying his achievement in light of the uncertainty of obtaining grant of the motion and, of course, all the other problems—Homer Rhodes, the world's worst witness; Ben Carpuchi, the lion of the courtroom, etc. But Zbrewski wasn't buying false modesty.

"Look, Shane," he said finally, "I do this for a living. All day, every day. At our level of deductible, we practically self-insure. And if you saw the shit the thousand idiots in this firm scattered all over the world get us into, then you'd know that I've seen my share of trouble. And I know a fix when I see one, and this is a fix. So don't be coy—sure it might not work, but it's great, and you can call me your Uncle Ed from now on."

At that point, Shane jumped on what he saw as his chance. "Well, Uncle Ed," he volunteered, "I'm coming to New York tomorrow, and I'm wondering if you would make some time to see me, say for dinner. My treat." Zbrewski was a bachelor who ate alone most evenings. Dinner with Shane Sullivan at the Brook Club on West Fifty-fourth Street was easily arranged for the following evening.

The two men, who had never met, liked each other immediately. Zbrewski saw Shane for what he was—a bullet flying through the air, someone who only needed to be aimed to be happy. Shane saw Zbrewski for what he could be—a Field Marshal who would support his combat generals through thick and thin.

"There's more going on at my firm than meets the eye, Ed," Shane said, after about an hour's conversation about Applied. Their dinner was being cleared away.

Zbrewski looked at him cautiously. "Well, every firm is up to its neck in horror stories—I mean, look at Weiner. But why tell me?"

"I'm telling you because I'm leaving Bondoc's firm, for one thing. Bondoc doesn't even know about my draft limine motion—that's how much distance there is between him and me right now.

"And when I tell you why I'm bailing out, if you'll let me, I think you'll understand. But parts of what I tell you are going to have to stay between us, and I'm going to trust you to have the common sense to understand that when you hear the whole story."

Ed Zbrewski had an instant headache. This was the last thing he'd expected from the bright younger man who'd sent him such a marvelous piece of legal work earlier in the week. Some bit of office politics dressed up as a cloak-and-dagger mystery. But he was trapped. It was his club, the coffee and port were on the way, and he hated scenes. So he just went way back into his familiar mental cave and nodded at Sullivan to go on.

Shane told the tale with the practiced ease of someone who'd had a long period of rehearsal at the United States Attorney's Office, complete with a reasonably verbatim recital of the Jones recording, which he offered to leave for Zbrewski.

When he'd finished, Zbrewski's coffee was cold and his glass of twenty-year old Croft port was untouched.

"He's finished," Zbrewski said. "Bondoc is finished."

"Seems to me."

"So why tell me?"

"Come on, Uncle Ed."

"You want his book?"

"I want Applied. I deserve it, and I can do the job for you. But there's one thing Bondoc can't know, and that's that anyone's got that recording. It might hurt that poor girl. I don't really think so—I don't think Gus is like that. But no one in our world should touch that, take any chance with that."

"But you're touching it, Shane. You're telling me about that recording—hell, you're giving me a copy of it. How do you know what I'll do with it? Is Applied so important to you?"

"I know I'm a prick to do it. My ethics professor friend and my daughter both told me to forget it, just quit Bondoc and go get some new cases. But I just can't see the real risk to Gina in what I'm doing here. I mean, I just can't see you doing anything to endanger anyone.

"So here we are. If I'm no good, I'm no good. If you're no good, you're no good. I'll have to live with all of that.

"Now you know what I know, anyway. I'm either going to be fired or quit Bondoc, all in a week or two at the most, and I don't know or care which.

"I want the defense of your firm's mal case with Applied. Bondoc is as good as dead professionally, so you're going to have to move things around with Applied anyway. If you don't want me, no hard feelings; it's been nice knowing you."

Sullivan then looked right at Zbrewski and smiled. "Don't look so glum, Uncle Ed," he said. "After all, I'm the one who's going to be out of work. Finish your port and cheer up."

Zbrewski took the Jones recording home with him that night. He played it several times before going to bed. In the morning, he had his assistant transcribe the thing, and, armed with the transcript, he then put his head, unannounced, into Thomas Gilhooly's magnificent corner office at around 11:00 a.m., brushing by Gilhooly's dragon lady on his way in.

Gilhooly was on the phone, and startled to see Zbrewski standing over him. Ever polite, however, he concealed his annoyance, and gestured his General Counsel onto the rich leather couch that stood to the right of the massive antique desk. With his free hand, he indicated his call would be over in a few moments.

A full twenty minutes later, the Chairman finally hung up the phone.

"Sorry, Ed, sorry. The bastard never stops talking, and about nothing, I can assure you. But he is a client, so how can I tell him someone so grand as yourself demands my attention, now tell me that?" Gilhooly said, with only at mild attempt to restrain his sarcasm.

Zbrewski, as usual, said nothing. Just studied the Chairman. Wondered how the man would react to what was coming. Wondered what he already knew. Not much, he thought.

Zbrewski had thought about what to tell Gilhooly, whether

to keep the recording from him as Sullivan had asked, so that the risk of Bondoc's learning the recording was out would be minimized. But Zbrewski knew his Chairman—Gilhooly was too tied to Bondoc for anything but the worst to possibly have a hope of dislodging Gus from his sinecure at Holliday & Bennett.

And even the worst might not do it, since Gilhooly thought—and not wrongly—that Zbrewski and the others on the management committee, Ben Laidlaw and Alice Greenberg, wanted him gone.

Zbrewski handed the Jones transcript to Gilhooly.

"Take a minute and read this, Tom. When you've finished it, we'll talk. I'm in my office."

Zbrewski got up and left. He smiled as he passed Gilhooly's crone. When she pointedly frowned back at him, he thought to himself how the firm had no meaningful pension plan for staff. Then and there, he resolved to beggar the woman as soon as Gilhooly himself was on the street.

Gilhooly called Bondoc as soon as he was through the transcript. It was only 8:30 a.m. in the Bay Area, and the call was patched through to Bondoc's car phone. The black Porsche was stopped cold in traffic on an approach to the Bay Bridge when the phone rang.

"Gus, it's Tom Gilhooly here."

"Good Morning, Mr. Chairman," said Bondoc cheerfully. "And to what do I owe this honor?"

"Cut the bullshit, Gus," said Gilhooly. "You're up to your ass in trouble and, because of you, so am I. This Haitian woman you slept with, this money that's been stolen, and this recording that might as well be on the radio.

"Zbrewski just came in here with a transcript, looking like the cat that swallowed the canary. Handed it to me and left. Told me to come see him in his office if I wanted to talk. Now, I don't even know where the little prick's office is, so what he's telling me is either there are some changes made or I'm out. Or maybe it's his way of telling me I'm out anyway. Because I backed the wrong horse. You. Because you, my friend are a world-class Typhoid Mary.

"Now, normally, we wouldn't be having this conversation. You would just be off my Christmas-card list. But you have fucked me up here so thoroughly, I have to let you have some time to try to fix this. Otherwise, I think Zbrewski may have me for real. So I will try and find out where Zbrewski's office is, and I will not let him fire you today or tomorrow. I will also try and find out who all else is fucking with both of us. But I am running out of oxygen fast, and I cannot believe that in an otherwise fortunate life I have had the misfortune to have ever heard your name."

Gilhooly hung up. Other than having said hello, Bondoc hadn't said another word. If he hadn't been sitting in standstill traffic, he would no doubt have run the black Porsche right off the road midway through Gilhooly's exposition of his impossible predicament. Only the insistent blaring of horns finally alerted him to a break in the traffic.

John Epimere was out when Bondoc, now at work, tried to call him. Gus then told Millie to hold all his calls except any return call from Epimere, and sat quietly trying to imagine how a transcript of the Jones recording could ever have wound up in Ed Zbrewski's hands.

Finally, after much thought, he buzzed Millie and asked her to have Shane Sullivan come and see him. When it was reported that Sullivan had left the previous morning for New York, for what purpose no one knew, and had not yet returned, Bondoc was quite disturbed.

Bondoc's next step was to call in the most junior member of the Applied trial team, a more or less permanent associate who'd been languishing there, hoping to make partner, for nearly ten years. That uncovered a copy of Sullivan's draft Motion in Limine Number One, the transmittal of which to Zbrewski without any consultation with Bondoc was obvious treachery of the client-poaching variety. At that, Bondoc attempted interviewing Millie Conroy and John LaBelle, both of whom refused to discuss Sullivan or anything related to Sullivan with him. They were escorted off the premises by security before noon.

Bondoc did manage a short interview with Bob Treister. He had kept all information about Gina from Treister and the rest of the partnership, of course, but now that it was apparent Sullivan had the recording it had to be better to beat him to the punch in exposing the truth. After explaining the basic facts behind the Jones recording to Treister, he explained his deep suspicion that Sullivan had somehow obtained the material, and was using it to try to move on Bondoc's book.

"Is this the guy you know, Bob?" Gus said, with a pained look on his face.

Treister was still trying to absorb what Bondoc's indiscretions meant for the firm—probably utter disaster, he quickly decided—and had little appetite for Bondoc's desire to psychoanalyze Shane Sullivan. Still, it was a legitimate question, in that they'd both made assumptions about what Sullivan would put up with that were proving wildly inaccurate.

"What I think about Shane is this—some people, better you don't push to see what's underneath. You push them, there's a whole lot of pain waiting to get out and bite you.

And you just got yourself bit. Bit bad, from what I can see. And it looks like we're all going to suffer along with you."

When Shane Sullivan returned from New York that evening, there was a letter from Augustus J. Bondoc, Esq., personally informing him of his immediate termination by Bondoc, Treister, Nimmer & Sourwine, a Professional Corporation, as well as of his potential liability for any past and/or future acts associated with interfering with relations between the law firm and any of its clients, specifically including, but not limited to, Holliday & Bennett.

No mention was made in the letter of the Jones recording. In a call to Zbrewski the next morning, Sullivan learned that Ben Laidlaw and Gilhooly, whose votes controlled the matter, could not be persuaded to fire Bondoc's firm. Despite the myriad problems Bondoc faced, Gilhooly had ultimately brushed off Zbrewski and Alice Greenberg by blandly expressing the hope that things would blow over.

"What a survivor that Gussy is," Sullivan said to Zbrewski. "My hat is off to the guy—there's just no silver bullet made that can kill him."

Zbrewski said nothing in response, just wished Sullivan well and promised to keep in touch. But privately, he wasn't as sanguine as Sullivan about Bondoc's longevity. There were just too many balls in the air for Gus to really have any hope of making it in the long term. That girl Gina was a major loose end. If she turned up dead or hurt, that was a forest fire Bondoc would not escape from unsinged. And Baby Doc was out a lot of money—surely, he would be heard from.

The meeting of the Board of Directors of Bondoc, Treister, Nimmer & Sourwine took place at Gerry Frank's law firm, Bass, Holman & Frank, back in the Embarcadero Center, from which office complex Treister & Sullivan had just recently fled. While John Epimere attended, he was there only in his capacity as Gus Bondoc's personal counsel. The sole issue before the board was the law firm's responsibility to report Gina's data theft to the client and the legal authorities.

Bob Treister had gone ballistic after his talk with Bondoc, particularly when it had been suggested to him that the unsuccessful cover-up, besides having ethical consequences, could invite criminal action against the firm and all its directors. This had made using Epimere as firm counsel, given his involvement in the cover-up, out of the question.

It was a tribute to Bondoc's continuing dominance over his co-shareholders that Frank, and not some true outsider, was retained to represent the firm. Treister, pointedly, had his own counsel present.

The meeting was acrimonious, mainly a pitched battle of threat and counter-threat between Epimere and Treister's lawyer, Tom Kagel, with Gerry Frank acting as referee. But at the end, Frank good-naturedly asserted control and announced the obvious.

"Look, my friends, all of you—Gus and John have done and will do what they think is right for Gus. Because of the way this young woman took advantage of him, Gus has been put under a unique cloud of suspicion with this unique client, who, unfortunately, has a history of great physical violence. That is not the firm's affair—we have no control over what Gus does to protect himself, practically speaking, other than just to fire him, which is a matter for a firm vote, and not a scheduled agenda item before the board at this meeting.

"From a legal standpoint, there are two things that must be done, and I hope John and Tom agree with me—but whether they do or not, this is my advice. First, you must, as an entity, report the data theft to the client through his

New York counsel and advise him of the nature and extent of your various types of possibly applicable insurance coverages, and you must advise your different carriers of the existence of potential claims. Second, you must, again as an entity, immediately report the data theft to the district attorney and the United States Attorney for this jurisdiction."

Frank's advice was voted on, and accepted unanimously, by the board.

BOOK TWO

EFFECT

26

Far Rockaway, Queens; Haiti; The Bronx
{August, 1995}

It was barely light when Gina left her apartment. She'd had another sleepless night. Bloated. The morning sickness had gotten worse. A passed-out junkie greeted her in the hall, a needle dangling in his arm. She had to step over the man to get to the stairwell. He'd shit himself, and the smell made her puke again right there.

Her project was two blocks from the water. I'll swim this morning, she thought. I'm just going for a good swim, and then I'll be clean, and I'll bleed again, and this damn baby will go away, and I'll be clean again.

Bondoc had worn condoms most of the time, she remembered. She couldn't know for sure, but he'd told her he was sterile. And she'd taken the pill and douched regularly. But she hadn't had her period since she'd left California in late April. It was early August now. Lately, she was sick every morning, and she was sure she was showing.

She'd spent three months hiding out here—junkies screaming in the hallways, gunshots ringing in the streets, and no period, always back to that, no period. Gina had no notion in any of this about the relationship between stress and hysterical pregnancy. All she could ever seem to really focus on was an image of Gus Bondoc's yellowed prick sticking into her, his sperm eating its way into her womb, making her life into something sick and wrong. Taking her over.

She made it from her Project to the oceanfront on Beach Twelfth Street without incident, brushing off panhandlers and johns just by staring them down. At the beachfront there were junkies and crackheads that'd slept overnight between the jetties, some wrapped in blankets, others just sprawled on the sand. She had on her house slippers, and there were so many needles in the sand that she jabbed herself several times on her way to the water.

The crowd paid little attention to one more bizarre sight that morning—a young woman throwing off her robe and diving straight into the breakers.

Gina was a strong swimmer. She'd learned to swim summers with her mom at City Island. She went straight out for five or six hundred yards. At that point, her head was clearing. She might easily have made it back to shore and back to her apartment in the Project, and she was already starting a lazy turn back towards shore. But a riptide, common in late summer off the Rockaways, came up and it took hold of her.

She was tired by then and the ripper pulled her under quite easily. When it was done suffocating her, it quickly propelled her body out into the Atlantic. Various bums later appropriated the housecoat and slippers Gina had left behind. No one noted her disappearance from the project.

That same month, Edouard Jones was called out of his cell and into a prison interview room. Once inside, he was confronted by his father. There ensued a long discussion about the older man's disappointment in Edouard's rumored behavior in the US and the negative effect of Edouard's idiocy on the Colonel's own brilliant career. This father-son chat ended with physical threats of the most lurid kind imaginable.

His father's rages often presaged torture and death for other men and women whose ends his son had himself witnessed. Edouard was found hanged in his cell the next day, an apparent suicide. His death went entirely unreported.

In August, Pierre Esclemond was shot and killed while working late at the paper. Two Guatemalan youths, high on paint thinner, walked in from the street, grabbed Pierre's own handgun out from its drawer while riffling his desk for money, and then shot him dead with it when he walked in on them.

They'd stolen less than fifty dollars, and were in and out in less than three minutes. No one heard the shot. From an NYPD standpoint, it was just an old dead black man sprawled across a beat-up desk in The Bronx. Wardling and his feebees took a look too, of course, but they found nothing more than NYPD had.

That left Israel to figure out what had really happened. His task was made impossible two weeks later, when the older of the two boys, aged fourteen, pulled Pierre's gun on an eighteen-year-old who was teasing him on a rooftop. The eighteen-year-old had been insisting that the boy "ain't never killed nobody." He quickly disarmed the fourteen-year-old, and then casually threw him off the edge of the six-story apartment building. It happened so suddenly that the fourteen-year-old had no time to scream before he was spattered in the alley below.

His ten-year-old companion heard what had happened later that day. He decided it was time to stop sniffing paint thinner.

27

New York; San Francisco
{September 1995}

Jean Claude Duvalier had grown wary of violence. It was much more complicated in Europe and the US than it had been while he was a king in Haiti. His drug use and sexual perversions now occupied ever-increasing amounts of his time anyway, and the handlers on whom he was increasingly reliant never recommended assassination or kidnapping.

When the matter of Gus Bondoc's sexual relations with Gina and his apparent hand in the earlier disappearance of sixteen million dollars was brought to Baby Doc's attention, he was filled with hatred for his former friend. It was beyond doubt that Bondoc was involved in a conspiracy of some sort against him.

But Baby Doc's attention did not linger long on Mr. Bondoc. The handlers were told to persecute the man by every possible means, but not to physically harm him. Spend what you please, bribe whom you like, imprison Mr. Bondoc if possible. At a minimum, do certainly ruin him. And then report back and be handsomely rewarded. Perhaps a half hour all told was devoted to the subject of

Mr. Bondoc's future. Numerous unpleasant things were then done.

Criminal allegations by Baby Doc were lodged with prosecutors in the Northern District of California against both Gina and Gus—against Gina for data theft, and as Epimere had predicted, against Gus for misprision on account of his failure to promptly report Gina's crime once Jones had reported it to him. Those criminal allegations by Baby Doc were referred back to Wardling, who had an active inquiry running in the Southern District of New York.

To make a solid point of Baby Doc's anger, his handlers had hired the most ferocious New York law firm in existence—Sklar, Ark, Slapp, Mead & Flood. At the truly astronomical rates charged by the Sklar Firm, it was clear Baby Doc's point was not to collect money. He was going to beggar the Bondoc Firm and every one of its officers, directors, and shareholders. All of whom, past and present, including Sullivan, were sued individually on multiple theories of liability, not all of them implausible.

Finally, Baby Doc's handlers filed a formal charge with the State Bar of California, seeking Gus Bondoc's personal disbarment. Bondoc had, according to their complaint, learned of a criminal data theft from his office by an employee and then failed to report it to his client.

As Gina's data theft was a felonious act under the federal Computer Fraud and Abuse Act, Gus's failure to promptly report it to a person in civil authority constituted the separate crime of misprision of such a felony. Under such circumstances, Baby Doc charged, Gus's disbarment was the only appropriate discipline equal to the gravity of his offense.

On Bondoc's side, the result of all this was chaos. Treister's continued threats to sue PW&S for Epimere's role in the cover-up quickly put Epimere in an intolerable position. He ended his almost thirty-year relationship with Bondoc in a two-minute telephone call one bright mid-September morning.

"Gus," the older man said, "John here."

"Yes, John." Gus knew the bullet was coming.

"Gotta go, Gus," Epimere said. "Wouldn't help anything to keep working on this for you anyway. You need some fresh insights. Sorry things didn't work out better and good luck."

That was it. Epimere was gone before Bondoc could say another word, his carefully worded letter of resignation arriving by hand a half hour later, a copy pointedly sent to Treister.

Gerry Frank's informal role as counsel to the Bondoc Firm was also ended. The only thing anyone could agree on there was to hire John Van Atta, the junior partner in Cotta & Van Atta, an up-and-coming litigation boutique. He would attempt to deal with the Sklar people, at least temporarily, at the joint expense of National Union and Lloyd's, who together held the employee dishonesty and legal mal covers for the Bondoc Firm.

The employee dishonesty coverage was very light, however—only $1,000,000. And there were big holes in the ten-million-dollar legal mal cover—the intentional nature of the cover-up, for one, was very troubling.

Gus, meanwhile, hired John Deronda, a Brahmin who'd been an AUSA in the Southern District of New York and knew Wardling well. Deronda's only job was to bird-dog the progress of the misprision complaint against Bondoc in New York, hoping to get a line on any indictment there before it was filed.

At the same time, Gus set to work convincing Gerry Frank

that Frank could and should represent him personally before the State Bar, pulling out all the stops on their friendship and arguing that Frank's brief flirtation with advising the Bondoc Firm presented no conflict.

"How could it, Ger?" Bondoc said, pleading with Frank at the other man's Stinson Beach retreat. "What good does it do the firm or that prick Treister for me to lose my ticket? What's it even got to do with any of them? Nothing. You know it. You're too big to be afraid of people like Treister. And I need you, Ger. You've been President of the State Bar—they know you down there on Frankin Street. They won't piss on you from a great height.

"My license may be all I have left when this is over, Ger. That and my ability to do the job. And I didn't do anything really wrong—I just wanted not to get killed by this savage Duvalier until I could figure out what to do next. I mean, I went to Epimere and followed his advice for Christ's sake."

Frank was embarrassed for Bondoc. If Gus would just think clearly, Gerry thought, then he'd already know his career was finished. Clients like the ones Bondoc had represented throughout his career would never forget or forgive the weakness he'd displayed and the public humiliation he was about to endure.

But Frank was a big man in bar politics, and he knew his presence in a State Bar case would help insulate Bondoc. And they did go way back, though what the attraction was Frank himself had never figured out.

Frank's own career had always been ever upward toward the light—the worst thing his firm had ever done was take defense money from the cigarette industry. And Frank had fought against taking that one tooth and nail, only to be voted down in the face of hard economic reality.

Cancer sticks and serial murderers, though, weren't quite the same thing. Bondoc just didn't have the intellectual horsepower—his thrust was driven by cunning. That type of talent took you over to the dark side awful easy. Poor bastard. Dead and buried at fifty-seven.

But Frank, unlike Epimere, was a mensch. He decided to step up.

"OK, Gus," he said, smiling genially at Bondoc. "There'll sure be a lot of unhappy people at my firm, but fuck 'em—I'll do it. Baby Doc and his boys can't do this to us, shit-eating motherfuckers that they all are."

Bondoc got home to Piedmont feeling good for the first time in months. The message on his home machine from Israel was brief.

"Both Pierre Esclemond and Edouard Jones are dead. Esclemond has been shot, assailants unknown. Jones is an apparent suicide. True nature of his death is entirely unconfirmable. Gina Costello is still missing. My bills will now be sent directly to you at your office. Make payment by wire transfer on a same-day basis as previously agreed with Epimere."

Bondoc walked to the bar and drank down a full tumbler of scotch, and then he drank another. At home, he was sick. Peg had gone to bed, but she awakened at the sound of his retching. Realizing it was him, she turned over and went back to sleep.

28

San Francisco
{October, 1995–March, 1996}

In early October, Lucy Lee at the State Bar's Office of the Chief Trial Counsel caught Baby Doc's complaint.

Lucy was forty-seven. She'd started law school at forty, trekking out to ABA-unaccredited JFK Law School in Walnut Creek, after her daughter had left the nest to begin her first year at college back east and her second child had started Miramonte High. Her then-husband, Bob, also a lawyer, practiced tax law in Oakland. He'd practically forced her out of the house and into the classroom once the kids were no longer underfoot.

JFK was only twenty minutes from their home in Orinda, and most of the other students were also baby-boom women trying to find their way back into the job market as something other than clerical workers or real-estate ladies.

In her third year of part-time law study, when Katie was a junior at Williams and Johnnie a junior in high-school, a guy came and repossessed her car while Bob was out of town. Quietly enough at first, he told her to fuck off when she tried to stop him. When she threatened to call the cops, he laughed out loud. Blaring now, so all her neighbors would hear, he said "Try paying your bills, lady—then maybe the cops will care." Then he drove off down the road in her minivan.

When the dust settled, it turned out bad old Bob had a cocaine habit, a gambling habit, and a chippie at the office to boot. Lucy wound up with half of the equity in Orinda, worth about $400,000 after the first and second mortgages, various judgment liens, the property taxes that hadn't been paid in years, and the sales commission.

She used it to get her daughter and herself through school. Katie graduated in 1991, and Lucy finished JFK in 1993. She passed the bar on her first try. Most of the $150,000 she had left she set aside for her son to go to a UC campus—she thought he'd be bright enough to get in, thank God. Then, with what little she'd budgeted of her nest egg to eat on, she went out hunting for her first job as a lawyer.

Almost immediately, she hit a wall. Criminal law horrified her—no matter what, she couldn't do that. And despite the fact that Lucy had gone to Vassar, graduating at the top of her class back when Vassar was all girls and the grades meant something, the prejudice against her lowly non-accredited law school meant she couldn't even get in the door at any business law firm.

It wasn't until six months into her discouraging job search that she caught a break. Her professional-responsibility professor at JFK—a male lawyer whose day job consisted mainly of defending other lawyers charged by the State Bar's Office of the Chief Trial Counsel with license-threatening offenses—sent her an e-mail. "Got a great lead, Lucy. Immediate trial-counsel opening at State Bar. You'd love it. But take it easy on me and mine once you're in. Call me. 510-622-5544. Prof. Phil O'Keefe." She never knew how

Professor O'Keefe did it, but she was interviewed and then hired within a few weeks. It was almost enough to make her forget bad old Bob and start looking at the male sex through new eyes.

Sure, it only paid $44,000 to start, and you'd never make more than $68,000, even if you lived to be a hundred. But it had dignity. You were a lawyer, you had cases. You went to trial, and you meant something in the world. And when you'd been as far down as Lucy Lee had, that meant something. She went out and leased a brand-new minivan her first day on the job.

But after two years, the repetitiveness of the work had begun to bother Lucy. It was always just bad old Bob, over and over. Coke or alcohol or a chippie or gambling or some other goddamn thing, or all of them together, and then theft, followed by disbarment. Hardly anybody who got caught up in the system was even at Bob's level, and Bob had worked for a six-lawyer tax firm. They were all independent operators weathering some sort of personal crisis. Few of them hired a lawyer or put up a respectable fight. They just tanked, and then disappeared.

But now Lucy Lee had caught the Baby Doc Inquiry off the wheel. It was a once-in-a-lifetime case for someone in her position, a real chance to show what she was capable of. So whatever fancy-pants lawyer Mr. Bondoc hired—and Lucy was somehow quite sure it would be someone in pants—that legal genius had better watch out. He was going to find out what a Vassar girl with a legal education could do.

In London, meanwhile, at One Lime Street, the Bondoc Firm's claim for legal mal coverage was not received enthusiastically. "Bugger was scared to death," said the elegantly tailored and thickly bespectacled Lloyd's analyst on the US desk, a slender man who'd seen every imaginable variant of American legal malfeasance over his long career with Lloyd's—all without ever having left the UK, even to go to Europe. "Not our rub, though," he told his chief assistant. "Intentional is intentional, and there's no cover for intentional."

What the Englishman meant was that all US liability insurance law, in California and elsewhere, denied cover for intentional acts. Otherwise, so the theory went, you'd be encouraging people to do harm to each other. It wasn't the end of the problem for Lloyd's, however. Since the Sklar Firm, in an excess of enthusiasm, had sued everyone associated with the Bondoc Firm for failure to report as well, Lloyd's would have to pay for the defense of a claim it would never pay any liability dollars on. And at the rate Sklar would run up the bill, that was meaningful in the context of a ten-million-dollar policy.

"Bloody stupid way to actually ruin someone," the Lloyd's man muttered to his assistant, both of them having grasped immediately what Baby Doc's handlers were really up to, "providing these Bondoc people with a free defense instead of making them pay for their own private lawyers."

The two Brits looked knowingly at each other. Lloyd's was tied in hundreds of ways into the Sklar Firm, which had a large City of London branch office not half a mile away. A discreet seafood lunch at Loch Fyne in Henley-on-Thames with a London-based Sklar partner gave the New York partner in charge of Baby Doc's case the indirect benefit of the Lloyd's men's years of experience, and a win-win situation for Baby Doc and Lloyd's was quietly arrived at.

Certain friendly amendments to the Baby Doc pleadings were made by the Sklar Firm, changes that cut the heart out of any claim to coverage by the Bondoc Firm under the Lloyd's policy. To do this Baby Doc limited his claims to allegations that the Bondoc Firm did not have either enough money invested in it or enough insurance purchased for it to justify allowing its corporate form to be used to protect its shareholders from personal liability. A Latin term, "alter ego," meaning that one legal person, the Bondoc Firm, should be treated as if it were the same thing as other legal persons, meaning all of its shareholders, was the literal name for this legal theory, which was not covered by legal mal insurance.

And, once that delicate pleading minuet was completed, so that all the Bondoc Firm shareholders were being sued for was alter ego, a separate declaratory relief case was filed in San Francisco Superior Court seeking exoneration of the Bondoc Firm's Lloyd's policy from any further obligation to defend the Bondoc Firm.

By January 1996, Bob Treister and Teddy Sourwine had hauled Kelly Nimmer in on the carpet for the umpteenth time to explain why the National Union policy covering employee dishonesty had only a million-dollar policy limit. The subject was an old one, but it had acquired a new urgency once the Sklar Firm had suddenly and precisely limited its pleadings to claims against the Bondoc Firm for failure to prevent employee data theft, which did not invoke legal mal coverage, and alter ego claims against the officers, directors, and shareholders.

National Union, whose small policy did cover, responded to the Sklar Firm's narrowed pleading by tendering full policy limits of $1,000,000. The Sklar Firm immediately declined. As the policy was otherwise wasting away under John Van Atta's legal bills, there soon would be nothing left to protect Treister & Co. They would have to pay individually for their defense, allowing their personal assets to be eaten alive by the Sklar Firm, just as Baby Doc's handlers had planned.

"Kelly," said Treister, glaring at Bondoc's henchman, "I always thought you had assets to protect yourself, and, really, I always thought you, of all the people involved in this firm, had a business head on your shoulders. So, why, if a ten-million-dollar employee cover would have cost just another $25,000 a year—why, for God's sake, didn't you just buy it?"

Teddy Sourwine was only a Bondoc shareholder because he'd routinely lent his class notes to Gus Bondoc during their three years together at Boalt. His tenure at the firm had been marked mainly by three unsuccessful marriages and multiple bouts of substance abuse, and his presence at a meeting about anything other than where to hold an office party was a marker of true apocalypse within the law firm. Teddy was now so frightened by the obvious end of all he held dear that even he felt compelled to lash out at Nimmer.

"Yeah, Kelly," he said. "You're so cheap, all the time, man—you're just squeezing the nickel, you know, you're just always the one squeezing it."

Nimmer ignored Sourwine.

"Bob," he said, "I admit, in hindsight, I've said it before, I say it now, I look like a complete dope here. I just never understood computers. I never understood how much potential for harm there was. I don't have what you have, asset-wise, but I could lose it all, what I do have—and that's, I don't know, seven or eight million. There's just nothing I can say—we don't have a plan."

Nimmer hesitated, looked at Treister, and then went on.

"By the way, Bob, what's that fucking Shane Sullivan doing about all this anyway? I know he didn't really cause any of this, but he sure didn't make it any better either. And I truly hate that arrogant, half-crazy motherfucker, I really do."

Treister looked bemused.

"Well, Kelly," he said, "I don't really know what he's doing about anything. I do know that John Van Atta's representing all of us, but once the insurance money's gone, and that should happen very shortly now, we're all going to have to agree on how to split John's bills up or it's going to be every man for himself. So sooner or later, we're all going to have to get in a room together.

"Right now, between Shane and Gus, Gus is roast pig and Shane is live pig. And I'll take my pig on the hoof in dealing with the Sklar people, because fucks like the Sklar people eat roast pig every day, and twice on Sunday. And I'll tell you one more thing about Shane; he was always full of good ideas about how to beat other people out of money. I think that talent might benefit all of us right now."

At the end of March, Lloyd's won its declaratory relief case on summary judgment. By then, National Union's policy was under $500,000, and Van Atta's bill was running over $100,000 a month.

29

State Bar Court, San Francisco
{June 3–5, 1996}

The State Bar Court was a modest affair, located in a high-rise Civic Center office building at 100 Van Ness Avenue. It reminded Gerry Frank of traffic court.

With Frank were his associate lawyers, Gene Kaplan and Sally Johnson, a paralegal, and his client, Gus Bondoc. On the other side of the courtroom, sitting all by herself in the prosecutor's chair, was Lucy Lee. Hunkered down.

Gerry had tried the David Boies/Dan Burt approach with Lucy Lee, the now-famous charm offensive in the CBS libel case that had left the inept Mr. Burt sure that Boies was his best friend in the courtroom. Lucy, though, wasn't having any of it. So, when his attempts at patronizing kindness failed him, Gerry hired an investigator to take a very thorough look at Lucy's background. That convinced him she had sharp intellectual teeth she was anxious to try out on him and his client both. So he'd known he was in for a fight before her first brief had hit.

Behind Frank, spread out in the audience section, was the media. This was a story too good to miss—$16,000,000 lifted from a scumbag dictator; a lawyer who'd been sleeping with the data thief and thought the dictator might kill him if he found out; the thief, by all accounts a beautiful mulatto, escaped and still missing. It was perfect for a public that loved to hate lawyers, and it was already selling papers.

On the bench was the entirely undistinguished but still Honorable S. Shulster. A time server, but very luckily for Gus Bondoc and quite untypically for the State Bar justice system, a time server who'd come from the defense side of the disciplinary bar. Here was someone who might listen to an explanation, thought Frank.

Solomon Shulster had never had more than six people in his courtroom at one time in his eight years on the bench. Crowd control was quite beyond him. He looked out at the unruly horde of reporters helplessly, bearing in mind what his wife had said to him as he left his Linda Mar home that morning.

"Look, Sol," Mae had said, "don't embarrass yourself like that asshole Ito did. I mean, make them show respect, but be nice too. You know what I mean."

He had nodded to her agreeably, since it was good advice. However, he had no idea how to accomplish it. Would they have the Judge Sol dancers? he wondered. Would he be on Letterman?

"Settle down, folks—this is a serious thing here. Please settle down or I'll have to ask everyone but the lawyers and Mr. Bondoc to leave."

To his utter shock, his audience took him seriously. He realized he could act like a real judge here. There was that guard outside, for one thing. Sure, it was just a minimum-wage private security guard, never the same guy twice, but if he sent his clerk out to get him Sol thought the man would probably come in and at least go through the motions of trying to throw these people out.

After Judge Sol had gotten over the novelty of it, he turned to Lucy Lee and said, "Ms. Lee, I've read your trial brief, and I must say, it seems to me, the Office of the Chief Trial Counsel is taking a rather aggressive view of Title IV, Part B, Standard 2.6(a)."

Frank couldn't have asked Judge Sol to say more. Right from the outset, the Judge was questioning why Lucy felt Gus's admitted failure to immediately turn Gina in to Baby Doc, an admittedly clear violation of California Business & Professions Code section 6068(m), was so serious in and of itself that it ought to result in Gus's disbarment.

"Your Honor," Lucy said, looking at Judge Sol like the old friend he had become after she had spent some part of nearly every day with him for going on two years, "this is not a normal case."

Sol was admiring, as always, just how good Lucy Lee looked in a dress, how much better she looked than Mae, the mother of his children. Mae no longer cared how she looked.

He drifted back to the case. So this is no ordinary case; you're right about that, Luce. But why should I hang this big shot? I know he'd spit on me if he saw me anywhere but in here. But I've read the charges, and what has he done? Taken money from a creep, a multiple murderer. So what? Tell me a big-time criminal lawyer in town that hasn't done that.

"The reason this is not a normal case," Lucy was saying, "is that Mr. Bondoc's conduct is not just violative of the reporting rule; it is also confessedly criminal in nature. It is misprision, as is demonstrated by the citations of federal authority in our trial brief."

Judge Sol quickly interrupted the prosecutor again here before Frank could spring to his feet.

"But Lucy, I mean, Ms. Lee, as I understand matters, you do not claim under Title IV, Part B, Standard 3.3."

This was what she'd been waiting for—a softball that she could hit hard.

"It is legally correct, Your Honor, that Standard 3.3 only covers already entered convictions. Thus far, Mr. Bondoc has been successful in getting the United States Attorney's Office for the Southern District of New York to exercise its prosecutorial discretion in light of the unsavory nature of Mr. Bondoc's client, Jean Claude Duvalier, who is a well-known serial killer of such abominable character that stealing from him or assisting those who steal from him is not deemed worthy of the attention of that office.

"But the underlying facts of Mr. Bondoc's misprision are not in dispute, and they involve a loss of $16,000,000 and the facilitation of the flight of a felon. And from the point of view of the Office of the Chief Trial Counsel—and please remember this phrase, Your Honor, because you will hear it throughout this trial—the client is the client, and if you behave in a criminal way toward your client, no matter how disgusting or evil your client is, you should lose your license under Standard 2.6(a)."

Lucy Lee was enjoying herself now. She looked over at Frank, and then at Bondoc, who glared back at her hatefully for a moment. She'd lead the afternoon Bay Area news, maybe go national. Maybe bad old Bob would catch her on TV in whatever rathole he was presently hiding out in.

"There'll be no excuses, no lucky breaks just because the government happens to hate your client. The Office of the Chief Trial Counsel will go all the way with this one, Your

Honor; it will go as far as it has to go in order to make an important policy point for everyone at all levels of the legal system to see. The client is the client. That can never change if the public is to be truly protected from lawyers like the accused."

Lucy sat down.

Judge Sol turned to Gerry Frank. "Mr. Frank," he said, "I did not mean to begin this hearing by asking for such involved speeches, but now that Ms. Lee has had her star turn before the assembled media, is there anything you'd like to add?"

"Your Honor," Frank said quietly, remaining in his chair, "this is, as Ms. Lee admits, not a Standard 3.3 case. Mr. Bondoc has not been convicted of any crime. If he is, he will be disbarred in the ordinary course on an automatic basis. It is merely an admitted failure-to-report case, where the only issue is the degree of punishment that is appropriate under Standard 2.6(a), a situation where disbarment is far from automatic. Judging the appropriate degree of punishment in such cases requires Your Honor to take into account Mr. Bondoc's prior lack of any disciplinary record and, more importantly, for Your Honor to become familiar with Mr. Bondoc's sterling record as a lawyer and member of the community during the many years he has practiced in the Bay Area."

Here it comes, thought Judge Sol—all these high mucky-mucks from Boalt and Stanford and Harvard and Yale, they all belong to this and they give to that. How do they find the time and yet screw so much money out of the system? He had never understood it himself. When Judge Sol had gone into private practice out of Golden Gate Law maybe he'd gross $100,000 to $125,000 in a good year, working out of a shared office near City Hall. It cost him $300 a month in rent, and he netted around $70,000 before income taxes after he paid for shared reception and secretary, and the insurance, which would kill you more and more each year—legal mal, health, you-name-it insurance. And then there were always deadbeat clients who you couldn't sue for fees for fear you'd get sued back and lose your legal mal coverage. The wife wants you to make more money, but how? Only going on the bench, where finally he was making a clear $126,000 before taxes, no hassles, had saved him from a nervous breakdown. And then this Bondoc jackass comes in here, money to burn, and like lady bountiful he's full of good works. How is it possible?

He knew how he, Lucy, and the media would be spending the next few days, anyway. Lucy would put Gus Bondoc on the stand and establish all she needed to hang him, short of ensuring Judge Sol was going to swallow this whole the-client-is-the-client business. For which there was no legal precedent, as Lucy knew very well, but still it was marvelous legal thinking. He had to give her credit— she'd scared Gerry Frank witless, no question about it. Win or lose, Judge Sol was proud of his girl. She always looked so good in a dress, too, and hardly ever wore pants to court, thank God.

Then, when Lucy was finished, Frank was going to march in every mainline San Francisco lawyer who owed him or Bondoc a favor, along with at least half the Boalt faculty, and they were all going to sing Gus Bondoc's praises to the sky. Sometimes things happen, they'd say; Gus was human, and being afraid of Baby Doc was not an unreasonable reaction.

It took three days. One beautifully dressed, usually trim, intelligent man or woman came in and recited their lines and exited stage left. By the time it was over, the media had lost interest in hearing how great Gus Bondoc was. Judge Sol pretended to take notes. Lucy doodled. She asked no questions of any one of Frank's character witnesses. Her case had a single thrust—the client is the client. Act in an admittedly criminal way toward a client, and actual conviction is unnecessary in order to fully justify your disbarment. It was new law, but it felt right. She never for a minute believed Judge Sol was going to go for it, but it might mean something upstairs at the Review Department.

At the California Supreme Court level, on the other hand, which was the court of last resort for disbarment appeals, where Frank frequently litigated, she realized she knew nothing. But just to get to that exalted level would be the ride of a lifetime.

30

Concordia Argonaut Club, San Francisco
{Early Afternoon, June 10, 1996}

There are any number of men's clubs in San Francisco. The P.U., where John Epimere was a regular patron, was one of the more famous. The Bohemian Club, the University Club, and the Olympic Club were all elite WASP institutions with long pedigrees. For the Jews and a few Irish, there was Concordia Argonaut.

On Van Ness, with a great buffet, Concordia was a home away from home for both Treister and Sullivan. As a result, the two men had continued to run into each other in the gym or at the pool.

Knowing Shane usually swam at lunch, Treister made a point of getting up to Concordia early one June day, determined to buttonhole his former partner. Bathing suits were optional at the all-male pool, and Shane was cranking along buck naked in the far lane. Treister, wearing a robe, waited for Sullivan to finish his swim and emerge up the steps from the shallow end.

"Shane," he said, "over here. It's Bob Treister."

Sullivan looked at Treister quizzically. "You sure you got

the right Shane, Bob? I thought we'd stopped talking to each other, except to politely grunt."

"Look, Shane— the wolf is at the door. Can we please talk about the wolf, for Christ's sake? The people I'm left with now don't know shit about wolves, besides how to attract them."

"You mean that fucking drug addict Teddy Sourwine?" said Shane. "Or Kelly Nimmer, the one who doesn't know what a computer is?"

Treister thought about what Sullivan would do if he knew how Treister had sold him out to Bondoc at the outset. Probably nothing, he realized. This guy already hates me forever. There's nothing left here but burnt bridges.

But one thing he knew about Sullivan was how much the man loved to solve complicated problems. You had to do it his way, though—if you fucked with his control, he would quit on a dime.

So this was going to be a one-decision deal. Treister would have to talk this through with Shane, see what Shane thought would work, and then either do it or not do it. There'd be no turning back after that.

31

Bondoc Firm Law Offices, San Francisco
{Mid-Morning, June 13, 1996}

On June 13 the shareholders of Bondoc, Treister, Nimmer & Sourwine, Gus Bondoc included, met in the firm's largest conference room. It was the first formal shareholders' meeting in the firm's thirty-five-year history, and it would also be the last. There was only one resolution on the agenda. The shareholders proceeded to authorize by majority vote, in lieu of a vote by the directors, the filing of a Chapter 7 bankruptcy petition by the firm.

What had brought matters to a head, of course, was Sullivan. The same afternoon as his long talk with Treister, the two men had flown to Los Angeles and hired consulting bankruptcy counsel for the purpose of declaring both corporate and personal bankruptcy.

The next morning, every individual defendant in the Sklar Firm lawsuit—other than Gus—who had a house or any other type of assets worth worrying about protecting was hurriedly invited to an early-morning breakfast session.

The bankruptcy guy was a typical cross between an accountant and an undertaker. He cut to the chase.

"The entity, it's a goner. You've got no meaningful insurance, so right now you're all working for nothing, and every dollar of future profit belongs to this Baby Doc creditor, whatever. It's all ego-driven to go on pretending you're in the law business anymore over there—it's just stupid, really.

"Now, the interesting play is this alter-ego thing. Many of you—Treister, Nimmer, some of the ex-shareholders who are also defendants like my old pal Shane, here—you file for the entity in San Francisco, then you can probably move all your personal cases here within the district as related cases. And in this division of this district you've got these two very fine bankruptcy judges, neither one of whom is likely to buy the kind of horseshit these Sklar people are putting out in the state court, and both of whom are going to control the cost of litigation— it's going to be old-fashioned bankruptcy-claims litigation, which is supposed to be cheap, because you're supposed to be broke."

There were a lot of questions, mostly stupid ones, many of which came from Teddy. He had a rich wife, so how could he be bankrupt? "You can't pay your litigation bills, Mr. Sourwine," the Los Angeles bankruptcy lawyer replied. A former Ninth Circuit clerk, he hated dealing with consumers and worked exclusively in the corporate bankruptcy arena, which this crazy deal was only on the cusp of. "When Johns Manville couldn't pay for all its defense lawyers, it went bankrupt; it's just a creative way of dealing with overwhelming litigation, among other things."

Kelly Nimmer asked the best question. "Whose lawyer are you, Mr. Chandler?"

John Chandler looked uncomfortable. "I'm not here soliciting, believe me, Mr. Nimmer. But Shane and I go way back, so I'm his lawyer for starters. He's asked me to represent

Mr. Treister as well, and as I see no conflict, I've agreed. I think it's logical for me to represent all the shareholders who want me and my firm, except for this Bondoc fellow, who presents some conflict issues and who I doubt would be interested anyway. For the entity, it's a short-term assignment; we'll get some local firm to do the dirty work."

Nimmer was amazed that Sullivan would include him and the others in what was obviously a very workable scheme to save their collective hides. And all they had to do was leave Bondoc on the burning deck, where Treister was clearly going to leave him in any case. One look over at Sourwine told Nimmer which side of the fence Teddy would be found on; Mr. Chandler looked like the safest thing this side of paradise to poor lost Teddy bear. Poor Gus, Nimmer thought. Had it really been such a big deal, putting the name Sullivan on the door?

32

United States Bankruptcy Court for the Northern
District of California (San Francisco Division)
{Early Morning, June 16, 1996}

Most of the good corporate-bankruptcy cases were filed in Delaware and New York. Corporate debtors could choose where they filed, and their high-powered lawyers usually took Manhattan or Wilmington, where they knew the judges and the judges knew them.

This left Charlie Rogers—an ex-PW&S partner hired by that august institution only after bankruptcy had itself become a semi-respectable legal specialization in the mid-'70s—bored stiff in his new job as the junior bankruptcy judge for the San Francisco division.

So when Charlie showed up for work very early one mid-June morning, he was visibly gladdened by his law clerk's news that he had caught the Bondoc Firm's Chapter 7.

"Here," he had delightedly said to his wife just days before catching the Bondoc Firm Chapter 7, "are people we actually know, doing disgusting things in ways we could not even have imagined."

The judge's wife, who knew Peg Bondoc slightly, shushed

her husband, putting her finger to her lips in reproof.

"Charlie," she said, "you go and be wicked about something or someone else. Why, that poor woman. The man is a swine, you know, just a swine, and all this going on with her children still there in their home, not yet even fully raised."

Of course, he knew the Chapter 7 would not mean much—just paperwork, really. The data-theft claim was obviously good, and a Chapter 7 Trustee would simply go about liquidating whatever assets the law firm had.

What was really brightening his day, and where he saw the fine hand of his old friend Shane Sullivan, was in the personal-bankruptcy cases filed by Shane, Bob Treister, and many of those they'd become associated with at the Bondoc Firm. The individuals involved had substantial personal assets, and were going to fight like tigers with Baby Doc to minimize their liability.

And best of all, these individuals were represented by John Chandler. First in the Boalt Class of 1979, a former law clerk to the very famous bankruptcy-oriented Ninth Circuit Judge Alex Kromansky, John, at only 40, had become the leading corporate bankruptcy practitioner within the Ninth Circuit. He was simply a boy genius, whose mind Charlie loved to watch hum along at high speed. Welcome, welcome, he thought, smiling brightly at his clerk. It was going to be a good day.

33

New York; San Francisco
{June, 1996}

The stunning and unexpected news of the Sullivan-precipi-
tated Chapter 7 bankruptcy filing by the Bondoc Firm had
hit Holliday & Bennett two days ago. It had forced an emergency meeting, as even Tom Gilhooly had grudgingly recognized the end of that law firm's representation of Holliday &
Bennett in the Applied case.

He and Zbrewski had been unable to agree on where the
Applied case should go next, however. For the first time in
recent memory, Ben Laidlaw was refusing to commit his vote
on an important issue to Gilhooly privately. Gilhooly had
the very uneasy feeling Laidlaw had been bought, and that
additional items, such as shortening his own present term,
might be on the unanimous-consent agenda today, but what
could he do? Bondoc was a continent away—he couldn't
strangle him yet.

Ben Laidlaw took the lead, obviously prepped by
Zbrewski. "This fellow Sullivan, who worked up the case
for Bondoc, has some very promising ideas. We've circulated
this motion in limine he gave Ed that apparently made Gus

think he was trying to lift us. Gus had been under a lot of strain, obviously. But Ed and I think the ideas in the motion may be sound. Comments?'

Homer Rhodes, of course, couldn't keep his mouth shut.

"Yeah, I've got comments. The guy has given up before he's begun—he's underselling my case. I don't know this guy Sullivan well. Only met him once or twice, but I didn't like what I saw. Obnoxious guy. No bedside manner. Probably too aggressive with juries. We must be able to do better than this."

Stan Wolmann looked at Rhodes, half in pity and half in sorrow. What a jerk, he thought. The man was lost. He himself had no ideas at all on how to get out of this mess. If the Applied case wasn't "undersold," then Holliday & Bennett would wind up paying Applied fifty or sixty million dollars. Shane at least had a glimmer of an idea, and Rhodes wanted to talk about the guy's bedside manner.

But Stan knew he didn't need to say anything here— this was the Ed Zbrewski show. Rhodes didn't have a vote. Laidlaw had the only vote that mattered; Alice and Ed always voted against Gilhooly anyway. So when the meeting started with Laidlaw praising Sullivan, it was game set and match.

At some point, in a very quiet place, Ed would explain to Rhodes that Rhodes was working for Sullivan now, and that although Rhodes' career at Holliday & Bennett was over anyway, if Rhodes ever wanted to work anywhere in corporate America again it would be best to do as he was told and assist Mr. Sullivan in keeping the harm done by Mr. Rhodes' misadventure in the Applied case to a dull roar. Wolmann was enjoying himself this trip a hell of a lot more than he had the last time, that was for sure.

Gilhooly knew which way the wind was blowing the

moment Laidlaw spoke first, but he'd done some homework. He thought he'd try a jab, at least.

"Ben," he said, "how can we turn over such a large matter to this Sullivan fellow when he has no support? And also, as I understand it, he and all of the people involved in Gus's firm, except Gus himself, have filed personal bankruptcy themselves, since they're being sued personally for the damages the data theft this young woman accomplished caused. Imagine the level of distraction? Shouldn't we just start over with a respected West Coast business-trial firm?"

Laidlaw and Zbrewski, not to mention Sullivan, had seen the Chairman coming.

"Of course," said Zbrewski, closing now, while winking over at Alice. "First, Shane has a very competent personal bankruptcy lawyer and assures me he will leave that aspect of things to him. Second, to help him with his work for us, Shane is going to associate with a firm named Baum, Baum & Cooper. John Cooper is a member of ABOTA, a close friend of Shane's, and we've checked him and his firm out completely. Shane and John will do Applied together, with the full infrastructure of the Baum firm underneath them, but with Shane exercising ultimate control, which I'm personally satisfied with. Shane, in my opinion, is a very bright man."

Gilhooly knew he was screwed. Frankly, he could care less about Bondoc, Applied, or, based on what he'd just seen, this asshole Rhodes, for that matter. If he was just polite, he sensed, Ed was prepared to let him live through the day. So magnanimously, if quite falsely, he said "Well, I did read this limine motion, and it was quite brilliant. Based on what's been said, I think Mr. Sullivan's a good choice and one I fully support. No need for a vote, I take it?"

Once again, Shane had what he wanted; now all he had to do was live with it.

It took about a week to get the Chapter 7 bankruptcy trustee for the Bondoc Firm to authorize the substitution of the Baum firm and Sullivan in Applied, and another two weeks to get all the files sent over to Baum's office in the Bank of America building, where they would all be kept. Shane had been reduced to working out of his garage after being tossed out by Gus Bondoc, and still hadn't found office space to set up his own shop.

He knew it was going to be an uneasy struggle for the wheel working with Cooper. They were ostensibly friends, and he'd brought the man not only this case, but several other meaningful cases over the years. But Cooper was, at heart, just a suit. His family background was all military—father and grandfather both West Point, father a Colonel, the grandfather a General on MacArthur's staff during WWII.

John himself was a graduate of the University of Virginia Law School. He had gone into the Army JAG Corps as a prosecutor for a four-year stint during Vietnam. Shane loved John for his toughness, but found him so conventionally minded that this toughness often became a source of frustration for Shane.

Yet John was a great sounding board—he would push back, hard, and the judges and juries were as conventional as he was, not to mention considerably dumber. So Shane put up with John's lack of imagination, even his insults, and sometimes he even let him imagine he was calling the shots. It always made him laugh, Shane meditated, the way everyone always assumed he was so intolerant. Given how crazy I am, he thought, I'm really pretty loosey goosey about a lot of stuff.

Applied was set for trial in November, and it was a hard

date. The only saving grace was that Carpuchi, true to form, was no more ready than Shane and John were. In particular, he still hadn't figured out what a shitty expert he had on damages. But also true to form, the first thing John was doing was digging in his heels at the notion of conceding the case hadn't been worth the candle to begin with. Like Rhodes, John Cooper didn't have any ideas of his own—suits never did. They only knew what they didn't like, and he didn't like the idea he was walking into a possible ten-million-dollar problem.

"Jesus, Shane," John said, "I know it's your case and all, but my firm's mal policy is on the line here, and look what you're asking me to do, right out of the box—make a limine motion that concedes that this client ran up a ten-million-dollar bill when the case they were prosecuting didn't have any chance of generating that kind of a damage award. I mean, Rhodes hates it and he's the fucking client, for Christ's sake."

Cooper, who had bit like starved trout when told the hourly rate and anticipated number of partner and associate hours that would be involved in defending Applied—all without reading anything or questioning anything, including Zbrewski's telephonic instruction that Shane would have control over all strategic decisions in Applied—had now read the file and spoken with Homer Rhodes, who, despite having had a lecture from Ed Zbrewski himself, had a difficult time with simple ideas like chain of command. Rhodes was also always happy to find an equally narrow-minded audience like John Cooper to speak with, and appreciated Cooper's bedside manner to the point he'd called Zbrewski and complimented Cooper on it. Zbrewski made a note that some sort of additional trouble must be brewing on the West Coast, but he was underestimating Sullivan.

"Look, John—forget your mal policy, and forget the idea that that doofus Rhodes is the client. You make nice with him, sure—that's what you're here for. You take him on direct. You make him act like a sweet little puppy dog. That's why I love you man.

"But the client is Zbrewski, who belongs to me. Who you never get to meet. Who I've been pumping full of sperm for a year, OK? You want it in writing for your Risk Review Board, you got it. This is money, my friend, big, big, money and it can walk across the street with one phone call, but that never happens, because every word I say, you believe, because you know I never lie, especially to you.

"Now look—as far as I'm concerned, we got one chance here. We keep the possible recovery down low enough just before trial so Carpuchi loses interest and it settles. Otherwise, it blows up and we eat it. That's how it has to be played in the end. Now we got, what, sixty days before we have to file my limine motion, and maybe in that sixty days you or one of the kids here spot some other way to deal with this thing besides what I say. Great, somebody's a hero, we'll have a parade."

John Cooper looked at Shane Sullivan. They had clashed before, clashed badly in a case where Cooper had brought Sullivan in. Cooper had tried ordering Sullivan to do something "or else," and catastrophe had resulted—for Cooper. Sullivan had brought in a mal lawyer to represent one of Cooper's clients. That guy then threatened to sue Cooper as a way of forcing him back into proceeding consistent with Sullivan's plan of action. Shane played rough when he had to.

Remarkably, the two men had reconciled. Not long after threatening Cooper with malpractice, Sullivan had him defend a large malicious-prosecution case brought against Sullivan when Sullivan had unexpectedly lost a jury trial. But after all their years together, Cooper knew it was always going to be Shane's way or nothing. And he also knew he didn't have a better idea and wasn't likely to develop one in sixty days. He just hated the way it all went so goddamn fast.

34

State Bar Court, San Francisco
{July 12, 1996}

Judge Sol's decision was filed pursuant to Title II, Division V, Rule 220, on July 12, 1996, by the Clerk of the State Bar Court. It was quite short, though Judge Sol had agonized over every word of it. It read:

The matter before the State Bar Court is the complaint by the Office of the Chief Trial Counsel against Respondent Augustus J. Bondoc, a Member of the State Bar of California. The facts are not in dispute.

Mr. Bondoc's client, Triton LLC, an affiliate of one Jean Claude Duvalier, was a victim of a data theft in violation of both state and federal criminal law by a non-professional employee of Mr. Bondoc's professional corporation. At some time after the data theft occurred, Mr. Bondoc commenced a sexual relationship with the non-professional employee. Later, Mr. Bondoc learned of the data theft. He failed to report the data theft, either to his client or the government, because, he claims, his client was extremely violent and might have assumed he was involved in the data theft.

Mr. Bondoc's client later was informed of the data theft by Mr. Bondoc's professional corporation. It submitted an Inquiry to the

Office of the Chief Trial Counsel, which filed a Complaint, seeking Mr. Bondoc's disbarment under Standard 2.6(a), which allows punishment, including disbarment, for violation of California Business & Professions Code 6068(m), failure to report significant developments in matters to clients.

Mr. Bondoc's counsel and counsel for the Office of the Chief Trial Counsel have both very ably presented their views of the case. They boil down to a single philosophical difference. Mr. Bondoc's counsel argues, and this court agrees, that absent a criminal conviction for misprision of a felony or some other felonious behavior, this case is nothing more than a normal, garden-variety Standard 2.6(a) case where Mr. Bondoc's lack of prior discipline and stellar character in the community are highly relevant, as is the fact that, by the time he learned about the data theft, all the financial harm had been done and the client did not suffer any additional financial harm as a result of his admitted failure to report. That deserves, and the actual sentence of this court shall be, a three-month actual suspension and the requirement that Mr. Bondoc take and pass the State Bar test on Professional Responsibility.

Put another way, while superficially appealing, the court refuses to accept the invitation by the Office of the Chief Trial Counsel to conflate Standards 2.6(a) and 3.3 and thereby effectively second-guess the decision(s) by the various governmental authorities holding prosecutorial discretion not to prosecute Mr. Bondoc, notwithstanding all the rhetoric about "the-client-is-the-client." Obviously, should Mr. Bondoc ultimately be prosecuted and then be convicted of any felony involving moral turpitude, that will invoke Standard 3.3 and lead to Mr. Bondoc's disbarment in the ordinary course.

Dated July 12, 1996

Hon. Solomon H. Shulster
State Bar Judge of the
Hearing Department

Gerry Frank was genuinely excited when he called Gus Bondoc.

"We did it, Gus—we shot that Vassar skirt right through the heart with a bow and arrow. And it wasn't as easy as it looked—that old State Bar judge was looking moo eyes at her like you wouldn't believe, and he has to live with her all through eternity, you know."

Gus was so distracted that Gerry's elated call hardly reached him. He'd been forced to leave his office in San Francisco just the week before by the Chapter 7 trustee, who was moving all the office files to dead storage, selling the furniture and other fixtures at auction, and trying to find someone to take over the lease. As a result, Gus's professional life was in utter chaos. Sure, he was interested in his law license, but he'd always had faith in Gerry, knew some low-life State of California lawyer couldn't beat him, for God's sake.

"Great job, pal," he'd said finally. "Just keep me informed." Then he'd rung off. No small talk. Not even a dirty joke.

As happy as Gerry was, that's how pissed off Lucy Lee was. Sol had actually been high-handed with her, the old fart. He needed to learn a lot more self-restraint, at least if he ever wanted to see her bare knees again. She had her petition to the Review Department seeking review of Judge Sol's order on file well within the fifteen days required by Title II, Division VII, Rule 300(b). It isn't over till it's over, she thought.

35

Far Rockaway, Queens;
Top of the Mark, San Francisco
{October, 1996}

David Israel and his New York operative both walked cautiously up the stairwell of Gina's Far Rock Project. Eric was openly carrying an automatic machine pistol. He was acting quite nervous despite the fact that there were four more guys covering them out in the streets below. And so far, it had just been junkies of various stripes and their associated very bad smells.

When they got to what had been Gina's apartment, it was still in the same locked-down condition Gina had left it in that last morning. Eric easily picked the lock, and the two men were treated to a horror of roaches still feasting on the paltry remains of what Gina had left behind more than a year before, as well as on their own past generations, long since deceased. The musty smell was as indescribable as it was overwhelming, and at first both men assumed Gina must be dead somewhere on the premises.

An immediate search showed the latter assumption to be false, but it did turn up three hundred and sixty dollars and change. Enough for Gina to have held out for another few months, at least. Shit, thought David, who had never had more trouble finding somebody than he'd had finding Gina.

He'd had to hire, if not fifty Haitians, then maybe twenty or twenty-five members of that expatriate community, and he'd ingratiated himself with another hundred or so. He'd learned more about Haitian culture over the past year and a half than he'd ever learned about Afghani culture during a similarly lengthy sojourn in that godforsaken country investigating a misdirected arms shipment, emanating from privately funded US sources, that had never made it to the mujahideen.

All before he'd finally found the one middle-aged Haitian mental-health-care worker who'd talked to Gina that day on the IND line and given her the address of the project apartment. And then it had taken weeks of patient cajoling to convince the woman that David's heart was in the right place, that David would never harm Gina, would only protect her from Bondoc, Baby Doc, the government, you name it. Ultimately, that was David's gift—he was the real deal. If it came to that, he was out of any assignment that involved hurting anybody who didn't deserve it, and fuck you, Mr. Client.

So here he was, ready to be of help, and the girl was gone. The money was here, but she was gone. Which meant, of course, only one thing—somebody must have taken her, because why would she ever leave without her money? Or her clothes, which also seemed to be here. There wasn't much, but there was the bag, as advertised—he'd gotten the details of the interviews with Pierre and Eugenia, eventually—and what you'd think a young girl would be carrying in such a small bag.

David knew, or at least he was pretty sure he knew, that

it wasn't Gus. And it wasn't the feebees—that he'd have heard about. So that left that fucking Baby Doc. My God, he wanted to toss. Just toss. Eric looked over at David and assumed it was just the truly unbelievably bad smell of the apartment.

"Pretty bad," he said, "but I've smelled worse, especially in training. They really make a point of bad smells in training. Sadistic about it, you know."

David ignored the remark. "Look, Eric," he said, "the working hypothesis is she's been lifted. Bring in a team. See if there's evidence for or against. Full report. Be careful, leave no traces of who you were, because after we look, we tell the feebees where to look, and they get the next sniff. Meanwhile, I'm going home. You stay here. Send somebody down below to take me back to my hotel. And listen, nice seeing you again."

Eric nodded, then spoke into his walkie-talkie. A few minutes later, another man, also openly carrying a weapon, walked into the apartment and took David back into New York to his hotel.

A week later, David had a report confirming his initial suspicions. Everything forensic pointed to a lift. She was just there one moment and gone the next, everything left behind, money, food, and clothes included. Given that she'd facilitated the movement of sixteen million dollars away from Baby Doc, this was highly suspicious. And so David gave up—he knew when he was licked.

His last act before getting on the plane to San Francisco was to pass along the fruits of his investigation to his mole in the New York office of the FBI, including a full oral summary of Eric's forensic study. "Look," he told the mole, "some bright boy may figure out Eric's been there, but they'll never know it was Eric, and there was no harm done, and Eric is better than the bright boy anyway. Bottom line is the girl's done for. Terrible story, but that's the truth. Tell your friend Wardling that there's no way to pin this on anybody that I know of, and I'd have helped him if I could, no matter who my client was. Just don't mention my name, all right?"

"Got it, David," the FBI mole said. "Too bad—a year and half of your life. I assume you got paid, at least."

"Of course—but I wanted to save that girl, and I was never close. She was kidnapped a year before I got there, maybe more. Dead in some basement somewhere. Tortured, probably. And the guy I'm working for, whose client did this, now he's scared of this client, but I just can't get behind feeling sorry for him. It feels to me like he ought to have been right next to the girl, yowling away with her when they killed her."

Kitty-corner from the P.U. Club is the Mark Hopkins Hotel. And at the apex of the Mark is the Top of the Mark, where there's usually a great jazz band and a nice meal to be had, not to mention a startling view of the City by night. David's apartment was close by there, and he had Gus Bondoc come over from the East Bay and meet him up there early, before it got crowded. He'd give Gus the bad news and then enjoy the rest of his evening, even if Gus was going to end his own by jumping off some other famous landmark.

Gus took it about as hard as David could have imagined. He wasn't a coward—David didn't see it that way. Gus was just calculating. Up to now, he'd been willing to assume that the deaths of Edouard Jones and Pierre Esclemond had not been caused by Baby Doc. But Gina's death—both he and David felt she had to be dead, the signs were too unmistakable— that was too much of a coincidence to be ignored, and Baby

Doc's penchant for violence was too well-known, the growing number of deaths too obvious, for Bondoc to feel safe going about his day-to-day life. And Gina had probably died in great agony—David had communicated that as well. Having to live with the uncertainty of being grabbed off the street and then tortured—at the thought of that gruesome prospect, Gus had almost lost control right at the table.

There was some satisfaction in it for David, no doubt. If the fuck had just avoided Baby Doc, just stuck to ordinarily ugly clients like every other scumbag corporate lawyer in town, none of this would have happened.

But no—this bright, bright man, with all his advantages, still just wasn't as smart as his two friends, Epimere and Frank. So he's jealous, and he wants to show off. And to do that he has to get in bed with a dictator, someone who likes to squeeze people's eyeballs till they pop out, someone who steals aid funds, who starves thousands of children to death. And that kind of BS attracts vengeful Bronx innocence, and so on.

Gus left. David ordered dinner and settled in for a night of excellent live jazz. He was glad to be back home. New York was okay, but there was no place like San Francisco. Period.

36

Superior Court in and for the
City and County of San Francisco
{Late Afternoon, Early Evening, October 22, 1996}

Things were looking up. Superior Court Judge Samuel Pollard was staring down gimlet-eyed at Ben Carpuchi, who was at that moment stuttering with indignation at the imminent prospect that Motion in Limine Number One, the last remaining pre-trial motion under submission, might shortly be granted.

Drawing Judge Pollard had itself been manna from heaven for Sullivan and Cooper as the Applied case had lurched through pre-trial preparation between June and October of 1996. In the state system, most judges are former district attorneys who have spent their time putting felons away and been rewarded with a pay raise and a reduced caseload on the bench, where they're "tough on crime." Many of these men, for these DA types are typically men, can't even balance their own checkbooks, and they haven't dealt with a civil contract case since leaving law school. These former DA judges do learn civil-contract law again, of necessity, on the bench, but their education takes years, and is costly for those they learn on.

The Ben Carpuchis of this world, the heavy-hitting plaintiff's business-trial lawyers with their outsize egos and their ingratiating personalities, count on such wholly ignorant state-court judges to "let them try their cases"— meaning, let them say any damn foolish thing that comes into their heads that an equally ignorant jury might buy, things that prey on jurors' suspicions about what corporate America must be up to in order to make so much money.

Carpuchi had used this technique to obtain overwhelming verdicts. His first big hit, for more than one hundred million dollars against Bank of America, had come while the Bank had been very weak generally, and had nearly caused the collapse of that fabled institution's stock. A former US Secretary of State had ultimately been brought in to argue the Bank's appeal, and Shane had been at the Bank's headquarters the day the reversal had come down. The entire executive floor had erupted almost as one man in loud cheers that seemed to go on for hours.

But Carpuchi had not lost every verdict on appeal, and he'd settled plenty of cases too. He was rich as hell, sloppy as hell, bombastic as hell, but mainly he was dangerous as hell, and the only way to live through the experience of trying a case against him was to either beat him on the papers or settle. Shane's strategy with Motion in Limine Number One was a little of both.

The problem in Applied, from Carpuchi's standpoint, was that Judge Pollard was not your everyday Superior Court Judge. He'd come out of Gerry Frank's firm, in fact he'd been Frank's senior partner, and he'd been a United States Supreme Court law clerk before that. He'd had a steady diet of business-law cases his whole career.

Funny, thought Shane, who'd had a very intense brush with

Sam Pollard when Shane had been a young lawyer, what going on the bench does to some people. Back when Pollard was a senior partner in Frank's firm, despite all the shine of Harvard Law, his clerkship to Chief Justice Earl Warren, and a host of other awards and prestigious governmental positions before going into private practice, Sam was a mean motherfucking street fighter. When Shane had unearthed a horde of extremely damaging documents in a hotly contested anti-trust case concerned with the nascent video-game business, he'd done everything but piss on Shane in order to distract him from asking the simplest questions in a key deposition.

Yet on the bench, the guy had always been the greatest. Smart, kind, never really wrong about anything. Even when Shane lost something, he still had fun with the judge. It was just pure pleasure. And if you tried big business cases for a living, dealt with the traffic-cop mentalities that so often made it to the Superior Court bench, you'd throw your body in front of a car to keep someone like Pollard from harm.

So Carpuchi was playing way out of his intellectual league. And boy was Shane enjoying watching Carpuchi sweat.

"It's for the jury," Carpuchi was saying, repeating himself for about the fiftieth time. He had let Ed Foley, his much more friendly Irish partner, argue up until about an hour ago, when he could see Pollard wasn't buying. Then Carpuchi had perforce thrown himself into the fray. He had only the slightest idea what Motion in Limine Number One was about— from listening there in court, he knew it meant he couldn't get more than ten million dollars from the jury. That he understood, and that he did not like. He had better things to do than spend, what, four months chasing a mere ten million dollars.

"Mr. Carpuchi," Judge Pollard broke in, "with respect,

that is not a legal argument. Everything in a court of law is not for the jury. In this case, we have the issue of whether your expert witness is qualified to give testimony as to damages or whether his testimony is too inherently speculative, especially in light of the rebuttal testimony offered by another faculty member from his own institution who, I must say, appears much more qualified to me. If I exclude your witness, all that is left as damages are legal fees and costs in the underlying case—simple as that. There's no jury issue there other than attributing fault as between plaintiff and defendant for the incurring of those fees and costs.

"Mr. Carpuchi, we have been over and over this with Mr. Foley while you listened, and now you've argued and have not said anything new, really, and I'm getting ready to rule. Though, everyone, please understand, this is a serious issue, and I have not made up my mind, as deciding in advance that damages are speculative, as opposed to waiting to see what a jury does—well, that's something that reminds me of the old joke about how there are old mushroom eaters, and there are bold mushroom eaters, but there are no old, bold mushroom eaters."

Pollard was looking right at Shane now, practically winking at him. Settle it, pal, he was saying—because you never know, you really don't. Sure you're ahead. Sure you should win. But now you go ahead and get this pig to go root in somebody else's trough. I've scared him good and proper for you, now you go kill him off for me. Then everybody's friends again. Actually, Shane reflected, it was really the same old street-fighter Sam—scare the shit out of Carpuchi, wink at Shane. They ought to make him a King; just being a judge isn't good enough. I don't care if he did piss on me when I was a kid—hell, it was good for me, taught me how to ask a good question. Taught me how to crawl through a minefield, if it comes to that.

At 4:30 p.m. Judge Sam Pollard went into his chambers to contemplate his decision on Motion in Limine Number One. And Ben Carpuchi swaggered over to Shane Sullivan and John Cooper and practically spit in their eyes.

"You little pissants haven't got a chance. I'm going to take your pants down in front of the first twelve we put in that box over there. Then I'm going to take out the biggest Italian dick you ever saw and stick it right where the sun don't shine. What do you think about that?"

These were the first words Carpuchi, who normally let the more diplomatic Foley do his communicating with opposing counsel, had ever spoken to either Shane or John. Shane was amused; John was not, and started to rise. Shane spoke quickly: "Look, Mr. Carpuchi—why don't we all cool off here. John and I both know your track record, and we both admire it. Let Ed and me see what can be done here, OK? Why don't you go down and have a coke or something? That judge won't be back out for at least an hour."

What Shane was really telling Carpuchi was that the superstar had plenty of time to go over to the aptly named Stars Grill, the only watering hole worth having a drink at within five miles of the old City Hall courthouse, an invitation Carpuchi readily accepted. He'd spent much of his lunch hour getting well planted there, and he was not at all adverse to returning early. Shane wasn't kidding himself, though—Carpuchi would not be drunk when the jury showed up. He would be freshly barbered, freshly tailored, he would smell nice, and the shittiest thing of all was he'd be so goddamn nice that butter wouldn't melt in his mouth. Every old lady, every working stiff, every minority, every gay, lesbian, transgender, every-what-the-hell-is-coming-next—they'd all think Ben Carpuchi was there just for them. No one knew how chameleons like Carpuchi did it any more than people understood why the Germans had listened to Hitler rant at Nuremberg or how Castro held the Cubans in thrall for hours in the streets of Havana. Demagogues, real ones, they just had it, and they made blood run in the streets. All Shane and John were doing was keeping the flow of blood down to a minimum for Holliday & Bennett.

Carpuchi had gone over to Foley and his female partner, Joanne Wharton. The three caucused for a few moments, and then Carpuchi and Wharton, a leggy, attractive brunette who seemed to have more than just a professional relationship with Carpuchi, left. Leaving Fast Eddie Foley facing Shane and John.

Fast Eddie was a trip. He had once made the Official Reports, where decisions of the Court of Appeals were reported, for sleeping with the legal secretary of an opposing counsel. Had confidences been exchanged? Unbelievably, especially in light of Fast Eddie's long-married status, the Court of Appeals had asked in response whether it was true love that had made Fast Eddie do it. For true love, apparently, meant no disqualification for Fast Eddie and his firm.

Fast Eddie had shown his stripes to Shane at one point in Applied by threatening to accuse Shane of some lie or other during a discovery road trip they took together. Shane had promptly threatened to call the private discovery referee the Superior Court had put in charge of the case and falsely accuse Eddie of having sent a prostitute to Shane's hotel room, just to see the little man jump in light of his earlier sexual peccadilloes. That had convinced Fast Eddie to lay off and play by the rules with Shane, more or less.

"So Eddie," Shane said, "you're a smart guy, and Ben, he's got better things to do than fuck around with Sam here. You drew the wrong judge. You know it, I know it. Hell, even Ben knows it."

Ed Foley had been fronting Ben Carpuchi a long time. He was no legal scholar, but he was a good guesser. His guess was Shane was maybe 80 percent right about where Sam Pollard was right now, and probably 99 percent right about where Sam Pollard was at the end of the day, which was worse, because that meant he'd have to keep Ben Carpuchi dry and humping through a four-month trial with this John Cooper asshole and a platoon of goons ragging on him every day only to wind up in the same place they were right now. And all they had to have done was get any one of fourteen other judges. But they'd shot their bullet on the law-and-motion judge when they'd been afraid they'd lose summary judgment on the standard of care on that other motion this dick Sullivan had filed, the only chance they had to challenge a judge for no reason, so they had no choice when this anthrax Pollard had shown up.

And then, out of nowhere, came this Motion in Limine Number One. No one on their side saw that coming, especially that sorry cunt Carpuchi was using to do the briefs. But Ben, at least, had had the decency to tell him to do whatever he thought best with the case before leaving to indulge himself. Ben had always trusted him to do the right thing with the money—to never waste his time, and to get the right price when and if their goose was otherwise cooked. Ben had never forgotten the Bank of America debacle, and had no interest in making the acquaintance of members of the diplomatic corps on appeal. Ben, God bless him, was all about the money. And what it could buy, including, of course, the very lovely Ms. Wharton.

"Twenty million. Take it or leave it," said Fast Eddie.

Since the last offer had been sixty million, this was progress, and both men knew it.

Shane did not hesitate. "Where's Louie in all this?"

He was referring to Louie Habash, the President of Applied, and quite a strong personality in his own right.

Eddie hesitated. He'd probably spoken too soon, but he didn't seriously expect any trouble from Louie Habash, as this was a straight-up contingency with all costs advanced by his office. Habash didn't have a dime invested—it was all gravy to him, and the contingent-fee contract said Louie would accept advice regarding settlement.

"He's outside; let me talk to him," Eddie said.

Half an hour later, he came back in, Louie in tow.

"Twenty million," said Eddie. "Take it or leave it."

Shane turned to Judge Pollard's courtroom clerk. "Please ask the judge if he will see counsel alone," he said to the woman, very politely. Always politeness to the clerks—they were the real killers in the court system.

Eddie looked at him, but said nothing. He knew what was coming.

Take it or leave it, I don't think so, Shane said to himself, let's all go see what Judge Pollard thinks about twenty million, Fast Eddie, which maybe I'll pay after somebody puts a flame thrower up my fat ugly Irish ass and lights it up.

An hour later, the deal was done, but only at twelve five, with final authority coming in from Ed Zbrewski in New York after a heated caucus was held by phone with the Holliday & Bennett executive committee.

Shane had argued hard to limit the settlement to the maximum of ten million in fees that had actually been paid his client, but Judge Pollard was having none of it.

"Don't forget the interest that's accrued on all that money, my boy. Not to mention the fact that there has been considerable legal incompetence on the part of your Mr. Homer Rhodes here, too. And also don't let's forget the Carpuchi factor. If I were ever to let that rogue elephant near a jury, why you'd be picking thorns out of your asshole for the rest of your life, boychick. So go back to New York, take your bows, and when you go to your RC church on Sunday be sure to count your blessings too." Shane smiled—the judge, as usual, was right on the money.

He left the Superior Court that night wondering if being in business was any easier than working within a legal profession that he'd stumbled into twenty-five years before merely because his LSATs had been so much higher than his GMATs.

37

Superior Court, County of Alameda
{Mid-Morning, October 31, 1996}

Peg Bondoc and her divorce lawyer were making their first appearance in family court. Gus Bondoc had taken every liquid asset he could lay his hands on and lit out, probably out of the country, two days after his meeting with David Israel at the Top of the Mark.

Gus had sat her down and explained his physical danger to Peg the day after he saw Israel. But he had made no attempt to tell her what he planned to do about it. She had a feeling it might come to this, but she thought he loved the kids too much to leave her and them high and dry financially, facing a default judgment for sixteen million in Baby Doc's civil lawsuit that would wipe out every asset he'd left behind, except—her divorce lawyer had explained—maybe her half of the equity in their Piedmont house, which was her separate property.

Anyway, the SOB was gone, the bank accounts she did know about, the securities at Deutsche Bank, at least seven millions worth, liquidated overnight and wire-transferred to the Caymans—the Caymans, for God's sake, and from there to who knows where.

Her very aggressive East Bay divorce lawyer, whom she got through a multiple referral from a network of divorced mothers at Head Royce, told her it was marital fraud of the worst sort, and the best thing she could do was start proceedings immediately. So she had.

By 11:30 a.m., there was a bench warrant for Gus Bondoc ordering him to present himself and account for the marital assets with which he appeared to have absconded, not to mention provide spousal and child support and start paying Edward Liebowitz's legal fees. But Ed Liebowitz knew this was no ordinary husband on the run, and he had only two words for Peg Bondoc as they left the Alameda courthouse at noon that Halloween.

"David Israel," he said .

"What?" Peg said. "That's the same man my husband's been working with—the one that warned him to leave the country."

"Maybe so," said her divorce lawyer, "but Mr. Israel also sometimes works for me, at least on my biggest cases, and I told him what had happened to you. He doesn't see a conflict—which, my dear lady, is the best news you could possibly have, because otherwise I guarantee you would never see Mr. Bondoc or any of your money again. With your permission, we'll see Mr. Israel later this afternoon."

38

Berkeley, California
{Mid-Afternoon, October 31, 1996}

Ed Liebowitz's office was in the old Wells Fargo tower on Shattuck, right near the downtown Berkeley BART station. He'd gone to Boalt and just never left town, lived on the North Side, walked to work most days. Ate in the restaurants in the Gourmet Ghetto, including Chez Panisse, several times a week. Went to Berkeley Rep. Voted to Ban the Bomb. Life was always good in the People's Republic, and over the years the college kids had all vastly cleaned themselves up, gotten good-looking and optimistic again. That was a kick in itself.

He had the top floor of the Wells building all to himself, usually hired two or three second-year Boalties cheap, no long-term prospects, just paid them eating money. They were fun to have around for company and to feel close to the school. He kept a couple of long-term paralegals to do the endless paperwork divorce law had become.

He knew both the Bondocs from before, but only slightly. His kids had gone to Head Royce, though they were older than the Bondocs' two kids. He gave to the same charities as they did, particularly Berkeley Rep, the real cultural gem of the East Bay.

David Israel he knew fairly well, though he knew he was not on David's A-list. He'd only called the man in desperation. Mostly when he called David, he got the old "I'm too busy, here's a name," and then the name didn't work out, at least compared to what happened when David said yes, which was uniformly amazing.

But this time, David didn't say no. In fact, if Ed was any judge of anything, David was actually anxious to get involved.

Peg was seated in Ed's office when David schlubbed in. She saw the same 5'6", slightly out-of-shape guy who introduced himself to Edouard Jones at the UN back in April 1995, but this time he was wearing his most approachable manner.

Ed Liebowitz sprang to his feet and made the introductions, describing David, to David's evident embarrassment, as a cross between Sherlock Holmes and Jesus Christ. Peg eyed her newfound savior more circumspectly.

"Mr. Israel," she said, "I'm a little concerned about your motive here. I know you worked for my husband trying to locate this young woman who caused all this trouble for him and then disappeared. And he told me how both you and he thought she might even have been harmed by this particular client my husband had. Now why would you want to help me find my husband after the information you gave him convinced him to leave me and my children?"

David looked at her.

"First, Mrs. Bondoc, there's no formal conflict here. I have no idea where your husband went, and my former assignment in no way involves this one under my own ethics, which aren't formal like a lawyer's; they're just what I'm comfortable with.

"Now, the rest of this is a little rough, but you asked, so I'm going to tell you. I assume you want to know, rather than just take what I'm offering." He hesitated. "Also, you should know, if you've got no money I'll wait till I find him to get paid."

At this point, Ed wanted to drag Peg into another room and tell her for Christ's sake to stop the whole process of putting David on the spot. But one look over at Peg told him he had no control over the silly bitch. As per usual when representing women divorcees, Ed thought—they all thought from the waist down. Money was always secondary to these women, no matter what they said on intake.

"OK," Peg replied. When she said nothing more, David resumed.

"I think your husband got this little girl Gina killed, and in a very nasty way too. Not directly, but karmicly. That may sound stupid to you, but I think he crossed a line when he took on Baby Doc as a client, and crossing that line led to a death here, maybe more than one.

"But the one death we know about, that little girl's death, that was probably a real bad death. And that death, well, it bothers me a lot. I think about it at night, and I see Gus's face, and I do not like him for it.

"And now he's gone, and he's gone with a lot of money, and you have next to nothing. So he should give the money to you—that feels right to me.

"Or forget everything I just said—let me make it real simple for you. Let's just say I don't like your husband very much, and so today's your lucky day, how's that?"

Peg understood none of this. Her husband, Gus, had been in the law business, just like their friends who were lawyers, just like his friend and classmate Gerry Frank was in the law business. Gerry and Gus were both very prominent lawyers, known at the law school, friends with the faculty and their wives. Sure, Gus had some clients who were always in trouble, but lawyers were supposed to help people who were in trouble. That wasn't illegal.

Then this young black girl had come in and stolen data—she'd been the one who'd committed a crime. And then she'd seduced Peg's husband and ruined their life together. And yet here was this apparently otherwise entirely pragmatic man telling her that her husband was a karmic murderer, whatever the hell that meant.

But Ed was actually all wrong about Peg—she wasn't thinking from the waist down at all. She *was* interested in the money. And all she'd ever wanted to get from Israel was a sense that he was sincerely committed to finding Gus for her. Anyway, she wasn't in the karma business. What she was in, as of a few weeks ago, was the flat-broke, two-kids-to-support, no-husband business.

So like Ed, when she'd heard that David would wait to get paid, Peg was ninety-nine percent sold anyway.

39

St. Andrew's Plaza, New York
{Morning, April 11, 1997}

Greg Wardling considered John Deronda to be among the best of the former Southern District AUSAs who'd gone private. A real trial dog, and no quitter. Witness this case, where this character Bondoc was long gone and John was still in here swinging, trying to prevent indictment in absentia.

What John didn't know, could never know, was the conversation that Greg had had with David Israel's contact within the bureau last October. The man, of about Wardling's age and seniority in government service, had walked unannounced into Wardling's office one day and told, not asked, Wardling to put his coat on and take a walk with him.

When they hit Foley Square together, David's mole looked harshly at Wardling and said "I know what you think of the bureau, Wardling."

Wardling said nothing.

Then Bill Jones laughed. "And," he said, "whatever you think of it, you can't think any less of it than I do, dick face. What I know about it, you only think you know."

Now Wardling was interested. There seemed to be a spark of intelligence at work somewhere in the meaty face in front of him.

"This girl you want?"

"Yes?" said Wardling, now quite alert.

"She's dead."

Wardling would have grabbed the agent by the throat or called a cop, but he realized how absurd that would be. And, he realized Jones wouldn't be telling him such an outrageously dangerous thing without a whole web of a story to support it. So he restrained himself.

The two men retired to a Blarney Stone Bar & Grill, part of a chain of only-in-New York saloons making half their money from funeral homes that got the calls from the bar for pick up of senior citizens dropping dead from inhaling the cheapest boilermakers in New York.

Jones, without naming names, explained his rise in the bureau on the tail of David's genuine investigative talents; David's sincere interest in Gina's well-being and his laborious efforts to find her; and, finally, the conclusion of his forensic team that she had been lifted and was dead.

Jones then gave Wardling the address of Gina's last apartment in the Far Rock Project.

"Believe me, Greg," he said, "there is not a man working for the government who could have done what this private guy did, and it took him more than a year. Now your guys want to sniff, sniff. No harm has been done to the crime scene."

"And what if I arrest you and sweat you and make you tell me who this guy is?"

Jones laughed. "Right. First, I forget I ever knew you. Second, I quit the bureau and go private, which I've been thinking I may do anyway. You know, we can't beat the Italians in the mob; we can't beat the Russians moving into Brooklyn. The Cold War's over, and I only hope and pray nothing else serious ever comes along in my lifetime, because we couldn't beat the girl scouts if they decided to stop selling cookies and tried to take over the government. You be nice and maybe, if you need me, I'll help you out in a real case with this guy sometime."

So Greg and Bob became friends, and Greg passed on the address to his captive feebees. A sniff was had, and in fact it sure looked like the girl was dead. That was all Greg knew as of April 12, 1997.

He couldn't prosecute Baby Doc—it was an absolutely clean lift, no traces. There wasn't anything on this long-gone scumbag Bondoc, who seemed to be running. And he wasn't going to indict Gina, not if she was dead in a cellar somewhere.

So he just looked over at John Deronda and said, quietly, "Stop yammering, John—there's nothing to fight about here. Your client is not, repeat not, the target of any current investigation by this office, nor is there any active case pending respecting the data theft in question.

"You'll have a letter to that effect that you can use in this State Bar proceeding, or whatever it is you're worried about, this afternoon. Now how about some squash sometime soon up at the New York AC? I'm tired of just beating your ass in the courtroom, you little mouse dick."

40

State Bar Court, Review Department, San Francisco
{Morning, July 7, 1997}

The Review Department had taken judicial notice of the "no target" letter from Greg Wardling, over Lucy Lee's vigorous objection. Gerry Frank was supremely confident Lucy's off-the-wall the-client-is-the-client theory wouldn't get any traction.

And then, bang, he (and Gus, though Gus was too far away to feel the bullet) were dead. The Review Department's Opinion came down like a rock on Ger, and it embraced Lucy Lee like a long-lost lover. The summary at the end said it all:

Thus, we come to a sad tipping point of this even sadder tale. An otherwise distinguished Member of the State Bar accepts the representation of a client who has been the subject of numerous verified reports by the United Nations Commission on Human Rights of extreme brutality and corruption resulting in the deaths of many thousands of innocent persons.

A young woman, barely out of her teenage years, then commits a federal felony directed at that client. A later in time and unknowing sexual liaison entraps the State Bar Member in what might well appear to the client as a conspiracy to take financial advantage of him.

Upon learning the truth and, according to his own testimony, fearing torture and death at the hands of the client, the State Bar Member then commits a federal misprision, itself a felony. But because he has thus far escaped actual prosecution, the State Bar Member has successfully convinced the court below not to conflate Standard 2.6(a) {governing failure to report the current status of active matters to the client} with Standard 3.3 {governing the effect of criminal convictions on the right to practice law}.

"If the law supposes that, then the law is a ass ..." said Dickens's Mr. Bumble in Oliver Twist, *and we agree. But "the law is not a ass." Rather, as is argued correctly by the Office of the Chief Trial Counsel, the client is the client, and the Members of the State Bar, at least, would all do well to remember it.*

A misprision of a federal felony, and thus an independent federal felony by a Member of the State Bar, undoubtedly occurred here, whether it was or ever is prosecuted. In this latter regard, we cannot help but note that if the State Bar Member accused here found the civil client in question—whom he had no ethical obligation to accept as a client—so frightening, then he should have thought about that before taking the client's money.

Our ultimate conclusion is that the federal felony of misprision's undoubted occurrence here must and should be taken into account under State Bar Rules governing breaches of ethical conduct. Thus, consistent with that conclusion, Respondent is ordered immediately DISBARRED *under Standard 2.6(a), given the seriousness of the conduct committed by Respondent as evidenced by the undisputed facts found in the record before this Review Department. The decision by the Hearing Department dated July 12, 1996, and imposing lesser discipline is* REVERSED.

Dated: July 5, 1997   *Edwards, J., Kanowitz, J., Stein, J.*

Lucy Lee was forgiving toward Judge Sol. After feeding him a steady diet of severe pantsuits for more than a year, she arrived on July 6 all decked out in a revealing new sundress she'd been saving for the occasion. Judge Sol had never been happier to have been reversed in his life.

On his side of the City, among the tall buildings downtown, Gerry Frank went steadily to work, doing what he did best, working away on a Petition for Review to the California Supreme Court that would knock those yokels in the Review Department back into whatever left field they'd come out of. Who did they think they were fucking with? he kept saying to himself, over and over again, getting madder by the minute. They can't do this kind of shit to me. This isn't in the books. Nobody gets this creative on one of my clients. Not in this lifetime.

If he could have hit his head against the wall in his office without attracting the attention of his partners, he would have done it. For, underneath all the hale fellow well met, underneath all the committees and the charities, why Ger was a very competitive lad, after all. Very competitive. And, boy, did he hate to lose.

41

California Supreme Court, San Francisco
{Morning, October 14, 1997} ·

Gerry Frank and his noted appellate team at Bass, Holman & Frank had outdone themselves. Their Petition for Review, made under Rule 952(a), California Rules of Court, protesting Gus Bondoc's disbarment on Lucy Lee's novel theory, had so lambasted the Office of the Chief Trial Counsel and the Review Department of the State Bar Court that even Lucy Lee had figured this was the end of the road for all her dreams of glory. Just one little-noticed oral argument before the Supremes, chalked up as a loss, and then back to Judge Sol slobbering over her outfits.

But Lucy was as competitive in her way as Ger was in his. She couldn't match him and his brain trust page for page in the time between the September 10 petition filing by Frank's team and her response on September 25. And she was humiliated by how easily her legal points were brushed aside by his final reply on September 30. And how haughtily, and how cruelly.

But one night, shortly after September 30, Luce was reading through all the Supreme Court shit for the umpteenth time when she realized that the verification which Rule 952(e) required was not actually signed by Brother Gus, but by Brother Ger.

Normally this was no problem. If the client happens to be out of town, the law allows the lawyer to sign for the client simply as a matter of convenience for everyone. But here Gus wasn't just out of town; he was plain gone, and she would bet her kids that Ger couldn't honestly tell the Supremes that Gus had ever actually authorized him to appeal.

Once she figured it out, she got so damn excited that if Judge Sol had been there, she would have pole danced for him nude. With no Judge Sol to tantalize, she just turned the radio way, way up and danced around the kitchen with an old broom, thinking all the while of that brilliant, arrogant, oh-so-nice white male, Gerry Frank, being so thoroughly behind the eight ball for once in his charmed life.

The next day, a letter demanding to know whether Gus had authorized the appeal went out to Frank. Twenty-four hours later, Frank hadn't responded—he'd foreseen the problem, but had never dreamed Lucy would catch it, and for once he was confounded. Lucy then swore out a declaration attaching the papers from Peg's divorce file in Alameda Superior, and now, on October 12, 1997, there was a one-line Order from the Supreme Court denying the Petition as unauthorized but depublishing the Opinion so that it had no precedential value for future cases.

Bondoc was toast, but the legal theory of whether the client was the client would have to wait for another less exotic case to have its day in court.

Lucy was sitting at her desk that afternoon when Ger called her. "Man," he said, "you kicked my ass and don't think I don't know it—I am a big fan of Ms. Lucy Lee. Listen, I think you're wasted big time over there. Ever think of selling yourself to the enemy?"

She couldn't believe it, of course. But within a few weeks, Judge Sol had to find something else to do with his days besides wait to see what Lucy would wear to court. And Lucy got herself a Miata.

BOOK THREE

AFTERMATH

42

Kuwait City, Kuwait
{December 10–11, 1997}

To say Gus Bondoc, who was traveling under a Czech passport, was angry with David Israel would have been an understatement of monumental proportions. Anticipating that, David had brought some friends: two ex-British Army types he'd known in Afghanistan who were still out in the Middle East, available for what might come up—which, as the Iraq-Iran war dragged on and Saddam became more threatening to the Kuwaitis, could mean a lot of things. David had asked them to tag along, and David was a good fellow, so along they came.

When he saw the muscle, Bondoc thought it was a lift that David was working for Baby Doc. He looked pale, sick. But rather than relieve him of his anxiety, David played him. "Look, Gus," he said, "hard or easy. All the same to me. All the same to them, come to that." He nodded to his backups, who like most beefy, lower-class Brits looked like they'd quite enjoy stepping on Bondoc's Adam's apple just for the sport of it.

The four of them retired to David's hotel, the Sheraton.

Bondoc appeared to be alone. He didn't say where he was staying, why he was in Kuwait City, or who he was with, if anyone. He just stared furiously at David.

When they were safely within the luxurious room— David liked to travel in style when style was available— David looked at Gus and said, "I'm not here for Duvalier. Not my cup of tea."

Gus, despite his anger, looked relieved. He relaxed slightly, and a few minutes passed. Then Gus spoke. "So who, for Christ's sake, is your client?"

"Irving J. Cornelius, Esq." said David, smiling.

"What the hell?" said Gus. "You mean that old crank that practices bankruptcy law out of some cellar in Oakland?"

"One and the same," said David. He went on to explain that Peg, acting on advice from her divorce lawyer, had hired a bankruptcy lawyer who, in absentia, had thrown Gus into an involuntary bankruptcy and then had Cornelius appointed his Chapter 7 trustee. Peg, in Gus's bankruptcy as a competing creditor, had then protested Baby Doc's sixteen-million-dollar alter-ego claim, just as all the other individual shareholders were protesting Baby Doc's claim in front of Charlie Rogers over in San Francisco.

Gus got it, of course; his firm specialized in bankruptcy-oriented litigation, so he understood the game. Thought it might work. Saw Sullivan's hand in it, too. A lot to admire in that boy.

"So what's the play, David?"

"It's so simple, Gus," said David. "Do I have to say what it is? It cheapens me. It embarrasses me."

"I think if you're going to criminally blackmail someone by threatening their life, yeah, you ought to have to say you're doing it before you take their money, yes I do," said Gus.

He'd stung David with that. And David came close to having the Brits beat him within an inch of his life. But David had never given an order like that, so all he did was shudder.

"You're a prick, Gus—I don't like you. And you should keep this in mind—there aren't many people in this world who can find you any time they want to. I'm one. Now you have a good deal of money that legally belongs to Mr. Cornelius. That same money, if it doesn't wind up going to Baby Doc, will eventually go to your wife and kids. So let's just say you're going to wire transfer, what, five million, today or at the latest tomorrow to Oakland, and I am then going to lay off. What do you say? Oh, and don't bargain with me, Gus—I know more than you think about what you've still got, and five million is generous."

Bondoc was caught. He'd been outsmarted, and not just intellectually—that he'd experienced before. No, here in this room was someone infinitely more cunning than he, someone who had outfoxed him without working up a sweat. Gus had never felt more like a limp dick in his life.

He looked over at David and said, weakly, "OK, so how do I know when I let go of the money that this little parlor game is over?"

David now broke into a wide smile.

"It's all a matter of talent, Gus. You, my sad friend, had eyes that were bigger than your talent. This made you unhappy and made you push your talent into some very dark places where nice people do not go. Now you are fucked. How fucked, I don't know. Whether you'll wind up in the same bat cave poor Gina wound up in, yowling your head off while they apply some instrument of pain to your carcass, that I truly don't know. I am leaving you with enough escape money so that horrible prospect is not on my conscience."

"My eyes are not bigger than my talent. I have a conscience to restrain my eyes."

"So now, listen to my conscience speaking. I do not fuck with people unnecessarily. I do no harm. I stay out of the way. I try to have a good time in life. You do the right thing here and you will not see me or hear from me again. I promise that, and there's nothing better you can rely on in this life than that."

"And I'll tell you one more thing for free here, Gus, just to get it off my chest, just for Gina. You crossed a line with this Duvalier character which no one with any sense of self would ever, ever have crossed. And all of this legalese crap about how everybody, but everybody, Hitler and Stalin included, they all should get a lawyer—that's just a fairy story. If that were really true, then you wouldn't be on the run. You must know it's a fairy story better than anyone. So let's just get our business done, and you get back to the business of staying alive."

A day later, the money was wire-transferred from an account in the Isle of Jersey to Oakland. Gus was gone, somewhere. David was on his way home. And the long-suffering Mr. Irving J. Cornelius, Esq. was the most surprised Chapter 7 bankruptcy trustee in the history of the Northern District of California.

43

United States Bankruptcy Court for the Northern District of California (San Francisco Division)
{July 15–16, 1998}

The last financial act of Gina Costello's data theft was played out in *Triton LLC v. Cornelius et al*, the consolidated-claims proceeding before Bankruptcy Judge Charles Rogers. It was designed to test Baby Doc's theory that Bondoc, Treister, Nimmer & Sourwine had been so mismanaged and under-capitalized that the shareholders ought, in equity, to have to pay all its bills out of their own pockets. Or, since each of those shareholders were now, including Gus, in their own personal bankruptcies, out of their otherwise solvent bank-ruptcy estates.

On one level, Baby Doc's scorched-earth strategy had already been defeated by Shane Sullivan's insistence that Bob Treister and his flock of sheep take refuge in the bankruptcy courts, where Shane had long operated and where Treister had previously feared to tread. The maneuver had stopped the Sklar firm dead in their tracks. Judge Rogers had seen the spend-them-silly tactic for what it was in a millisecond, squashed the battalion of Sklar lawyers sent out from New

York to intimidate him, and put the whole claims-resolution process on ice until, as he put it, the Chapter 7 trustee handling the liquidation of the Bondoc Firm itself could liquidate the receivables and other assets belonging to the entity and one could see "what was what."

With the avid assistance of many of the shareholders—Teddy Sourwine was pathetically diligent—"what was what" wasn't bad. The Chapter 7 trustee had wound up sitting on about four million cash. But there were two million in other creditors unpaid, and there was the indisputable sixteen million owed to Triton LLC, the Baby Doc front that had had its data lifted, with only $500,000 in insurance left to cover that loss. Which meant, if the bankruptcy judge found an alter-ego claim was going to stick here, a $13,500,000 shortfall. Plus maybe interest, plus attorney's fees, plus the expense in everybody's individual bankruptcy filings, plus try and get a credit card or a mortgage in this lifetime.

And for what? Nobody in the room had slept with Gina Costello. And I was never exactly a Baby Doc fan, thought Shane, though I guess I did know he was on the premises when I was in love with this stupid deal. What the hell is the matter with me?

Judge Rogers took the bench. Shane was not at the counsel table—that was John Chandler's and his hammer Franklin Truman's job. But looking at Charlie always made Shane feel better about life. Rogers had a wicked wit, and he used it on Shane more than most, perhaps because Shane didn't hesitate to sink a barb or two back. But, like Judge Sam Pollard, Rogers was another example of that rarest breed of trial judges—both fair and smart. Rare because, while most judges of all stripes tried to be fair, given the vagaries of the political appointment process, the vast majority simply lacked the intellectual firepower to get out of the forest before dark when confronted with any truly complicated civil matter.

So even though it was his own personal ass on the line in the most intimate possible way imaginable, Shane felt relaxed. Not that he hadn't tried to stack the deck against these poor rabid fucked-up New Yorkers in every way possible, including, in particular, home-towning them with Charlie's absolutely favorite fair-haired boy, John Chandler, whose mere presence in the courtroom made old Charlie's brain sing opera. Shane was a survivor, after all. Charlie would have done nothing less to him had their roles been reversed. Would have kidded him about it later, too. Because there was nothing better than graveyard humor in Charlie's book. After all, he was a bankruptcy judge, not a milkman.

The lead trial lawyer from Sklar stood up. He didn't look like any trial lawyer you'd ever see outside a bankruptcy court—a large man, overweight, with a heavy beard. Not especially well tailored, although it may have been that no suit, no matter how expensive, would have looked good on such an awkward, aggressive body. He looked like an offensive lineman forced into a tuxedo for an awards dinner. But it didn't matter, really—bankruptcy law was all in the imagination, and the judges didn't hold appearances against the bankruptcy lawyers that practiced in front of them. Though Shane wondered—his boy John, after all, was svelte, handsome, charming, and cold steel from an analytical standpoint.

If Mr. Rude over there got nasty, then Frank the Hammer would bite fast enough, but John was a whole different package, and Shane thought much the better one.

"Your Honor," said Lester Swartz, the offensive lineman.

"Yes, Mr. Swartz?" said Judge Rogers.

"Triton LLC is ready to proceed."

"And for the various respondents?"

"Also ready," said John Chandler, rising politely and smiling at his mentor. Lester Swartz glared menacingly at Chandler's friendly manner toward the judge. He knew everything about the myriad connections between the two men, but there was nothing illegitimate about any of it. In the federal system, disqualification is near impossible. Being forewarned did not make the sight of it any less painful.

The judge saw the interplay and smiled inwardly. If only it were so simple: decide every case based on which lawyer you like the best. Why, Mr. Swartz, to look at you, how could you ever win a case? And yet from your position of power in the best firm in the country and everything else I've read about you, you've won quite a lot. And your briefs here are excellent. This case is a horse race.

So relax. Let's get down to the evidence and let me do my job. Don't make poor John have to unleash that goddamn Franklin Truman fellow on you—that kind of shit I don't need in my courtroom, not today. For God's sake, if we start that, Shane Sullivan will probably wind up jumping the rail, too.

Not for the first time he wished they'd assign a US Marshall to the bankruptcy courtrooms permanently, just to settle some folks down a bit. Money gets people so excited, he would tell his wife.

"Let me give you my preliminary thoughts here, gentlemen. This is an unusual case. While there is no reason I can think of, no statute that says a legal professional corporation cannot be the subject of an alter-ego claim, there is no reported case that has ever involved such an entity's being held one, either. That is correct, is it not?"

Both lawyers agreed.

"However, as one would expect in a law corporation, all the paperwork is in absolutely apple-pie order, articles, bylaws, minutes, all perfectly typed, bound, preserved, sealed, stamped. The shoemaker's children all had shoes here, correct?"

Again both lawyers agreed, although clearly Swartz was straining to say more, and felt he was being railroaded by the judge.

"But Mr. Swartz argues this is much more than a mere corporate-paperwork case. What he is saying is that the Bondoc Firm was big business. It had massive liability exposures, day in day out. It had a ten-million-dollar malpractice policy, and even that may have been light. In particular, it was massively underinsured for employee dishonesty, a mere one-million-dollar policy, and, overall it was badly undercapitalized, which is reflected in the fact that, at the end of the day, its bankruptcy estate has liquidated at four million and left unsecured debts, including Triton LLC, of eighteen million, less the five hundred thousand dollars that will go to pay Triton LLC from applicable insurance."

The Judge paused.

"So," and here Judge Rogers looked right at John Chandler, "Mr. Swartz says the only fair thing is to make the people who ultimately made all these horrendous business mistakes, the shareholders, the ones who elected the people who underinsured and the ones who themselves undercapitalized, foot the bill. And from a review of the assets in the shareholders' personal estates, it looks like there is the money to do it. So the issue before me is whether that fits within the precedent of what's appropriate under alter-ego doctrine. Right, Mr. Chandler?"

There were a lot of unhappy people in the bankruptcy

court when Charlie Rogers finished that little speech, and one happy one. Lester Swartz, smiling slightly beneath his beard, sat down and sank back in his chair. A colleague patted him on the back. The judge had practically quoted his trial brief.

In the audience Bob Treister glared at Kelly Nimmer, whose head had sunk between his knees. The reference to underinsurance had been utterly condemning. Nobody adequately capitalized professional corporations—whatever the hell that meant, anyway—they were all emptied like piggy banks every year. But Kelly's abysmal failure to grasp the implications of computer technology, and to properly insure against the massive employee dishonesty that it enabled, that failure had put himself and every one of his colleagues at the literal end of their financial ropes. Listening to a bankruptcy judge explain why you were fucked on the opening day of your trial in a bankruptcy court was an abysmal experience.

John Chandler, however, was not at all perturbed by what he'd just heard. The world, to him, was a series of interesting and mainly solvable problem sets.

"Sounds correct to me, Your Honor," he said cheerfully. "I might phrase it a little differently, though. The real issue is whether the Bondoc Firm did anything unusual here, which it didn't. Nobody gets punished under alter-ego theory for not being a pioneer in the fight against crime, Your Honor. After the publicity surrounding this case, the next law firm that comes in here, maybe they should have their shareholders pay, but not these poor fellers."

Charlie Rogers sat on his bench and looked out onto his courtroom, stone-faced now but inwardly delighted. This is why I'm a judge, he thought. Six feet of paper filed in this mess. And I get up here and give old John a lecture that would make most young guys go throw up, if their clients didn't lynch them on the way to the men's room. A lecture that makes that New York asshole over there sit back like the cat that ate the canary. OK, so I really don't like him, I admit it—he's way too New York for me—and it's an ugly suit.

And what does my boy Johnnie do? He stands there and he throws it right back at me. And I do agree that if they just acted like everybody else, if they carried normal amounts of employee-dishonesty insurance for example, then they're okay. If they can prove that, then they can keep their money and this disgusting Baby Doc can go hang.

The trial took two days. Frank the Hammer and Mr. Rude got into it about every hour. Shane's examination was a farce; he was the world's worst witness, wouldn't answer a single question straight. Kelly bled all over himself apologizing for being so stupid about computers and all. But John Chandler's expert had done a comprehensive survey of Bay Area law firms of not more than thirty lawyers having equivalent revenue streams to the Bondoc Firm, and the most employee-dishonesty insurance coverage carried was five million. One firm carried only a hundred thousand, and the average was exactly a million. Moreover, capitalization ratios were all uniformly lower than what had been caught in the Bondoc Firm bankruptcy, no doubt because in the Bondoc Firm the piggybank had not yet been emptied in 1996 when bankruptcy was filed.

The closing arguments on July 16, 1998 came late in the day. Mr. Swartz, sensing the case had gotten away from him, focused on the unfairness of such wealthy lawyers hiding behind a screen of legalisms to escape a lawful debt. He carefully avoided any mention of who was behind the screen of Triton LLC. John Chandler had the last word.

"Your Honor," he said, "there is no jury here, and I will

not waste time by stooping to ad hominem attacks on anyone, other than to note that, as usual, there are plenty of unpleasant people here on both sides.

"Alter ego is equitable. Bankruptcy is equitable. What Gina Costello did to start the ball rolling here could never have been anticipated. Certainly the Bondoc Firm was not prepared for it. No one else Triton LLC might have gone to for legal representation that in any manner resembled the Bondoc Firm in terms of size or financial structure would have been prepared to pay for the financial side effects of it. We've proved that. It would therefore be inequitable to make my clients pay personally."

Judge Rogers asked, "Matter submitted?"

The lawyers both said yes.

Judge Rogers said, "All claims of Triton LLC are denied." Then he left the bench.

Shane Sullivan quickly ran up and kissed John Chandler. Kelly Nimmer wept. Bob Treister quietly left the bankruptcy court without speaking to anyone. And life, finally, went on for Teddy Sourwine, not to mention Gilbert Levy, Andy McGlynn, Joe Sarone, and all the other Bondoc Firm shmucks who had always held it as an article of faith that being associated with a professional corporation meant peace and security in an otherwise uncertain world.

44

Europe
{2003-2005}

Gus Bondoc had been in Eastern Europe for several months, traveling as a tourist. He no longer seriously thought anyone was after him, with the possible exception of the IRS—he hadn't filed a federal income-tax return since fleeing the US, for obvious reasons. His days of obsessing over Baby Doc were long gone.

He'd even managed to start up a desultory e-mail correspondence with his estranged children, whom he'd been relieved to find had been saved from penury by Judge Rogers' decision denying Baby Doc's last effort to penetrate the Bondoc Firm's corporate shield and get at Peg's interest in their marital assets. The whole thing was an unbelievably shitty deal, but he was alive, he had some bucks, she was alive, the kids were doing well, and here he was in Budapest. Maybe he would even get laid.

He'd just come out of the Buda Castle when it happened. A taxi came right at him as he crossed the street. He swore he had the light. The son of a bitch just ran him over and kept on going.

Gus didn't wake up for three weeks. When he did, he'd lost the use of his legs and some of his brain. Eventually, he recovered enough to travel, and the hospital authorities e-mailed his children, who prevailed on Peg to see to his affairs. He'd been put, under an assumed name and on a pre-paid basis, into the German Center of Gerontology, located in Berlin. It provided excellent long-term skilled nursing care to accident victims with the multiple types of cranial and other injuries Gus had suffered.

Now in a wheelchair, Gus had difficulty speaking coherently for most of the time he remained alive at the center. One day, however—the nurse noted it as December 5, 2004—shortly before he passed away, he did rally. At that time, he gave his favorite nurse an account of what had brought him to such a sorry state, alone, in a foreign country, a cripple.

"At first I blamed this girl, you know—she tricked me. And then I blamed my client, who was trying to hurt me, who may have hurt me; I can't be sure. All I really know is this: I went further than I needed to. Most people do, so I'm no worse than a lot of others. But I had more opportunity, so I got in more trouble. Made worse enemies than most people do. It's not much consolation, understanding things. But there it is."

The nurse noted Gus had started to cry at that point, had asked to e-mail his kids, which he did. They e-mailed him right back, and that had seemed to calm him down. The nurse always said Gus seemed like a nice man.

Index of Law Firms and Individual Players

I. *Book of Business* Judges (in order of first appearance)

II. *Book of Business* Law Firms (in order of first appearance)

III. *Book of Business* Law Firm Lawyers (in order of first appearance)

John Epimere .... *Senior Partner, Patton, Welts and Sims*

Ben Laidlaw.. *Senior Partner, Holliday & Bennett*

Alice Greenberg .... *Senior Partner, Holliday & Bennett*

Thomas Gilhooly.................................. *Senior Partner, Holliday & Bennett*

Ed Zbrewski... *Senior Partner, Holliday & Bennett*

Sol Weiner.. *Senior Partner, Holliday & Bennett*

Stan Wolmann...................................... *Senior Partner, Holliday & Bennett*

Homer Rhodes .... *Senior Partner, Holliday & Bennett*

Tom Martin... *Junior Partner, Holliday & Bennett*

Shane Sullivan .... *Senior Partner, Bondoc, Treister, Nimmer & Sourwine*

Robert Treister .... *Senior Partner, Bondoc, Treister, Nimmer & Sourwine*

Gil Levy .... *Junior Partner, Bondoc, Treister, Nimmer & Sourwine*

Andy McGlynn .... *Junior Partner, Bondoc, Treister, Nimmer & Sourwine*

Joe Sarone.. *Junior Partner Bondoc, Treister, Nimmer & Sourwine*

Kelly Nimmer....................................... *Senior Bondoc, Treister, Nimmer & Sourwine*

Teddy Sourwine .... *Senior Bondoc, Treister, Nimmer & Sourwine*

John LaBelle... *Junior Partner, Bondoc, Treister, Nimmer & Sourwine*

John Cooper .... *Senior Partner, Baum, Baum & Cooper*

John Van Atta .... *Senior Partner, Cotta & Van Atta*

Lester Swartz .... *Senior Partner, Sklar, Ark, Slapp, Mead & Flood*

IV. Lawyers Not Working for *Book of Business* Law Firms (in order of first appearance)

Ben Carpuchi... *The Lead Lawyer Suing Holliday & Bennett for Legal Malpractice in* Applied v. Holliday & Bennett

Jack Rose.. *Gus Bondoc's Vanquisher in the Sol Weiner Case*

Mary Jo White .... *United States Attorney for the*

Southern District of New York

Greg Wardling .... *Assistant United States Attorney for the Southern District of New York*

Joseph Abrahams .... *Shane Sullivan's Criminal Defense Lawyer*

Pete Brad... *Shane Sullivan's Ethical Advisor and a Professor at NYU Law School*

Sid Lorand .... *Federal Public Defender who defends Eugenia Costello*

John Deronda .... *Gus Bondoc's New York Criminal Defense Lawyer*

Lucy Lee .... *Gus Bondoc's State Bar Prosecutor*

Ed Foley .... *Ben Carpuchi's Partner*

Joanne Wharton .... *Ben Carpuchi's Associate*

Edward Leibowitz................................... *Peg Bondoc's Divorce Lawyer*

John Chandler .... *Shane Sullivan's Bankruptcy Lawyer*

Irving Cornelius .... *Gus Bondoc's Bankruptcy Trustee*

V. Non-Lawyers (in order of first appearance)

Nancy Frehen .... *The Plaintiff in the Weiner Case*

Peg Bondoc .... *Gus Bondoc's Second Wife*

Sammy Bondoc....................................... *Gus Bondoc's First Wife*

Francesca Hernando............................... *One of Weiner's Victims*

Louie Habash... *The President of Applied, Ben Carpuchi's Client*

Gina Costello... *The Haitian Woman Who Steals Data From the Bondoc Firm and Becomes Gus Bondoc's Mistress*

Pierre Esclemond................................... *Gina Costello's Mentor*

Francois Duvalier ("Papa Doc").............. *Dictator of Haiti*

Jean Claude Duvalier ("Baby Doc")......... *Also Dictator of Haiti and a Client of the Bondoc Firm*

Tony Costello .... *Gina Costello's father*

Eugenia Estime .... *Gina Costello's mother*

Millie Conroy .... *Gus Bondoc's personal secretary*

Edouard Jones .... *a Member of the Haitian Diplomatic Mission to the United Nations*

Col. Francois Jones .... *Father of Edouard Jones*

Carla LaBelle .... *the Wife of John Labelle*

Claire LaBelle .... *the Daughter of John LaBelle*

Thomas Bondoc.....................................*the Son of Gus Bondoc*

Elizabeth Bondoc..................................*the Daughter of Gus Bondoc*

David Israel...*a Detective*

Eric Andresen.......................................*a Security Operative Working for David Israel*

Sean Hennessey ....*a Member of the San Francisco Police Department*

Grace Sullivan ....*a Daughter of Shane Sullivan*

George Higgins.....................................*Greg Wardling's Immediate Desk Supervisor at General Motors Acceptance Corporation*

Peter Johnson ....*a Member of the New York City Police Department*

William Jones ....*a Senior FBI Agent*

VI. Alphabetical List of All Individual Characters With Descriptions (arranged by last name first)

Abrahams, Joseph..................................*Shane Sullivan's Criminal Defense Lawyer*

Andresen, Eric.......................................*a Security Operative Working for David Israel*

Bondoc, August.....................................*Senior Partner, Bondoc, Treister, Nimmer & Sourwine*

Bondoc, Elizabeth.................................*the Daughter of Gus Bondoc*

Bondoc, Peg ....*Gus Bondoc's Second Wife*

Bondoc, Sammy.....................................*Gus Bondoc's First Wife*

Bondoc, Thomas....................................*the Son of Gus Bondoc*

Brad, Pete...*Shane Sullivan's Ethical Advisor and a Professor at NYU Law School*

Carpuchi, Ben.......................................*The Lead Lawyer Suing Holliday & Bennett for Legal Malpractice in Applied v. Holliday & Bennett*

Chandler, John ....*Shane Sullivan's Bankruptcy Lawyer*

Conroy, Millie ....*Gus Bondoc's personal secretary*

Cooper, John..*Senior Partner, Baum, Baum & Cooper*

Cornelius, Irving ....*Gus Bondoc's Bankruptcy Trustee*

Costello, Gina..*The Haitian Woman Who Steals Data From the Bondoc Firm and Becomes Gus Bondoc's Mistress*

Afterword

There are few heroes in life. But life is not bereft of heroes, and neither is the law. Book of Business is not written up as entirely lacking in heroes either. Among the judges and lawyers in Book of Business who, in the author's view, qualify as heroes are Superior Court Judge Sam Pollard and Bankruptcy Judge Charlie Rogers, along with lawyers Gerry Frank and Lucy Lee.

The fact many of the other law related characters portrayed in Book of Business are sullied with the muck of human fallibility—financial, sexual, and otherwise—should come as no surprise to any reader who lives in the real world. Most of us are, and so what? No one goes to jail for it, and the same thing holds true in Book of Business.

Finally, David Israel is not just any hero; he is the author's hero. But remember, David is a trick character. He is burdened with neither a college degree nor a law degree; he is made smarter than most everybody else; and, most important of all, he is given the virtue of a good heart.

If I ever write again (unlikely), it will be about detectives—about whom I know only a little—and not about lawyers—about whom I know much. Believe me, lawyers are entirely depressing to describe. David the detective, in contrast, was a pleasure to write about from beginning to end.

Acknowledgements

First, this Book of Business is dedicated to Mrs. Will Nathan, and the four now grown little Nathans, who make up the next generation of the tribe of Nathan, and without whose loving support over the past thirty plus years nothing would have been possible.

Next, as this Book of Business was begun in 1995, and had been moldering untouched in a desk drawer since 2002, this Book of Business is also dedicated to—and the author's most profound thanks go out to—one JS, prominent lawyer, diplomat, author, and poet, who, in 2006, charmed and cajoled the author into believing there was worth in both the writing and the message of this Book of Business. Any errors, or other sins of omission or commission contained in the writing of this Book of Business, whether literary, legal, or otherwise, remain exclusively those of the author, and not JS.

Finally this Book of Business is dedicated to the late, great SM, HPL, and CG as well as to EM, JM, JK, BL, SVE, RB, JV, BG, BH, MH, TT, MB, NB, LOK, JH, CH, WH, LH, JN, WN, RS, CD, EK, RC, JF, RM, JS(#1), JB, RW, EM, RD, HL, PS, RT, SP, DM, JT and, especially, DF. Among them are relations, friends, law professors, law partners, law colleagues, judges, and, yes, indeed, a certain private dick. No full names, please. Thanks for the ride, each of you, folks.

Additional Comments Regarding Use of Hyperbole

In addition to the standard Publisher's Note that appears in the frontispiece of this edition of Book of Business, the author wishes to add the following additional, but not inconsistent, comments of my own. With the exception of the two infamous Duvaliers (though large parts of the Duvalier plot here, are, of course, entirely fiction) and other such obvious historical personalities as Adolph Hitler and Josef Stalin, no person(s) who may otherwise be found to have been somehow depicted in this novel by way of any other possible similarities, are in any manner intended by the author to be portrayed in anything other than an entirely hyperbolic—and thus fictional—manner, and this novel absolutely does not purport to portray any such person(s), whomever they may be, in any manner in a factual way, as there would be and is no basis, in fact, for any such assertions by the author.

About the Author

Will Nathan is the pseudonym for a 2006 Norcal Superlawyer who wishes to remain anonymous.